ALSO BY RIVKA GALCHEN

Atmospheric Disturbances

American Innovations

Little Labors

Rat Rule 79

Everyone
Knows Your
Mother
Is a Witch

Everyone Knows Your Mother Is a Witch

Rivka Galchen

Farrar, Straus and Giroux

New York

Farrar, Straus and Giroux
120 Broadway, New York 10271

Library of Congress Cataloging-in-Publication Data
Names: Galchen, Rivka, author.
Title: Everyone knows your mother is a witch / Rivka Galchen.
Description: First edition. | New York : Farrar, Straus and
    Giroux, 2021.
Identifiers: LCCN 2020058349 | ISBN 9780374280468 (hardcover)
Classification: LCC PS3607.A4116 E94 2021 | DDC 813/.6—dc23
LC record available at https://lccn.loc.gov/2020058349

Our books may be purchased in bulk for promotional, educational, or
business use. Please contact your local bookseller or the Macmillan
Corporate and Premium Sales Department at 1-800-221-7945, extension
5442, or by email at MacmillanSpecialMarkets@macmillan.com.

www.fsgbooks.com
www.twitter.com/fsgbooks • www.facebook.com/fsgbooks

1 3 5 7 9 10 8 6 4 2

for my family

Everyone

Knows Your

Mother

Is a Witch

Herein I begin my account, with the help of my neighbor Simon Satler, since I am unable to read or write. I maintain that I am not a witch, never have been a witch, am a relative to no witches. But from very early in life, I had enemies.

When I was a child, our cow Mare at my father's inn was cross and bitter toward me. I didn't know why. I wouldn't hesitate to put a blue silk ribbon on her neck if she were here today. She died from the milk fever, which was no doing of mine, though as a young child I felt it was my doing, because Mare had kicked me and I had then called her fat-kidneyed. Was she my enemy? It takes time and experience to gain a cow's trust.

Now I'm seventy-some years old. I'll spend no more time on the enemies, or loves, of my youth and middle age. I'll say only that I've never before had even the smallest run-in with the law. Not for fighting, not for cursing, not for licentiousness, not for the pettiest theft. Yet attributed to me in this trial is the power to poison, to make lame, to pass through locked doors, to be the death of sheep, goats, cows, infants, and grapevines, even to cure—at will.

I can't even win at backgammon, as you know.

IF MY DEFENSE fails, a confession will be sought through torture, first with thumbscrews, then with leg braces, then with the rack—or something like that. It depends who the council hires for the job. If mercy is taken upon me, I'll be beheaded and then burned. If no mercy is taken, I'll be burned without first being beheaded. That happened to seven women last year in Regensburg. My children, with some help, have been coordinating my defense.

There are two things a woman must do alone: she does her own believing and her own dying. So says Martin Luther. Or so you say that Martin Luther says, or said. I was born the year Luther died. I took Catholic Communion only one time, in error. My daughter Greta is married to a pastor who says that's okay. My son Hans agrees. I hold Luther in highest esteem. He, too, was vilified. Again, I'm grateful to you, Simon, for sitting with me, for writing for me, for being my legal guardian.

This is my truest testimony.

On a Tuesday midmorning in May of 1615, four long years ago now, there was a gentle knock at my door. A freckle-faced young boy, with eyes downcast, said I was to follow him to see the ducal governor Lukas Einhorn. The boy had light eyes and wore clean, short trousers. It was hot out. I offered him a cool, weak wine, but he blushed and refused. Why was I being called? I asked him. He said it was an official summons. But he didn't know for what.

You'll remember, Simon, that it was a rotten spring that year. The beets were wrinkled, the radishes spare. The rhubarb, usually a celebration, was like straw, and same for the asparagus. The preceding winter had been fierce. One snowy eve a goat had turned up at my door, a beggar like Christ, I thought, and so I let the goat in, and he was so frozen that when he knocked his head against the leg of my table, his chin hairs broke off like sugar plate. I met a shepherd from outside Rutesheim whose nose fell off when he wiped it. The months had been ominous. The price of a sack of flour had nearly doubled. Half the town was having to borrow from the grain stores.

But it was a sunny day that Tuesday. I put on my boots, kissed my dear cow Chamomile, left behind my washing.

And I had a smug guess as to why I was being summoned. You'll laugh at me when I tell you this. I thought that Lukas Einhorn wanted my help. Mine! On account of the dark and difficult seasons, you see? He was a new ducal governor and he had no idea how to manage. I suspected that Einhorn wanted me to ask my son Hans to prepare a horoscope for him, or even to prepare a whole astrological calendar. I began to be annoyed, assuming Einhorn would expect the work to be done for no pay. So many of the so-called nobles petition Hans for astrological calendars, for weather predictions, for personal horoscopes. Even Emperor Rudolf had asked him: What do the stars say for war with Hungary? And even the Emperor never got around to paying. The new emperor is no better. It's always the same with some people. They may as well ask him to mend their hose. Hans was already living in Linz then. He had just remarried, and was teaching at a small school. He had been denied a job at his university in Tübingen on account of some nonsense about what Commu-nion wafers are made of, and though Hans is known at all the finest courts, he is paid only in insubstantial status. That May he was caught up in all sorts of conflicts with printers, and also he was trying to find a suitor for his stepdaughter. I was seen as having Hans's ear. But the man only has the two ears same as God has gifted the rest of us.

I get so little acknowledgment here in Leonberg of Hans's place in the world, and that's good—who wants to bring out the devils of envy? But I suppose I was waiting for the chance to dismiss a compliment, to say that Hans's accomplishments were his own, and not mine, though Hans does say, and I don't disbelieve him, that the mother's imagination in preg-nancy impresses itself upon the child. And Hans does look like me, not like his father, may he rest in peace or whatnot. As I followed that boy, I thought: Okay, I'll ask Hans for the horoscope, or whatever this ducal governor wants, it will be good for my son Christoph, who had only that very year pur-chased his citizenship, who wanted to move up in the world, as Hans had, and why not? We passed one of the small civic gardens where hurtsickle and blue chamomile had been left to overcrowd each other. A white rabbit crossed my path.

Outside of the ducal governor's home, a stone engraving of Einhorn's shield was being finished by a young mason. The shield showed a unicorn rearing up on its hind legs, like a battle horse. A vanity.

In the cool front room of the ducal governor's residence, the boy showed me to a seat next to a vulgarly stuffed pheasant and then left. The pheasant had green glass eyes. The feathers looked oily; the pheasant looked evil. Turned to evil, I will say, as opposed to born of evil. I was thirsty. I waited there, next to that unmoving pheasant.

Well, Kath-chen, I said to myself, you're not a child, you must be your own source of light. You can say yes to asking after a horoscope, or you can say no, but if you say no, you should say so politely.

I DON'T REMEMBER how long I waited. Then a woman walked into the room. A woman I knew. It was Ursula Rein-bold. Had she also been summoned? Her hair was falling from its bun. Her curls were sweaty. Her face was flushed. She was laughing, crying—both. Ursula has no children, looks like a comely werewolf, is married to a third-rate glazier. It's her second marriage. Two of Ursula's brothers, to my great misfortune, have come up in the world. One serves as Barber Surgeon to the Duke of Württemberg, the other as Forest Administrator here in Leonberg. The barber I call the Barber. The Forest Administrator, Urban Kräutlin, I call the Cabbage. It suits him, right? If you speak with people from Ursula Reinbold's hometown, as my son Hans has done, everyone there knows that as a young woman Ursula took powerful herbs given to her by the apothecary—the apothecary with whom she had an affair before her first marriage. Also widely known is Ursula's later affair with Jonas Zieher,

the freckled coppersmith, an affair that preceded her second marriage. Zieher was recently before the court for calling an honorable man a "devil's godfather" and was fined
five pfennigs. I am getting ahead of myself. What I want to
say is that Ursula's brother the Cabbage was there with her.
He was wearing a green hunting cape, and his posture was
poor, and his cheeks were red. Behind him was the whis-
kered ducal governor Einhorn, unkempt, and with a spotted spaniel in his arms. They smelled of drink. The crowd
of them looked like a pack of dull troubadours who, come
morning, have made off with all the butter.

I KNOW YOU'LL think it's not wise, Simon, but I'd like to
say something about Ducal Governor Einhorn, whom I prefer to call the False Unicorn. He's not from this area. He was
brought in by the marvelous Duchess Sybille, may she rest
in peace. The False Unicorn was to defer to Sybille's judgment in all matters. Then Sybille died so suddenly. The Duke
was distracted—with counting soldiers, signing treaties,
commissioning lace shirt cuffs. He was paying no attention
to affairs in Leonberg, and so the False Unicorn usurped
powers that should have reverted to the Duke. He began to
puff up, Einhorn did. He wore his hair longer. He had a new
collar made. He went around telling anyone who would listen that he was very bored in Leonberg, and that the women
in Stuttgart were more attractive. I will say that the False
Unicorn looks like an unwell river otter in a doublet.

   This manuscript is for after my case has ended, whatever the outcome.

   In Duchess Sybille's time, people traveled long distances
to see her medicinal garden. It was often open, for walking or festivities. There were pinks and bitter oranges and

a bright coltsfoot for cough. There were aromatic rhizomes for teething, rare scurvy weeds. There was a sesame plant that Sybille grew near hellebore. The two plants, if brewed together, could help with certain forms of madness, or so Sybille suspected. Even the downy thorn apple was tended in her garden. I could go on. Many mornings, with Sybille's permission, I took home cuttings. She was a woman of substance. I will add that she showed considerable interest in my research into herbs for St. Anthony's fire. She took even a peasant like me seriously. Not because of Hans. But because she was a woman of science. Sybille's garden is now all but a goat's grave. Einhorn has neglected it.

Simon, I understand your point: I don't want to make enemies where there are none. But I am laying out basic and indisputable facts about a man who, almost idly, as a pastime, became my persecutor.

THE FALSE UNICORN was slouched in a chair behind his desk. He scratched the chin of his spaniel, cooing, smiling. "It's a curious thing, how much God leaves behind for us to do. Well, whatever mistakes we make, he'll correct them in the end, so maybe it doesn't much matter what we do. Still, we have to look like we're making an effort, am I right?" This sermon was directed at his spaniel. Then he looked up. "Well, then. So. Where was I? Oh yes. Frau Kepler. That's you, yes?"

I said it was.

"It has come to my attention that you've used your very considerable dark powers to make this fine glazier's wife"—at this he looked over at Ursula, who nodded encouragement—"to make her moan, weep, cringe, writhe, be barren, and cackle."

"No cackling, sir," Ursula said. "But the other stuff—yes."

"All right, then, never mind about the cackle, Frau Kepler. But the rest."

"It was a poison she gave me that did it," Ursula said. "It was a bitter wine, a witch's brew."

"Don't interrupt him, sister," the Cabbage hissed. "Our apologies, sir."

Einhorn was kissing his spaniel's head. The spaniel licked his face. He set the spaniel down. "Sorry, so much going on," Einhorn said, with another smile. "I never thought when I was posted to a little backwater like this that there would be so many . . . tasks. This one wants alms, that one wants foraging rights, the carpenters don't want the stain of building the gallows. Where were we? Here: With the force of my office, I ask and insist and demand that you remove the curse or wound or injury or make an anti-poison using whatever powers devilish or whatnot are needed. I give you permission. I insist. So as to help this poor and kind and humble woman here before us today."

I looked around. Was he really speaking to me? The glass-eyed stuffed pheasant was silent. I turned to Ursula, who was looking into her lap. "This is silly," I said. "You're all drunk."

The Cabbage, rising from his seat, said, "We'll stop telling people you're a witch. Just remove the curse. Please. We won't ask for unreasonable compensation. Only for what's fitting. You're not going to get a better deal than this." It was like he was bartering for buttons. "What's done by sorcery can only be undone by sorcery, I have looked into it," he said. "She can't urinate without shouts of pain. She cries in front of important guests. Her husband says she doesn't function for him anymore. What did my sister ever do to you? If you hate the glazier, why not attack *him*? Don't you have any pity? You've had children of your own. She's my own mother's child—"

Suddenly he was on his knees, pulling at my skirts, begging me to cast my undoing spell, telling me she suffered terribly. I should have been more afraid, I know that now. But all I could see that Ursula had suffered from was grease stains on her blouse and hair that needed re-pinning. Unfortunately, I said as much.

Look, I had once upon a time enjoyed a laugh with Ursula at the market. She used to do a good imitation of the cheesemonger's stutter, and also of the old pastor's sermonizing. Her laughs were always mean, now that I think about it. When Duchess Sybille was building her summer palace in Leonberg, she hired many contractors and craftsmen in town. She hired my own son Christoph to make a magnificent pewter bathtub, for which she paid him one hundred and eighty thalers. Ursula pressed Christoph for an introduction for her husband the glazier, but Sybille didn't hire the third-rate glazier.

"You have to help her," the Cabbage said. "His Honor the ducal governor has ordered you to help her."

Ursula was weeping, or at least pretending to weep, and my own heart was moved, as if an infant were crying. I reached out toward her. I had an impulse to fix her hair. "You'll feel better soon," I said to her, stupidly.

At that, the Cabbage rose unsteadily to his feet and pulled his sword from its scabbard. It was a vain sword, made to look like rope at the grip, something a nobleman might commission and then reject at the last moment, leaving the sword maker in a bind. "Un-curse her, you toothless witch."

I have most of my teeth, and have lost only the most superfluous ones. But I didn't say that. Fear had finally made its way to me, where it belonged. It was as if God had forgotten where I was. There came to my mind the image of the severed thumb of a woman from near Augsburg. Her thumb had come off under the screws and rack. She was being tortured for her confession. No confession came, and she was sent back to her cell. The next day, she was cleared of the charges of sorcery. When the officers went to release her, they found her dead. No one contributed funds for her burial.

CONTRARY TO WHAT my children might believe, and though I was very afraid, I said only exactly what was proper. I said that it was wrong to surprise an old woman with such fantastical and abominable charges. And it was also not legal. Charges should be made before a court, not at the edge of a sword on a midday afternoon when an old woman is meant to be in her home. I didn't even have a male guardian with me. I repeated this, that I did not have a guardian.

In so many years of living one learns a thing or seven.

The Cabbage shook his sword.

I said I had done nothing to injure Ursula, and could do nothing to cure her.

"That's not true," the Cabbage said.

"Your brother is a proper surgeon to the Duke," I said. "If he can't help her, why would I be able to?"

"What's done by a devil can only be undone by a devil—"

"You're asking me to call the devil—"

"I am—"

"You'll have to call on the devil yourself—"

The Cabbage stumbled and stepped on the tail of the spaniel, who yelped.

"Now this is getting disorderly," the False Unicorn called out. He picked up his dog. The absurdity of my peril! At the same moment, the Cabbage pushed the tip of his sword against my chest, jingling a pewter bauble my son Christoph had made for me. The fabric of my dress tore. I screamed.

"This squabble is getting boring and dangerous," the False Unicorn said, stepping forward. "Put away the sword, please," he said to the Cabbage. Then he turned to me and asked me couldn't I just give the two what they wanted, just a little un-cursing, was it really so much trouble?

I said I was a poor widow called in recklessly against the rule of law.

"What law?" Einhorn said, as if waking up. A paper on a nearby desk interested him suddenly. Something had sobered him. He set down his dog and approached me. "What a stupid mess of a morning." He inspected me. "Your dress can be easily repaired." He reached past his waistcoat, pulled out three pfennigs. "This will cover the mending. Or you can mend it yourself. Whatever you want to do." He held the door open for me, and told me that I was welcome, more than welcome, to go. He said that all of us should go. Then to me: "It's true that you have no guardian. This encounter is, well, it is void. It hasn't happened. Under the eyes of the law, and therefore of the Lord, this afternoon is invisible."

Once when I went mushroom hunting, I came across a large elk missing the main part of its left antler. One of its eyes was swollen shut, crusted with pus. The elk's gait was unsteady. It smelled of yeast. Its grunts were unearthly. As that elk moved, the forest around it seemed transformed: the leaves had become eyes. I was being tested or invited or was about to die. Then the ill elk made another lowing sound, louder: as if dispossessing itself. Oniongrass tickled my ankle. The elk walked away. I walked home.

No, Simon, I didn't tell my family right away. I told no one right away. I didn't even tell you, as you know. I gathered some chicory on my way home and brought it to my cow Chamomile, who was looking well and unaltered. The next hours were curious, unsettling, dreamlike, ordinary. Maybe what happened had been meaningless. Maybe, as Einhorn had idly announced, it hadn't happened. I finished my washing, kissed Chamomile goodbye again, and then walked over to my son Christoph's home.

"I'm not in a good mood, and I don't want any advice," my son said when he opened the door. "No opinions, no takes, and no guidance, and no naysaying."

Okay, I said.

"A man wants to eat a whole sausage now and again."

His guild taxes had been increased. This had been announced at the guild meeting that very day.

He went on, "Of course, being junior, I said, Yessir, thank you very much and I agree completely, and I don't need to hear anyone acting as if another option was available to me."

Christoph's wife, Gertrauta, was near the stove, preparing a simple meal of dumplings in soup. "If they told him the sky was green, he would say, Yes, it is, sir, a lovely emerald." She was adding a lot of dill to the soup, which I hoped Christoph wouldn't notice, as he isn't friends with dill. "He'd say it was emerald and then he'd come home and complain to me about the price of tin."

"No one is hurt by saying the sky is green, Gertie," Christoph said. "No one goes hungry."

"He's a field mouse, Mama Kepler."

So I resolved to sit at this meal without making mention of my encounter with the Werewolf, the Cabbage, and the False Unicorn. I would put it out of my mind.

This resolution was, however, shortly challenged. Gertie had that very day read a pamphlet on the recent witch trials in Eltingen. "The three women were executed together, all on one platform. It's cheaper that way, you see, for the town. But they don't just use a knacker, they pay for a real executioner." Gertie loves to hear about the miser whose heart was found in a chest with his jewels after he died. About the holy nun who married the Moor who kidnapped her. She'll read any pamphlet she can get. It makes me not mind that I can't read myself.

"Two of the three women executed were named Barbara," she said.

Christoph wasn't listening, which was fortunate. He had a pile of receipts he was thumbing through with irritation, in between slurps of soup. Little Agnes, six years old, was playing nearby, moving beans around with a spoon.

"Two Barbaras?" I said, trying to do my part. "Must be an unlucky name."

"Maybe," Gertie said with a frown.

"Who's Barbara?" little Agnes asked from the floor.

"Oh, there are lots of Barbaras," Gertie said. "Don't worry about it."

Gertie told me that the executioner, a certain Jeronimas Breuning, had been hired from his regular place of work, in Nördlingen. This Breuning fellow let the women speak one last time at the end, "which is proper form, you know. You can't just knock people off with no word, like some knackers do." The first Barbara begged that her children be taken care of. She couldn't remember what she'd confessed to. She said she had no acquaintance with the devil. And that she hadn't been fed, making it difficult to think, and also that her legs had been broken.

"It's like I'm eating flowers here," Christoph said.

"There's no dill in it," Gertie lied.

"Did the Barbara cry?" Agnes asked.

"The pamphlet didn't say," Gertie said.

"Why do you believe everything you read, Gertie?" Christoph said. "Wasn't the Barbara standing there? If she was standing there, then her legs weren't broken—"

Gertie dismissed him with a hand wave. "Mama Kepler, I want you to hear this, because this is what I really wanted to tell you. That first Barbara confessed to only one wrong in her life. She said she had used a powder for mites in her young daughter's hair, and that the powder was too strong and that the powder had killed the little girl—"

"What little girl?" asked Agnes.

Gertie chopped on: "She'd used the powder on the advice of the apothecary. Can you imagine? Now, if that doesn't open your heart to the woman—"

"Did you know the Barbara?" Agnes asked.

Gertie told Agnes that no, she didn't, the Barbara had lived outside of town, beyond the Metzger farms, and it was said she had never been one for community, or weddings. "I did recognize the second Barbara. She sold soap at the market. An odd woman, smelled of pickle. When it was her turn to speak, all she said was that God knew her. That God knew her and that she knew God, and that there were no other words to say. Okay, but who doesn't God know?"

Christoph set down his receipts. "Gertie, is there any mustard? This isn't a soup, it's a sheep's meadow."

I said quietly that dill was very good for fertility, and also for bones. Gertie got the mustard.

Then Gertie told me she was about to get to what she called the good part. "The third woman had red hair," she said. "You know how that can be. That redhead was a real show. She stepped onto the platform laughing, saying that the executioner looked like a bumblebee."

Simon, I imagine that you're like me and have always avoided executions, but I have heard that all the executioners dress in bright and expensive colors; they make a lot of money and they show it. Gertie went on to say that the laughing redhead then confessed that she had killed seventeen mules, forty-three hens, six goats. She had made eighty-six cattle ill, of whom seventy-one had died. Or the numbers were something like that. She also claimed responsibility for the death of eleven infants. She had first met the devil when she was tending sheep. He was dressed in green. He was wearing a fine black wool hat with an unusual feather and was the most handsome man she had ever seen. The fiendish lover proved to be coldhearted, but he had made her promises.

I felt suddenly very tired. Agnes asked for more soup, which I fetched for her.

"The redhead contested only one point of her conviction. She said she had never danced at a witches' Sabbath. She didn't like dancing, and had always been against it."

"Huh," I said.

"Say what you will, but I love dancing," Gertie said.

Christoph was scraping the bottom of his soup bowl with the spoon.

Agnes's dress was wet with soup.

Christoph said, "The only important questions are how many thalers were seized from those women, and who did those thalers go to?"

When Christoph and Gertie got married, the match was

seen as a good one, with Christoph's handsome looks contributing to that evaluation. We must be honest and recall that Christoph, for all his qualities, was the son of a widow of little means. He had worked as a journeyman. With admirable swiftness, Gertie's father, a pewterer, had introduced Christoph into the Pewterers' Guild. I will add that Christoph did not disappoint him. I will not speak ill of my daughter-in-law. But I could not drink my soup. During the whole of her chatting, I had not managed more than a sip.

"You're not hungry?"

The milk of my cow Chamomile had been particularly rich of late, I said. The unseasonable heat had sapped my appetite, I said. Also the soup smelled delicious. I, for one, loved dill, which was also good for the blood. I was sure I would be regretting my abstention later. I asked if I could borrow a needle and thread. I stitched up the tear the Cabbage's sword had made in my dress.

Simon, you can probably imagine what it was to leave that harrowing, silly meal. And when I returned to my home, Jerg Hundersinger was there. Eighteen months earlier, Jerg had borrowed twenty-five thalers at a rate of five percent. He came to me now with a basket full of apricots, a clutch of woodruff. That was how I knew before he spoke that he would not be making his payment. No one likes a lender. No one likes a borrower. It hasn't been simple to be a widow for so many decades. It is sad that inheriting my dear father's house was good fortune for me.

I offered Jerg a cool drink.

He said no, thank you.

It was the second time that day my offer of refreshment had been refused.

But Jerg did take a seat. "I heard one of the pigherds came across two full bags of fine flour. Out in the west forest," he said. "What a trick."

"Luck of the woods," I said.

"Would you call it that?"

I ate one of the apricots. It was tart and tasted of lavender. I again offered Jerg a drink. It was hot outside. He was sweating.

He didn't respond to my refreshment offer. "I can't pay you this month," he said.

I said I wasn't surprised.

"But you can count on me," he said. "Before the grape harvest is over."

My mind was elsewhere. Little did I know how soon my

expenses would soar, the revenue from my fields frozen, the meager assets of my home seized.

"Funny thing with that pigherd and those bags of flour," Jerg said. "*I've* never found two bags of fine flour in the woods. I've never found a ribbon. I've never found a coin."

"I found a key once," I said.

"A key to what?"

"This was when I was a girl. I soon lost it again."

Jerg ate three more of the apricots he had brought. "I've never had that kind of luck," he said. "I was born with an extra thumb, you see."

He showed me his spare thumb. I'd seen it before, of course. Though I had rarely given it thought. You would think an extra digit would really stand out and command your attention.

He said, "You'd be sad to lose a finger, and even more aggrieved if you lost a thumb, yes. But this thumb has brought me nothing but trouble. When I was younger, I considered asking the barber to remove it, or even the butcher. In the end I lacked courage."

"You run an excellent bakery, Jerg," I said. I could see he felt low. "As did your father. His egg cakes were top. As are yours."

"The business is stuck in an endless drought," he said. "Maybe it's the thumb."

"I think it's the price of flour."

He finished the final two apricots. That was fine with me. Through the window, I saw the blacksmith's oldest daughter was walking by. Jerg went to the window, then knocked on the glass gently. "It's a very clear pane," he said. "Very nice quality."

It wasn't nice quality. It had been done by the third-rate glazier Reinbold years before, back when I had even shared a drink now and again with Ursula the Werewolf, who would ask after Hans's connections, who would compliment my knitting, who would show me what mushroom powder she now believed was her cure-all. "Why did you refuse a drink?" I asked Jerg.

"I'm not thirsty," he said.

"What do you think of the glazier Reinbold?"

Jerg didn't answer right away.

"What do you think of the glazier's wife?"

He looked at me. "You know her brother serves the Duke now. A doctor."

"Are you afraid of Ursula Reinbold?"

He shook his head. "They're half-formed people, if you know what I mean. They're hungry people spiritually." He knit his fingers together.

"Are you afraid of me?"

He sighed. "Kath, my wife calls me a devil at least three times a day. Do you think I then go checking under my hat for horns? It's a fallen world. Some of us are unlucky. Three years of bad crops. I've done nothing wrong. I suspect you've done nothing wrong, either."

"What am I accused of?"

"It's those of us who do nothing wrong that get into trouble. I don't listen to them, but some people do, Kath. Half-formed people, like I said. And greedy people. And people too proud to take a loan. Envious people. You know—the usual monsters. I'm sorry to say."

My time in the town hall was no dream. The unreal quality of the day was the illusion. The pronouncement by the ducal governor that what had happened had not happened—that was not the case.

I grew up in Eltingen, where those two Barbaras and one other woman were executed. I had no connection to those women, Simon, I want to be clear about that. I moved to Leonberg at the age of nine. I don't look down on the people of Eltingen, or on my daughter-in-law, who is also from there. My brother, Jeremias, a well-off peasant, still lives there. That said, it's not without meaning that the River Glems, which proceeds so comfortably through Leonberg, makes an uneasy turn at Eltingen, growing more narrow and vicious before then doubling again in width, lending a disturbed atmosphere to the whole area. Even as a young girl I recognized this. Several times I came across revenants in the forest there, but because I was a child, I didn't understand what I saw. The marigolds that grow in that section of the Glems have small leaves and almost no scent. Job's tears grow there in abundance, too. Do you know Job's tears, Simon? It's an odd plant, with no flower, and I've seen walkers make rosaries from the hard seeds, not that the rosaries bring them peace—they remain an anxious and fidgety bunch. God writes the gospel, Luther says, not only in the Bible but in the woods and in the stars. Some people worry about being born under an unlucky star. I don't. I worry about being born in an unlucky place.

I hurried back to Christoph and Gertie and Agnes, feeling foolish shame, and I told them what had happened to me. I hoped they would laugh at this old woman and say it was nothing. Christoph said, "That glazier is a despicable, lazy, half-witted ass of an ass with less heart than the smallest fish. I'll bet you a thousand thalers that talentless flea is at the center of this."

The glazier Reinbold of course was not even present at Einhorn's.

"But who put the idea in his silly wife's head?" Christoph continued. "That flea did. He's been speaking ill of me at every opportunity ever since he missed out on a commission from the Duchess. Am I the Duchess? I'm not. He told the fishmonger that I'm a hothead. Me, a hothead? And of course it's the fishmonger he tells, since he works with everyone and has no inhibitions. That little beetle wants to ruin my business at the very moment when I've taken on a loan to pay for this home. Duchess Sybille is dead! If I couldn't get him a commission then, I sure as hell can't get him a commission now. I don't know what we should do, Mama."

Christoph has been brought to court for disrespectful language more than once. It wasn't too bad. The parties met up, the words were declared as if never said, a fine was collected that went to the public works, and the dishonorable words are not even noted in the court documents, or so I'm told. A reasonable reconciliation. When made with people of honor.

"We should file for slander," Gertie said.

"Someone always thinks she's the sausage maker around here," Christoph said.

"Mama makes very nice sausages," little Agnes said.

"I'm not saying anything about sausages," Gertie said. "I'm saying simply: You need to file for slander. The guild won't be pleased to have a member suspected of being a witch's son, I can promise you that."

"And I can promise you that Einhorn doesn't want to be reminded of a drunken morning of extralegal accusation," Christoph said. "He looks totally incompetent in the situation.

Even criminal. And we're bound to file through his office—
how's that going to go? He'll make sausages of *us*. It'll be a
great big picnic of Kepler sausages—"

"We're not accusing Einhorn," I said.

"But it all goes together, Mama—"

Gertie said, sausages or no sausages, we absolutely could
not *not* file for slander, because she had read a pamphlet—

"I don't want to hear about your pamphlets—"

"With God and Mama Kepler as my witnesses, I am going
to tell you about this pamphlet," Gertie said. There was an
elderly woman in Sindelfingen, Gertie knew of the woman,
it was a true story, and this woman, who was known as
Martin's wife, had considered it beneath her to counter the
claims that she was a witch. The claims were made by liars beneath her station, she said, they were ridiculous and
she would not dignify their villainy with a formal retort,
that sort of thing. It was two young nurses who worked
in the elder home where she lived that were making the
accusations. And Martin's wife, despite her being above it
all—she found herself on trial. And what did the judges find
most suspect at the trial? That Martin's wife had never complained about being called a witch.

"What happened to her?" little Agnes asked.

"Her head was mounted on a pike at the town's edge.
Children threw stones at the head."

"Gertie, please," Christoph said.

In truth, Gertie's contributions were highly informative.
"They can only torture you for confession if there are two
reliable accusers, not only the one," she said. "I don't think
the Cabbage counts—he never said you hurt him, only his
sister, right? Now, if you have a relative who's also a witch,
well, then that *is* a problem. You don't have such a relative,

do you? If you do, I think then they can torture you for a confession straight off, but—"

Agnes said, "I know about witches, too."

"Go outside, Agnes," Christoph said.

"The butcher's boy said I was a witch from a family of witches," Agnes said.

"Which butcher's boy?" Christoph asked.

There was a terrible loud knocking at the door then. An image came to my mind, of my sickly grapevines being cut, and bleeding.

MY DAUGHTER, GRETA, looks not a day older than twelve, Simon, though she's over thirty, but still without child, though she has tried many remedies, but her husband, the pastor Binder, has refused to take fennel seed, and Greta doesn't push him. She's nothing like me, Greta. Leonberg had schooling for girls by the time she was of age. I prepared a biscuit with bacon bits for her each day. She told me as a girl that she was close friends with the number eight, and also was fond of eleven. Greta lacks the unhappiness and difficulty that has helped me so much in my own life, Simon. She thinks well of the world and everyone in it. Her father left to find fortune as a soldier when she was too young to remember, so at least she has that on her side.

The knock at the door turned out not to be a werewolf, or an imperial guard, or a beggar. It was Greta. She embraced me. "I know in my heart it will be okay," she said.

"Is there already a broadsheet about this?" Gertie asked.

"I overheard the tanner's children talking in the market," Greta said. "I ran over."

"You're too thin," I said to Greta.

"It's the season, Mama," she said.

"A small waist doesn't let the blood flow," I said, but she paid me no mind.

"The whole way running over I was thinking that they couldn't have meant witch when they said witch. Maybe they aren't fond of you, or they fear you, or they were drunk, but let's not grow problems. If we approach them with love, if we see God's reflection in them—"

"Then they'll know we're weak—" Gertie said.

"If we behave with grace, then they will behave with grace," Greta said. "I really believe that. If we show kindness and forgiveness, so will they."

"That's a deranged idea," Christoph said. "But I certainly would buy a round of cakes and beer for our enemies, if I thought it would help. That's what I was arguing toward before you came."

I asked, "Doesn't anyone want to know what the witch thinks?" None of them laughed or even gave me a half smile. Greta said she hoped I didn't make comments like that with others, that wasn't something that I did, was it? I said no, it wasn't.

"But what are you thinking?" Gertie asked me. "Is it that you're thinking we should ask for Hans's advice?"

I hadn't been thinking about that.

"Bringing Hans into this would go poorly," Christoph said.

"He invites envy," Greta said quietly. "People have strange ideas about him."

"It's more than that," Christoph said. "I remember when I was four years old I asked Hans for one of our pears, and what did he do? He said: It's not a pear, it's an apple. I said again that I wanted a pear. He said again that it was an apple, not a pear, and then told me that if I used the correct word then he'd give it to me. I screamed and shouted for the pear, and he still didn't give it to me."

Gertie said, "Christoph, none of us know what you're saying this for—"

"My point is he doesn't relent."

"Did you relent?"

"I was four years old!"

"I'm still confused—it was an apple, or it was a pear?"

"See, even though he's miles and miles away, he's making you ask the wrong questions about a pear."

"About an apple."

"And this isn't a situation for being unrelenting. Greta, Mama—tell Gertie I'm right about Hans, please. All respect to Hans. He's my older brother. But he's made his way in the world the easy way, through his studies. We're the ones who have stayed behind and managed. I'm beginning to think clearly now. If you want to take sausages out of the mouths of foxes, you don't fight the foxes. This is a sausages-from-the-mouths-of-foxes kind of situation."

＊ ＊
＊　None of us mentioned Heinrich. Hans, Christoph, and Greta are all still here. I had a fourth child who lived into adulthood, too, but who is now in heaven. You never met Heinrich, did you, Simon? Christoph didn't blame Heinrich. Nor did Greta. Even Gertie in her straightforward way didn't darken his name. No one in our family points blame at Heinrich. Not even, later, Hans. My son Heinrich is not the source of these accusations. But given the way Heinrich's final months have since been maliciously deployed by a growing number of enemies, I should like to clearly describe the sad details surrounding my Heinrich's return to Leonberg. This was in the winter before I was accused.

To do so requires saying a few more words about Ursula's brother the Cabbage.

Over these past three difficult years, the Cabbage, in his role as forest administrator, has halved the legally permitted hunting of stag. He has cut allowances for wild boar. He did this even after frosts had ruined vines not only in the mountains but in the valleys, too, and even as Leonbergers were especially stretched buying wood to keep warm. The rope maker was fined for serving a humble acorn coffee to guests, as the Cabbage charged that the acorns had been illegally foraged, though this is an eccentric and extreme interpretation of the pannage laws. The Cabbage jailed the widow Kircher, who returned with forest morels in her pockets, shortly after curfew. There are so many stories like these. It's discouraging to list them. When I gather branches to keep my cow Chamomile warm, I do so in very small batches, and only at midday.

During this time of austerity and greed, the Cabbage has had two new capes made for himself. One is made from a fine linen that catches the light. Another is wool, though it's trimmed coarsely in a cat fur, a distinction falsely claimed. I know this from the tailor Schmidt, who was later a cause of so much distress.

HEINRICH WAS BROAD-SHOULDERED, and handsome, and had a mole on his right cheek. He had an adventurous spirit that was ill-fitted to his actual life—like his father, for whom he was named. Heinrich's feet and hands were large, his stride was beautiful, balanced, and strong. He didn't get on well with the apprenticeship I set up for him with the cloth-cutter. I paid a fee for the ruined selvage. The apprentice-ship with the mason went better, at first. But Heinrich ended up in court for fighting. Heinrich didn't like to be corrected, or admonished, or disagreed with, or disliked, or, really, instructed or supervised; sometimes he didn't even like being spoken to. Such qualities are suitable ones for an emperor. Heinrich was excellent at threshing. Though often he slept in the field. At sixteen he ran away to become a soldier—another resemblance to his father.

I'd rather not talk about sad things. But it's been said that the Reinbolds were not the first to call me a witch—that before them, it was Heinrich.

What they're talking about is the winter of 1614. It now feels so long ago. This was the winter when Einhorn and Cabbage, both newly appointed and unusually stupid, sent officers to patrol the forest to protect the chestnuts. They hoarded them as feed only for the pigs of the nobility. My nephew's son went to prison for digging up wild ginger. These same officers also counted and monitored the hunting of the stag. No, Simon, I am not repeating myself, I'm being clear.

Heinrich had been away from Leonberg some twenty-five years, when, that winter, he returned. No advance word was sent. His two children were still in Prague, by the account of his wife, who also hadn't seen him, or heard word, in years. But when Heinrich arrived at my door on a Friday afternoon, I wasn't surprised. I knew he was alive. I don't have the words to explain it. The adder, born alone from its egg, knows how to catch its prey. It was like that. Heinrich's coat was torn and unclean, he looked shorter, his face appeared uneven. He was hungry. My heart was a spring sparrow's.

I had a loaf of spelt bread baking in Rosina Zoft's oven. Back then she let me make use of her oven, as she lets many make use of her oven. I went to Rosina—who I now understand is suggestible, and vicious—to fetch my bread so I could offer it to Heinrich. Rosina said she would as much expect a snowstorm in August as to see Heinrich Kepler back in town. I didn't pay her comment any mind. I didn't even know what she was getting at. I also am accustomed to taking sausage from the mouths of foxes, as Christoph says. At home I had some butter to offer Heinrich. And apples. But I wanted to offer him some milk. My own dear Chamomile was at that time dry. I had to ask Rosina for milk. Rosina is the wife not of Jerg, the six-fingered baker, but of Martin Zoft, the black-eyed baker. She gave me the milk begrudgingly. She said she was not the rich woman so many thought her to be, and that when everyone comes asking day in and day out, even a saint has only one liver to give. I didn't interrupt her complaints. I'm not much good at begging. I'm too proud. Or is it that I'm not proud enough?

I was later to suffer greatly for having begged that milk. Rosina was among the first to fall in with my enemies, as you know.

I gave Heinrich all that I had.

"This is nothing, Mama. I need meat."

I promised to get him meat as soon and as best as I could.

Heinrich sat at my table sullenly. His stories weren't easy to follow. He complained of the slender cut of the clothing of Spaniards. Including of the soldiers. He said that the songs of Gypsies were irregular, and yet people gathered round for them, and paid him no mind when a Gypsy was within a mile. He also said that Gypsy sweets were not sweet at all, and that their marzipan was bitter. He hated sticks for playing drums even more than he hated Gypsies. The sticks left his skin raw and were impossible to find before midday. The sticks still carried the spirits of living tree dryads, he said, spirits that had never helped him, had never answered when he knocked, had never kept him safe. And he was tired of the cold. Wherever and whenever it was cold. Cold was a devil. And worse than cold were monks, who served a false god and refused care to noble, tired soldiers.

It wasn't easy to obtain meat. I eventually got hold of a leg of goat. When I asked Rosina if I could use her oven again, for the goat leg—the whole neighborhood makes use of her oven, that's what it is to be a baker's wife—she shouted at me even as she shoved it in carelessly. When I came home, Heinrich shouted at me, too.

He wasn't well. When he slept, he ground his teeth. He had never done that as a child. At night he paced. Then most mornings I found he was already out. I didn't know where. Later I'd come home to find him quietly sharpening a knife at my table. In those moments, he spoke to me in a loving and sad way. By the week's end, he moved to his sister Greta's home. He died there a few weeks later, following fevers and confusion.

Even in the intensity of his confusions, Heinrich never called me a witch. People hear what it pleases them to hear. And whose policies were responsible for the shortage of meat in the first place? The Cabbage is worse than a fool. I never hurt his sister, the attender of many wedding feasts, the bearer of no children. I never hurt her in any way. Meanwhile, the Cabbage murdered Heinrich. He murdered him through his hoarding of the supply of stag and wild boar. And now Rosina works to murder me, through malicious rumors. The greedy misuse the world by striving to acquire it, said Martin Luther. Luther also spoke of those who misuse the world by struggling to renounce it—but of that trouble, Ursula Reinbold and her crowd have no understanding.

It was decided that a complaint of slander against Ursula and her brother the Cabbage should be filed as soon as possible. When I say it was decided I should say, rather, that I decided. I said to Christoph that I could see very well the logic of saying the sky is green if it pleases another, but I couldn't see the value of saying that I was a witch, to please another. Greta's sunny pleadings I ignored altogether. Gertie was on my side. But I couldn't file the complaint myself, nor would I have wanted to.

Christoph agreed to come with me to the court office as my guardian. It was his feeling, as the third son, that when there was manure to move, he was the one to move it. If there was a sausage to be forgone, he would forgo it. He wasn't complaining, he was being honest, he said—and I agreed with him. I'm not proud to say that on the walk over, another rabbit crossed our path. Was it an omen? Christoph kicked at the innocent creature, but the creature was faster than Christoph. Christoph was then stung by a bee. He cursed the Lord, but of course he meant nothing by it.

When we reached the offices of the court, a very short peasant was in line ahead of us, filing a complaint. I can see the man in my mind even now. His eyes were watering. His hands trembled. His fingers were blistered. A poultice of wolfsbane would likely have helped him.

A sweaty clerk asked the peasant to kindly speak up, please.

Startled, the man took a small step back.

I didn't recognize the clerk. His shirtsleeves were frayed,

but he wore a handsome dark doublet, and had a bright green kerchief with a violet embroidered on it.

The short peasant whispered more loudly, with some emotion. His employer, he explained, a certain Basilius Beserner, had, in a fit of anger, taken his hat from off his head and thrown it in front of pigs. The pigs were being moved to the market, and—

"What a man does with his hat is no business of this office," the clerk said with a sigh. He wiped his forehead with the kerchief. "This is outside the purview—"

"It was my hat—" the quiet man said.

"He was wearing your hat?"

"The hat off my own head, sir."

"Let's start again at the beginning," the clerk said.

The man was close to tears. "My name is Lucas Banft. I'm a pigherd in the occasional employ of—"

"He's been insulted sir," I said, trying to help out.

"You're not his legal guardian, are you, young lady?" he asked.

"Of course not," I said.

"She doesn't mean to offend," Christoph said.

Legal guardians are men, of course. And I'm an old woman, also of course.

The clerk said, "I'm going, if you please, to ask complete quiet from you. I'm watery in the hearing. It's a small thing from a fever that started on St. John's Day, but I won't let it set me back. I'm interested in serving our citizens and aim—"

The peasant started up again with his story about his employer throwing his hat in the mud, in the path of the pigs. As I myself was there to lodge a complaint about being slanderously and perilously accused of witchcraft, you might think that I would look down upon the pigherd's hat complaint. But that is in no way the case. It only fortified my feeling that one has to insist on justice. At that point in time, the threat of torture and execution did not feel real or possible. I wasn't at the court offices from fear, I was there from anger. It was the terrible incorrectness of the accusations that had me out of my home.

When the pigherd finished stating his position, I suggested he add, to the case of being dishonored through the muddying of his hat, the point that ungratefulness is theft.

"Now, now, step back," the clerk said. "Summary judgments are reserved for the part of the chancellor, not for the part of idle bystanders."

"It's not a judgment," I said. "It's a simple truth."

"I'd like to add it," the pigherd said.

The clerk sighed. His ink smudged. He said he was new to the job; he had thought it would be an easing off his former work as a scribe; his wife was lame but of a good family and this work had been arranged through her people and he had been asked, in ways both direct and not, to be grateful in various forms. He agreed, then, that ungratefulness is theft, in the eyes of enough people. He appended it to the pigherd's complaint.

I'M THINKING, WHAT happened next? Oh, I know. Christoph has a pipe with the face of a bearded man on the front that makes him appear vain and unwise. When I say "him," I mean Christoph, not the man on the pipe, who looks reasonable enough. I asked Christoph who gave him the pipe. I didn't think he'd spend his own money on a vanity like that. He dismissed my inquiry. Anyhow, when the matter with the short peasant was concluded, Christoph lit up his silly pipe.

"Ah yes, if you would be so kind as to extinguish the pipe, sir," the clerk said. He covered his mouth with his curious green kerchief. The clerk, who as you know later proved to be a kind man, was named Sebald Sebelen. I can hear his strained politeness even now.

Christoph barked at Sebelen that he'd never heard such a feathery request, and was everyone against him, too, now? Was the whole family going to be maligned? He would smoke as any other man might smoke, wherever he might smoke.

Whereas I thought this would be a moment when Christoph elected to display his much-talked-about agreeable approach.

"I've got sensitive eyes, sir, I beg of you, it's no special treatment. Also a cough. My wife says in another life I was a hummingbird—"

Christoph refused.

Sebald took a scarf from a drawer and tied it over his face.

We filed the complaint of slander, with some difficulties.

Sebald asked Christoph questions, which Christoph relayed to me, which I answered to Christoph, who would then rephrase what I had said to Sebald. I wouldn't call the process efficient. And when the clerk spoke, his speech was muffled by the scarf. And even so, Christoph wouldn't extinguish the pipe.

"When will the case be heard?" Christoph asked the clerk in closing.

"I'm new here," Sebald said through his scarf.

"Jew here?" Christoph said.

"*New* here," I said.

"I don't care if he's pumpkin stew or the blood of Christ," Christoph said. "I want to know when the case will be heard."

As it turned out we were in court by the soonest available date, in October. But we weren't in court for my slander case. Instead we were in court in October for a case involving Christoph, who had gotten into a bloody tavern fight with three men from Eltingen, one of them the third-rate glazier's cousin. The men had insulted his mother, of course. The Werewolf Ursula and her brother twice failed to turn up for their questioning, and this was delaying my slander case indefinitely. I was born during the Schmalkaldic battles, my father told me. He said that even his one-armed uncle was at the town wall with a scythe, that all the Lutheran armor multiplied the sun. I think that sense of fight has stayed with me. Christoph spent three days in prison and was fined four thalers.

Since the glazier and his wife have succeeded in reversing Katharina's civil case against them into a criminal case against her, I thought it would be clarifying if I, Simon, explained myself here. I stepped in as Katharina's legal guardian after Christoph's intemperate first performance. That was more than three years ago, almost four. I am an old man, and ill-suited to the position. And to think that I had expected everything to be resolved within a season, or two at most. Certainly I hadn't expected the situation to escalate as it has. I will stand by Katharina nonetheless, as to stand by is fundamental to my character. However, calumny has a broad shadow, and since I am a friend to Katharina—I think it's fair to use that term—that shadow has reached my doorstep, though hopefully it has not made its way into my home. If someone were to interrogate me as to my motives or knowledge, I would like to be prepared.

Let me start with how I first came to be acquainted with Katharina.

I try my best to like people. To expect good from them. If you see someone as a monster, it is as good as attaching a real horn to them and poking them with a hot metal poker. I really do think so. In order to avoid turning people into monsters by suspecting them of being monsters, I do my best to keep myself mostly to myself. Even as I live and work, here, quietly, in a city, surrounded by people. A monk without a monastery, that was my hymn for many years. Even a monastery—too much of a crowd. Monasteries may as well be called prisons or dens of sin, I'm told. Living in

Leonberg allowed me to be unseen, in plain sight. Customers see me as they might see a water pitcher or a hammer or a patch of shade—as a thing for a particular use. That's how I like it. A home in town is preferable to a home in the countryside for another reason: in the countryside, you have no choice but to take care of whoever is passing by, but in town, there's always another house near enough. Also, here in town, I live near a church. The piety of the building extends beyond its walls. It can seem as if I've attended sermons even if I don't leave my kitchen table. I'm nearly there. I'm an annex.

As long as I am speaking too freely, I'll share my one small rebellious conviction: Luther said man has an independent and direct relationship with God. If he had really followed his ideas out, or if the rest of us had, shouldn't there be no church left at all? But he didn't follow that idea out to where it leads. Instead, he married one of the nuns he liberated. He lost his way. A bit. No, I take that back. I have the utmost respect for Luther. He must have followed through his idea in his own way. I believe very much in following through. Standing by, and following through. And not seeing people as monsters.

Still, to be wary of a neighbor, or of anyone, is simple good sense.

Katharina, when she moved into the house next door, disrupted my peace and quiet.

BUT NOT AT first. She had moved into the house next door about two months prior to my first speaking with her. I respected that she, like me, kept herself to herself. My new neighbor was to all appearances a busy old woman, who had grown children assisting her in her move into the house.

The most fuss was made over that cow, Chamomile. Katharina set up Chamomile's quarters with much more attention than I saw given to the rest of the home. Over the next days, I was greatly reassured, as I saw my new neighbor was not one of these older women who sit at their window knitting or washing or whatnot and watching all who come and go. She was busy. She had visitors. She often had her back to her window. Early evenings she cleaned Chamomile's quarters meticulously. In one or another lively way she was always doing something other than paying attention to me.

Now I will say, so that I don't seem eccentrically attentive to her not paying attention to me, that, although it was a long time ago now, I have in my past had trying, even life-threatening attention paid to very small and minor actions of my own. I've nothing to feel guilty or secretive about in life. But a fear of being misunderstood has stayed with me for a long time, for a lifetime.

So Katharina and I exchanged no words and that was wonderful.

Then, in April, early, on a half-moon, she came knocking at my door. Midday! Holding a clutch of cowslip with flowers of pale purple and inky blue. "A lung is a sheep," she said to me. She walked past me, and into my home, uninvited.

A sheep?

She indicated the white spots on the leaves of the cowslip.

"They don't look like sheep," I said. 'They look like spots."

She shook her head. "That's not what I mean."

This was what sheep eat, and she thought my lungs would do well to eat the same. She said these cowslips had the right density of spots, which is rare, and that when she saw them on her walk back from the Junker's eastern fields, she knew she would bring them over, God may as well have pointed his finger at them. "I hear your cough day and night," she said. "It's a wet cave; you've been using syrups. You may as well lick a sow, it's not going to help. Have you seen how full and healthy the sheep in the east valley are? These cowslips are from the east valley. The sheep do well on them, are kept healthy by them, and a lung is a sheep. Your lungs are sheep, my lungs are sheep—that's what lungs are. Every gravedigger knows it." She set the spotted leaves down at my table, where I was working on a buckle. She looked at my buckle. She looked around my home.

"I'm no good with plants," I said.

She told me to soak the leaves in wine and drink the brew five times a day, on its lonesome, without meals—she said that was what she came to share with me.

Yes, I said.

Then she said she had moved into the house next door to mine.

Yes, you have, I said.

She said that she had bought it with the inheritance from her father, Melchior. Had I known him? He had run an inn in Eltingen. Maybe I had known it?

I said no, I had not known it.

She looked at me as if I were speaking a strange language. "Everyone your age knew it," she said.

I was out of practice speaking with people about anything outside of saddle-making. Though I also had a lot to say about stirrups and buckles. But even in labor: my best business came in the form of written requests. My reputation is separate from my personhood. I didn't want to become more practiced at talking to people. I'm a happy person. When a soup tastes good, leave it alone. I didn't need a friend.

I said to Katharina simply that I was sorry if my cough had been bothering her. Myself, I hardly noticed it.

AS KATHARINA WAS hopefully leaving, my daughter, Anna, came through the door. I haven't mentioned Anna. Anna is twenty-five. She had smallpox when she was fourteen years old, and her face still has the scars. I don't know if she is shy of this. It's not a subject of which we've spoken. Anna curtsied politely to Katharina, then turned and gave me a look of fire. She does not like to have visitors.

Anna's mother was twenty years younger than me, and she died in childbirth. I should have remarried, for Anna's sake, but I sometimes am astonished I managed to marry the first time.

"The pastor gives a dispensation for wearing powder," Katharina said to Anna.

"What?"

"It's not wrong to wear powder, if it's to good purpose," she said.

Anna shook her head.

"It's a little thing and you shouldn't be ashamed. These days people talk about makeup as if it's for loose women and for men playing girls in plays. Or for Italians. Maybe rouge or lip paint would be too much. I respect humility. But I wouldn't leave my life behind in a cave on account of some new idea about face powder. I used it as a young girl and it set my shoulders back, and my own daughter, whom everyone says married very well, married at twenty-seven, her virtue unquestioned."

Even I could see that Anna was as close to tears as a full

moon. But I didn't want to say anything. Knowing Katharina as I know her now, I imagine she saw herself as giving motherly advice to a motherless girl. However, I believe that all Anna heard was that she was correct in hiding her face from public view.

After Katharina had left, I said to Anna, "She's just an old, old lady who lives alone."

"She's a prune," Anna said. Which is unusually unkind for her. "You have to be more clear with people, Papa. She probably feels welcome here. She's going to come over again and again, if you're not clear. You have to be clear. You can't just not say something and hope for the best."

"She looks even older than me," I said to Anna. "She'll likely not be our neighbor for long."

MAYBE KATHARINA'S HERBS would have helped my cough. I didn't take them. They remained on the table in a pretty decay. The flowers were various colors rather than one color. In that way, they looked to me like a family. One reason I may have made errors and failed to understand Anna is because I myself came from a family of eleven children, of which I was one of the many middle ones. I was the pale purple bud, the weakest—but I lasted the longest. Not through merit. Once Katharina's herbs were wilted, I went out under the slim moonlight and buried them in the garden.

A few months later, there was that terrible flood. My home is set rather lower than Katharina's. And lower than the church—lower than all around me. The water came all of a sudden, and was rising. Three bags of grain were ruined before I had even paid mind. Anna was away at her aunt's home in Linz. I could have waved down help, or called upon the closest neighbor. But I didn't. It's contrary to my character. I had once nearly drowned in a lake, because I'd been too embarrassed to call out or wave my arms. By chance some perch fishermen passed by, and they saved me.

My workshop floor was transforming into a pond. I was facing the ruining element alone. I was ready for the destruction. I felt queerly at peace. Oh, I would make a small effort, so that I could argue before the angels that I wasn't a suicide.

But then it turned out I wasn't facing the rising waters alone. Before I could even properly account for how many of my tools had been washed away, and where I could find a high place to transfer my leather cuttings and my favored jacket—there was Katharina. That old woman. Three young men were with her. They dug a channel for the water to run out. One hung a line to which we clipped the leather skins. Another led out my goats and lambs, talked the pastor into sheltering them in the church through the storm. Through all this, Katharina was decisive as a ship captain: calling out plans in what I now recognize as her usual off-putting way. Her intrusive nature had this resplendent underside.

I slept in Katharina's home for about three weeks, as I repaired my own.

That was when we started playing backgammon.

She was a frustrating opponent. She leaves her tiles unprotected even when not forced into that position. That said, she does have a charismatic attack. I've pointed out how this doesn't go well for her. Except against children. But she didn't change her strategies. Well, a relationship developed. The rough breeze of her blew life back into the dying ember of me. I am not speaking of love, or of any of its pale shadows. What we had was a sturdy and practical fellowship.

When I was young, women often took me into their confidence. Single women, married women, widowed women. Also girls. I knew about their flirtations, their anxieties, their physical pains, and much more. I lived elsewhere at this time. What did those women read in my face? I'm not an unusually nice or understanding person. I'm easily confused by people. I'm unusually bad, for example, at predicting who will love, or despise, whom. My own father's fondness for me—I found it mysterious. What I remember thinking as a child about this was that I had done nothing to earn his affection. He said often that I was like my mother, who was dead.

When Katharina needed my help, I told her I would stand by.

After Christoph's humiliating run-in with the law, then we did decide to write to Johannes. To Hans. Greta penned the letter. She's more gracious than Christoph or myself. That was October. October of almost four years ago now, my God.

We heard nothing back. This was shortly after the feasting of the pigs on acorns. Do you remember that? The summer had been very dry and one might have imagined the acorns would be small, but that wasn't the case. One of the rope maker's pigs ate so much that the beast became wild and disorderly and was seen walking in circles, and was later found dead in the furrier's fields to the south. No one knew why the beast had chosen there to die, of all places, but there he was. I thought of the short peasant whose hat had been thrown in front of the pigs. I had run into him in the market. He had received his writ of apology, for which he had paid twenty-five pfennigs to keep a copy for his home.

Christoph also had paid for a copy of the settled agreement from the fight between him and the men from Eltingen; the names he had called them he had retracted, formally; and they retracted their words as well, formally. The whole event became as if written in water.

Why hadn't my case advanced, as theirs had? I didn't speak to you much of these worries of mine at the time, Simon. I felt I had asked enough of you, and I found our evening backgammon a relief.

One chilly Tuesday afternoon, Jerg, the six-fingered baker, knocked on my door again.

"Their bread is very lightweight," he said. He had a squash

with him, which he set down on the table. It was a green and yellow squash, with a long neck; it resembled a heron, but a sad heron.

"Whose bread, Jerg?"

Rosina and her husband's. Their bakery. The bakery closest to us. I will remind you that Rosina had begrudged me the milk for Heinrich, and also had been miserly about making space in her oven for his meat.

Jerg took a seat again at the table, petting the neck of the squash he had brought over. "They never get fined for selling underweight loaves. I've been fined six times, and my bread is heavier, and I'm quick to give a thirteenth loaf. The scales can't be trusted. They mess with them, you know."

I thought he was next going to explain why he wasn't able to pay me back that month. Instead, he looked down at the floor and said, "She says you rode a goat backward to death. The wife of the baker. She's saying it to anyone who will listen. And she says that you poisoned Ursula with a bitter wine. I don't like to bring bad tidings, but I thought it was wrong, and that you should know."

I laughed. They may as well have been saying I was a young bride, it was so absurd. I reassured him that I knew all about her treachery, her small heart, her viciousness and envy and stupidity and tendency toward falseness and evil. But no one would listen to her.

Jerg shrugged. "Maybe it's nothing, maybe it's something. There was another person, too. Not a fellow I knew. He said twelve years ago, you asked him to help spread manure in your fields. You were alone. He refused you. And that after that, he felt a pain in his legs."

"Who said that?"

"A thresher. I don't know his name. Crooked nose and half-bald."

"And why was he saying that? What else was he saying?" These tidings bothered me more than Rosina. Rosina was a nothing with which I was already acquainted. This other mystery vulture—that was more distressing.

Jerg shrugged again. It seemed to be all he knew how to do. "He has been heard to say that his leg pains—that they were caused by your witchcraft. That you punished him for not helping."

"Who was he telling these stories to?"

"Whoever was there. He was proud. As if he'd battled a dragon. It was told in that kind of way. The baker's wife, she was excited, too. As if she'd outwitted a goblin."

I took the heron squash the six-fingered baker was offering in place of his payment; or maybe it was the gossip he was offering in place of his payment.

Do you understand that any false testimony you knowingly give will provoke God's great anger in your earthly life and will deliver your soul unto Satan upon your death?
That sounds right.

What is your name, age, and profession?
Martin Vollmair. I work as a gravedigger in Rutesheim.

Can you tell us about the unusual request that was made of you?
The people I meet aren't out to buy a loaf of bread. They're often in a peculiar mood. Though not always. I receive many unusual requests.

We want to speak to you about Katharina Kepler.
Okay.

Eighteen years ago, Frau Kepler asked you to dig up her father's skull?
No. Not exactly.

Seventeen years?
No, I mean not exactly asked me to dig up.

You are under oath, Herr Vollmair.
It is my habit to tell the truth at all times.

Okay. Tell us what happened.
Frau Kepler was visiting a different grave. Not her father's grave. She was visiting the recently dug grave of one of her

grandchildren. The wreath on her father's grave was dry and old. She brought over some blessed thistle, some holly, and made it into a fresh wreath for her father's grave. Not the most regular of wreaths. But it was nice.

Then what?

I had not dug the grave for Frau Kepler's grandchild, but I was digging another grave nearby, for a shoemaker. I see so many things. You never think of a gravedigger as a great witness of life, people treat me as if I'm not there, but then this woman, Frau Kepler, she was calling me. Turns out I was working not far from the grave of Melchior Guldenmann—that was her dad. I had known the man somewhat.

And Frau Kepler made an unusual inquiry?

She said she'd heard it was a fine thing to have a skull covered in silver, that you could drink from that. She asked me: Could I dig up her dad's skull? She wanted to send it to her son the astrologer in Prague.

Do you often receive such demonic requests?

I was once asked to dig up the liver of a dead infant. I didn't do it. But the person didn't mean any harm. Another time I was asked to bury a beautiful shepherd dog. Not just anywhere, but in the main graveyard. You want to know who asked that? I'm under oath. I'll tell you. The Duchess made the request. Dogs aren't allowed a Christian burial. Now, that seems obvious to me, even uneducated as I am, but of course grave-digging is my expertise. I learn not to judge but to explain. Very simple. Also common is people come digging to retrieve brooches. Or rings. These might be common thieves. Or it might be someone who comes from love. Someone who regrets their decision of what to bury with the dead. It's often the gravedigger who's blamed! But

I ask you: Would a man risk his good name and employ for a crime so easily solved?

Let's return to Frau Kepler.
There are different opinions on whether a man may choose to come back for his wife's ring. Or a mother for her child's toy. I'd like to give a sermon one day, on what I've observed of the nature of humans. I tell you it would be very engaging to the public. Much more engaging than the pap usually served on a Sunday.

To confirm: the accused asked you to dig up her father's skull.
No, but close. She asked me both if it would be possible and how much it would cost to dig up and—

How did you answer?
I said I'd need to ask my boss-fellow, who at the time was Pastor Graf. He's the fellow who was making the majority of decisions about the graves, about their location, all the questions in the rare circumstance of someone being moved, and so on.

She persisted?
She saw it would be a whole back-and-forth and round the bend—she said to never mind about it.

She feared your boss, Pastor Graf?
That wasn't my impression, no.

A skull is a legally recognized tool of sorcery.
We all have skulls, sir. This was many years ago. I'm willing to talk as long as it is useful to you sirs, all of you, but I find this all very strange to have so many people interested in this conversation. Of all the different conversations I've

had in my years of digging graves, this was not one of the remarkable ones.

Thank you for your time, Herr Vollmair.
It's a funny thing being called up like this. I've enjoyed myself, all told. How did you find me, again?

Now, Simon, of course I worried that Hans wasn't answering Greta's letter because he feared for his own work and life as the son of an accused mother. You told me he would stand by. But did I want him to stand by? Greta and Christoph tried to hide it from me, but they, too, were being threatened, in ways about which they are still secretive. Hans had not written saying he would stand by. But nor had he written saying he would not stand by.

But I was still me, wasn't I? I was cleaning and feeding and grazing my animals, I was cutting my grasses, spinning, sewing, reaping, even dreaming. I dreamed of awaking from a rising chatter of locusts. I looked down at my hand and saw it become young and smooth, then wax old again, and back to young, its appearance cycling like the moon. In another dream my husband, Heinrich, had returned. He was furious with me, he wanted money, he called me ugly names; then in another moment he had a quail in his hand, and he put an arm around my waist, and whispered kindnesses into my ear; then he was my son Heinrich, and was throwing dishes in the kitchen; and then he was again a baby in my arms. It was unpleasant, and tiring, to have to go through so many feelings each night.

One cold November morning I was tending to Chamomile, bringing branches in to warm her, and she looked at me very directly, very deliberately. I asked her, What is it? She leaned her head against my neck. She was telling me something, that was my strong sense. I didn't need to wait for the stars or even my children to clear the brambles around me. She expected something of me.

So on that Tuesday, a day so clear and blue that I suspected no one else would want to attend to troubles, I went in directly to the town hall, to look in again about the matter of getting my trial on the schedule. The slipperiness of the Werewolf and Cabbage could not delay things indefinitely—there were rules, if only they would be enforced.

And you, Simon, were kind enough to escort me as a guardian.

The same clerk, Sebald Sebelen, was there. The one who had the green kerchief with the violet on it, who had taken down the pigherd's complaint, and never raised his voice in asking Christoph to stop smoking.

Sebelen was resting his head on the desk. He was sweating, though outside there were flakes of snow. I cleared my throat to alert him to our presence.

"Ah, the astrologer's mother," he said. He appeared startled. He wiped his brow. "You're not out among the puppets?"

"Puppets?" I thought maybe he meant townspeople, who, sure, they had indeed become puppets of a kind.

"The market," he said. "I passed through there this morning as they were setting up." He blew his nose in his beautiful kerchief. He was speaking of the market where the Dutch and Italian traders set up their stalls selling vanities none of us need, and fill the children with wants they didn't have before. I do like the musicians there, however, and am especially fond of the viola de gamba, which has no false sweetness to its sound.

I said I wasn't someone with a strong interest in puppets.

"I so like the way they move," the clerk said, wiping more sweat from his forehead with a small dirty handkerchief he had. "I always wanted one as a child, but my mother was afraid of them."

"Herr Sebelen, I'm here because I've received no update on my case."

"Is that right?"

"Do you know when it will be heard?"

"I can write your concern in the log," he said.

"It's been nearly half a year," I said. "The pigherd's case was heard. Dozens of cases have been heard."

"Well, I will most certainly write that in the log, then."

"If I came here to tell you a barn was on fire, would you write that down, too?"

"Oh yes, that poor man! That fire was because he was doing his threshing by candlelight, you see."

"What fire?"

"Peril is ever-present," Sebelen said, wiping his sweaty brow. "I thought you were speaking of the fire at the Hochsfeld barn. It's difficult times. Attendance at sermons has dropped. I myself have been too ill to attend. I haven't taken Communion for twenty-one days."

"I'm sorry to hear that, Herr Sebelen. To hear all of that. Really. But I'm asking you: if you know something about my case, I'm begging you—give me some clue."

He now wiped his neck with the green kerchief. "I'm disappointing a higher number of people than at any other time in my life," he said with a little laugh. "I would've loved to have spent this day at the fair, among the puppets. My wife says she should have married my brother. If my luck continues this way, maybe she'll have the opportunity. I'd love to meet your estimable son one day. I'm sure he can tell me something wise. Would he do a horoscope for a little guy like me?"

"Maybe. Probably. I can't really say. He's very busy." It was painful to be reminded of Hans's silence.

"Now, is this your guardian with you?" asked Sebelen.

Simon, you will recall you were shy.

"He is," I said. "He is my legal guardian and also my neighbor."

He liked you, Simon. I saw the look pass between the two of you. Then you gave that nervous sneeze and cough. He produced a second of those beautiful handkerchiefs, from another pocket, and offered it to you. That one handkerchief became two. It was like he was a magician.

You said, "She's asking only to know if the case is scheduled. She means no trouble." You returned the handkerchief to him. You took off your gloves and set them at the table, as if you meant to stay.

Herr Sebelen looked around the hall, which held only the three of us. "The matter is above me."

Above him was the mounted head of a stag. With weird painted glass for eyes.

Herr Sebelen wiped his brow again. He was seized with another very strong cough, covered his mouth with his green handkerchief, turned away. We waited for the cough to pass. "My apologies," he said, catching his breath.

Then you spoke again. "Please, Herr Sebelen. You've got ears. You must know something. You can trust my discretion. I think you sense that. What is the status of Katharina's case? I'm asking you not in your role as an official, but in your role as a man here in a room with us."

You touched his hand then, and I mean no slander when I say it was like you were a wizard. Sebelen changed. He looked down at his log: "Well, it's very discouraging." He lowered his voice. "Someone might say to you that if you had spent many hours in this dim room, you might have heard that the ducal governor was advised that his involvement in your being called to accusation was, well, less than would be smiled upon by the legal offices in Stuttgart. A close examination of the proceedings would not flatter him."

Simon, here you asked the question: "He wants to hide his role?"

"It would be an embarrassment," Sebelen said. Then he started coughing yet again. "More than an embarrassment. It might put his position at risk. Very much at risk."

"You're saying that he made a mistake, and that I will pay for his mistake," I said.

"Yes, I would say that is a fair summary of the situation." Sebelen then stood up. His face was sickly yellow, I could see that now that the daylight fell on it fully. "I wish you hadn't filed that slander claim. Maybe things would have gone differently. If I had understood the situation, I would have advised you." He then looked at you, Simon. "I worry for you as well, sir. But whatever you do—whatever both of you do—I ask you to consider not adding me to the list of people likely to pay for the ducal governor's mistakes. A criminal case is now gathering force every day, against your gracious self, Frau Kepler. I expect that case will get to the courts before yours ever does. I'm not suited to this position. Not at all. Not suited to any position, really. But this job is of more than the usual value to the well-being of my family. I would recommend you leave. I hear the yipping of the ducal governor's spaniel."

I mention here, as it is the way with the world, that I heard that the clerk—who had been kind to me, in truth—was down with what some said was the plague a few weeks later.

Linz, January 2, 1616

Solemn, prudent, wise, and especially reasonable
gentlemen, I duly lend you my service to the best of my
ability, with joyful New Year's wishes.

On December 29, my heart racing, I read a bewildering
letter sent by my sister, Margaretha Binder, dated October
22. From what I could gather, your court is investigating
several persons implicated in the raving fantasies of
a local housewife, a woman hitherto considered to be
totally unserious, and who now has surely lost her mind.
My dear mother, an honorable septuagenarian, has been
brought under suspicion by this demented person and
now stands accused of giving her an enchanted potion,
which is supposed to have caused her insanity. This
same suspicion has spread in the form of baseless slander
among the townspeople, who've let themselves be blinded
by the devil—the deity of all darkness, superstition, and
misunderstanding. Forgetting God, they sought the help
of the devil and his occult devices, of which they claim
to have some blameless understanding. They did this
to determine whether their alarm was justified, though
it's well known by legal scholars who've written on this
horrid subject that the use of sorcery against sorcery
(*maleficium contrario maleficio solvere*) is equivalent to
a pact with the devil. Such a blasphemous offense is

punishable by torture, especially when used against an innocent person. The devil manifests himself in superstitious fears.

I've heard this account not only from my sister, but from other trustworthy relations as well. My heart is shattered by the thought that such underhanded measures have been taken against my kindly and beloved mother, increasingly forlorn in her old age. The authorities have even gone after her son, my brother, threatening him with imprisonment or worse if he refuses to pay her expenses. What's more, under the pretense of royal authority, my mother was seized and threatened with weapons as if they meant to kill her on the spot. Finally, using flattery, empty promises of harmless intent, and all other villainous tricks, they pleaded with her to perform the alleged ritual even as it went against God; and so it's they who've openly condoned the use of sorcery, and they who deserve the most severe punishment.

Taking all of this into account, it's no wonder that my distressed and frightened mother put her ire aside to perform what has been described, to save her own life. She was forced to do it, notwithstanding that the Almighty forbids it, and although she acted innocently, a judge without sufficient understanding of codified law recommended torture, which would surely end in a gruesome death. The books are full of such vivid examples. And yet, now that God himself has mercifully restored the health of her undeserving accuser, these devils continue to attack my poor, innocent mother, and dishonor her good name, wanting nothing less than to cut her throat.

All the while, she's supposed to believe they're helping her by using fear and superstition to banish one devil with another.

From my sister's letter, I'm further given to understand that in addition to claims against an old woman's life, honor, and property, they're also prosecuting her entire circle, including my sister, her landlord, and my brother. It wasn't made entirely clear, but it seems that I, too, may be subject to investigation. Through others I've learned that two motions have already been filed, although I'm not sure whether they implicate me or my siblings, or whether I'll need to act in defense of my own property and endangered reputation, should they try to claim that I myself practice forbidden arts. Such overblown and ludicrous allegations could blight my fifteen years of imperial service, which would surely break my precious mother's heart.

By reason of my double connection to the case, I hereby petition the court to provide copies of all relevant documents and communications submitted thus far, as is within my right. My personal courier will deliver these to the Cannstatt post office, to be sent to Prague. If my health allows, I'll apply for leave to return home. Meanwhile, I humbly request that the court take heed of my interests and considerations. It's not my intention to hinder a lawful course of action; yet because it implicates my siblings (and our family name), I will not be left unaware of any proceedings or sentences, nor shall I waive my right to be informed of motions made against any party under Leonberg's jurisdiction, on behalf of my honorable, widowed mother and her property. Together with my prominent friends and benefactors, I will defend her until the matter is concluded according to the written law.

Herewith, gentlemen, we anticipate your customary protection and the fulfillment of the requested actions.

With respect and deference,
Johannes Kepler, Imperial Mathematician

Do you understand that any false testimony you knowingly give will provoke God's great anger in your earthly life and will deliver your soul unto Satan upon your death?

I do.

Tell us your name, age, and if you are married, and any work you do.

Endres Leutbrand. Twenty-one. Not married. I no longer work as a bathing master's apprentice.

You say you had an unfortunate exchange with Frau Kepler. Can you tell us about it?

She seemed real friendly-like and knowledgeable in that old lady sort of way. I'm someone who has loads of respect for older ladies, I was in no way expecting harm or trouble, and I also liked Frau Kepler because she wasn't demanding like some older people are, or groveling and teary and asking for help with every little thing like they're a rabbit who lost a leg in a trap or something. I feel a little bit shy about explaining how Frau Kepler and I came into contact. I had a problem with my skin, mostly on the tops of my legs. It was bumpy like a tree bark and hot as fire. The blacksmith's daughter said to me that Frau Kepler had been helpful to her when she had near on the same thing. She said that with Frau Kepler's help what she had went away before the moon went from half to quarter. I thought my rash came from my not being grateful. I won't go into it. I lost my mother when I was very young and maybe that is part of my openness to older women.

Let's stay with what happened with Frau Kepler.

Yes, she gave me a poultice that burned even worse than the rash was already burning. The poultice was to help with my rash, but it didn't help. It smelled of vinegar. My skin peeled. I was crying. I saw how I had been wrong, but I didn't say anything to her, I was too ashamed. I walked out of there not wanting to tell anyone about the stupid devil's cure I had taken.

How old were you at this time?

I was twelve, sir. But a woman.

Do you understand that any false testimony you knowingly give will provoke God's great anger in your earthly life and will deliver your soul unto Satan upon your death?

Yes.

State your name and age.

Severin Stahlen. I am thirty-two years old according to my mother, and thirty-one years old according to my father.

You have something to share with the court about Frau Kepler.

Yes. I had a pig as a child. Not my pig alone. The whole family's pig. But the pig had a special liking for me. This was twenty or so years ago. But it is more vivid to me than last Wednesday's market. I knew the pig would be slaughtered in October. But I was a child and I also believed this pig would grow with me, like a sister. Sorry, it makes my chest hurt to think of times past. I hadn't thought back to that sister-pig of mine until Ursula came round talking about Frau Kepler, and I am very grateful to Ursula for her bravery in explaining to me all her pains and difficulties, and all that Frau Kepler had done to her with the poisoned wine. She was talking on and on about the poisoned wine and everything, and I was thinking, My pig! My dear pig, Clover. Frau Kepler was already an old lady when I was a child. She had the face of a hungry bird. I saw it. She was talking to my father's helper, a young man with a big nose. She was talking to him and that was when she touched my pig's hoof. Frau Kepler did. I saw it, clear as the sun going down. It was the left hoof of my pig. I didn't like Frau Kepler's face. But I didn't know why I didn't like her face.

In what way did you suffer?
Clover died after that. Not in the slaughter. She was hit by a cart full up of apples. It was awful. It was only with all this chitchat around town that I made the connection to Frau Kepler. Once I knew, I realized: I knew all along. Children know things. They see things. They have special powers. I had that power back then, and it took me all these many years to get that power back.

Any false testimony you knowingly give will provoke God's great anger in your earthly life and will deliver your soul unto Satan straight after death—you are aware?

I am. Very much so.

State your name, age, and profession.

Hans Benedict Beitelspacher. I will be fifty years old by Christmas. I am employed as a schoolmaster.

How did you come to know Frau Kepler and Frau Reinbold?

Ursula Reinbold? I don't know her well, but I know Jacob Reinbold, the glazier. I don't know if Frau Kepler offered Ursula a poisoned drink. I can't speak to that. I do know that Ursula suffers terribly. It's tied to the moon. The pain subsides when the moon moves from one cycle to the next. I don't know more about it. And no, I don't know anything about whether Ursula has had previous dealings with the law. I have never heard that she was in prison for licentiousness.

But you have known Frau Kepler many years, right?

Katharina Kepler, yes. I've known her since I was a kid. I was in primary school with her son, the astrologer, Hans. She sent him in with heavy biscuits, butter, jams. He then went on to other schools. There was more money on Hans's father's side, but the father's parents didn't like Katharina. They didn't help pay for Hans's schooling, and Hans's father was already dead, or presumed dead. Instead, the grandfather on Katharina's side helped with the school fees. I believe he mortgaged his land. Still, Hans complained that they sent him to seminary instead of law school, that was what they could afford. Hans was full of himself always. Sorry I drifted. Frau Kepler was not on my mind as a child. Her son was proud and secretive but also he was fine. I have no complaints about Hans. Other than the usual complaints among children.

After Hans went away—that's when I had more dealings with Frau Kepler. Even when he was a married man, and I was a married man, still Katharina bothered me for favors. She often annoyed and unsettled me. One time, for example. It was summer. I had been working in the field, a long summer day. It was an unusually early grape harvest. I came back, to my own home. I was with my wife. She had been working in the fields alongside me. The doors of our house had been locked while we were out, of course they were locked. But then there she was, sitting at our own kitchen table. Katharina Kepler, near a jar of pickles. I was astonished, as was my wife. Why was she inside our home? Passing through locked doors like that—it was dark magic. We stood there like blockheads, my wife and I, I am sorry to say. Frau Kepler greeted us like we were children. Then she begged me to write something for her. I should have asked her to leave. She often came to me asking for favors, especially to help her read something, or write something. Usually she was asking me to read letters Hans had sent to her. Or to write letters in response to Hans. I'm happy to help, I like to help others. But it was as if I was the only person she knew who could read. Why did she always have to come to me? That day she came in through the locked doors, she said she had a letter she wanted to send to Hans, that it was urgent. Okay, but again—why me? She wanted to make me feel his success over my own. That's why. Here I have worked so hard in my life, and faced so much adversity, I won't go into it, and I had my wife and my home, and Frau Kepler comes in, begging me to help with her letters to my old schoolmate, as if he's a prince. Although I don't know Ursula Reinbold well myself, I am glad to have finally been asked about the Kepler family. It is something heavy inside of me.

What was the letter she wanted you to write that day about?
I don't remember. The letters were never of interest. There were a number of them. This was some seven or ten years ago. When my wife was still alive. Before I was walking with sticks as you see me now.

You understand that if you are hiding the truth then God will punish you?
That's why I'm here. To tell the truth. There was another incident I can tell you about. This was seven years ago. The astrologer's mother hectored me on a Sunday. I wanted to go to vespers. She wanted me to read some letters from the astrologer. She kept me from going to vespers. She was begging me and hectoring me. No, I don't remember what the letters contained. I remember only that she went on about his appointments. Often she was worried about him. He served in Catholic territories, and with weird people. This was not long after he was working with the aristocrat from Copenhagen, the one with the moose and the false nose. God knows what he was doing there.

I helped her with the letters, I read them to her, and then I wanted to go out. She said she had a very good wine in her cellar that she wanted to share with me, as a gift. I said no, thank you. I wasn't thirsty. She begged me and bullied me into waiting while she went to get the wine. My wife and I had to sit there like two cabbage heads, waiting.

My poor wife. When she returned, I took a small sip to be polite. It tasted of hyssop. She pushed me to drink more. I said no, thank you.

I'm so relieved to be able to speak about this.

Now, this time with the wine, Bastian Meyer's wife, Margretta, she was there, too. Have you spoken with Bastian Meyer? He and his wife lived on the other side of the Glems. Frau Kepler also pushed the wine on Margretta Meyer. Margretta wasn't a drinker. She often went a whole week without a drink; she was odd and drank mostly water, and also milk. That was the way she lived her life. She was a nice woman and I always liked her, she never said a mean word to others. I'm sorry for my tears. Frau Kepler pushed the wine on Margretta, too. At first a little, then even more. Frau Kepler served it to us in mugs made by her son the pewterer. She is a braggart.

I read the letters out to her. She made me read them several times, I remember that.

Margretta drank a whole mug. Over the next months, she became thin and weak. She is dead now.

As for myself, I felt a pain in my leg the next day. Soon in both legs. You see the state I'm in now, requiring crutches.

You must have been frightened.
I did not give it any thought then. I took it as it came. But as I am now, I see the situation differently.

Are you sure you can't remember the letters?
The second time, Hans was no longer with the rich Dane anymore; that man had died.

A lot of people die in the proximity of the Kepler family.
Maybe that is true. You see the state I'm in. I'm a widower and lame.

If Katharina has been so frightening to you for so many years, why didn't you speak out earlier?

I'm even becoming lame as a man. I no longer function as a man should. I hardly find life worth living, I am close to tears every day.

Please, Herr Beitelspacher, the question is, why did you not say anything before now?

I haven't always had God in my top pocket. I've done things I regret in my life. I believed that God was punishing me for them. Maybe Katharina was God's means for doing so. I don't know. I don't want to speak out against God's will. I am not speaking out now. I'm sharing the information that I have and letting the court decide.

✦ ✦ ✦ I wasn't going to leave town like a reprimanded dog, Simon. Hans wrote insisting that I come as soon as possible to stay with his family in Linz. Greta read the letter to me three times over. Hans was in a panic. I'm his mother, not his child. A winter journey is no small thing. Linz is outside of the duchy, a different legal district, and I would appear to be fleeing—I suppose I would be fleeing. Also Chamomile wouldn't be able to come with me. She's very attached to me. I'm very attached to her. His plan was absurd. Living so far away, Hans had lost sight of how my accusers here are fools. He had confused me with his grand friends, or with himself, having to flee because they're the tallest poppies in the field. I was no estimable mathematician to be burned for saying that cabbages might grow on other planets, too. Hans himself had had to leave Tübingen, had fled Graz—he had developed a habit of leaving. That was my thinking. Myself, I wanted to go about my life as normal. I'm no more trouble than a goose. I'm innocent, so I should conduct myself as innocent. I told Greta I would not be leaving.

She said, "Your enemies aren't evil people. But they are your enemies."

I've always had an enemy here and there, I told her.

She said, "I am trying to see the good in everyone. All people are made in the image of God." She lost a pregnancy in that time. That made me suspect the others of sorcery. But sad things are so commonplace. And as you say Simon: see no monsters. Greta said, "I don't want to be less than honest with you, Mama. I'm fearful." She began crying, which enraged me.

MY PLAN THAT January afternoon had been to help Gertie with her spinning, and I wasn't going to alter that plan. Gertie always had some idea or another preoccupying her, and she could chat about it unbidden for as long as one needed the sound of a human voice, and also, she never seemed to fear much of anything. She was birdsong, if you tuned your ear correctly. I wouldn't feel pressured to leave Leonberg while listening to her.

On the way across town, I deliberately did not avoid the central market. It was my market as much as anyone else's. I saw a young boy gathering snow into small piles, gathering twigs. It looked like a little village. I complimented him. The boy jumped up from his efforts and hurried away.

I continued on. The butcher Topher Frick had sausages hanging at his stall, with small bouquets of dried sage and thyme as well. I know now that he later gave confused testimony about me, but this was before then. I often bought from Herr Frick. He has that broad moon face, like a child. I sometimes thought that he pressed down on the scales a bit. But I will say he always yielded if I asked him to weigh the purchase one more time. He is like a child trying his luck, really. I greeted him. Maybe I greeted him aggressively, as a test, to see where I stood with him. Greta's tears had gotten to me.

"Oh, I hadn't seen you there," Frick said. He had his hand at his heart, he looked anxious. His young son was at his side, pretty as a daffodil. "You appeared all of a sudden."

I said good afternoon.

"Isn't it terribly cold?" Frick asked.

I didn't think so.

"It feels like a north wind, but it's coming from the east. Very strange." He was looking at me like I was a specter—or was he?

I should try to think well of him, I thought. I had Greta's voice in my head, telling me that all people are the image of God. Why not all voles, then? All fleas? They were God's creations, too. "I suspect it will be calm tomorrow."

He shook his head. "I see storms coming."

"Storms?"

"I'd say so. Purple skies behind you. You must know that."

That made me feel his butcher knife at my throat. "You think I'm the cause of storms?"

"I didn't say that, Katharina."

"Everyone knows your mother was a witch—"

"It was my aunt," he said.

His little boy was staring at me. I felt gray and rotten. "I'm sorry," I said. "I don't know what I was talking about."

"Please don't hurt us," he said.

I apologized again and hurried on, and nearly bumped into Hans Beitelspacher, the schoolmaster. He was drinking a beer at a nearby stall. I've known Beitelspacher since he was seven years old. When he worked as a brickmaster, I encouraged people to hire him, even though he had been a weak-minded and envious child, but he had no mother, and I had worried for him.

"I don't need anything, Frau Kepler."

I wasn't offering anything.

"You shouldn't sneak up on a fellow like that," he said.

"I'm in a rush," I said, walking on.

A trio of girls selling candles parted to let me by. I began to feel as if I were some furry clawed thing walking among quail.

AT CHRISTOPH'S, GERTIE set me up at the spinning wheel while she sat nearby on a stool embroidering something. What was she making? It was still a half round, waiting to resolve into a shape. Christoph was at another guild meeting, she said. Darkness came early, so we lit candles to continue our work. Little Agnes was in a deep sleep. She kicked now and again, like a dreaming dog.

"Greta is being asked to pay a year's rent up-front," Gertie said.

"She didn't tell me that."

"Of course she didn't," Gertie said.

"But why?"

"It's difficult to get details from Greta. Also, they executed three more women outside of Stuttgart."

The wool Gertie had given me to work with could have been better, the crimp varied from section to section, but I was making do. "When I was a girl, only the Catholics spent time on so much murdering and drama."

"It's difficult times," Gertie said.

I disagreed. I thought the times were not difficult enough, since people still made time for telling lies. "The Reinbolds are moving up in the world, not down," I said. "Some birds build their own nests and raise their own baby birds, but cuckoo birds take the nests of others and knock out the better eggs."

"Two of the Stuttgart women were pigherds," Gertie said. "But the third was a pastor's widow."

"You're saying I should go to Hans?"

"No. I think that makes you look guilty. But Christoph may think otherwise." Gertie continued her needlework on her not-quite-a-thing. "And even if those women were witches, it's like killing foot soldiers, what do they know, really, most of them? If I ran the world, I'd cut off the head of the beast, not a talon here and there. All that snipping only strengthens the beast," she said. She switched from a yellow to a pink thread. "They put a bag of gunpowder around her neck."

"Whose neck?"

"The pastor's widow, like I was telling you."

"I see," I said. Though all I saw really were lightweight bread loaves from Rosina Zoft. I pictured them floating away, out the chimney. Then I pictured new loaves, pulled hot from the oven on a wooden pallet. In my vision Rosina sliced into a loaf and inside were bleeding hands.

"It's a clever solution," Gertie continued. "The gunpowder explodes early in the burning process. So the heart explodes. Which is so much better than watching and waiting through the whole long goodbye."

I said nothing. I felt as though the devil were in the room with us. He was laughing at us. He was a small man with a mustache and no beard and wearing a blue knit caftan. "Are you listening, Mama Kepler?"

"I didn't know that about gunpowder," I said.

"Here, what do you think of this?" She held up her needlework, which had transformed into a tiny dress. "It's for a doll for Agnes."

"It's beautiful," I said. As you know, Simon, that very night I asked if you would take care of my dear Chamomile. I would go to Linz.

I hope it is not inappropriate for me to include my own thoughts here, alongside Katharina's. I sometimes feel as if we are writing to God. Even as he wouldn't need the report, would he? He would already know. I must be writing to someone . . . smaller. Perhaps it doesn't matter. I find that, whatever happens, I want a true account that exists outside of my mind. Let me say: a curious coincidence is that around when Katharina was thinking of whether to go to Linz, my daughter, Anna, had been staying with her aunt not far from Linz. Anna stayed with her there through the celebrations of the new year. Anna returned to Leonberg a short time before Katharina departed. And upon her return, she looked different.

I hardly noticed it at first. Yet it was as if my liver or kidneys noticed, while the rest of my body went about its business as per usual. Had she gained weight? Lost weight? At moments it even seemed to me that she was a different height.

"Papa, I have something serious I want to talk to you about," she said over breakfast porridge. Nearby on the table as we ate was an open backgammon game.

I said go ahead, tell me.

She wouldn't tell me. She said she needed a little more time. Maybe over the evening meal, she said.

I was occupied that day with scudding a batch of hides. Scudding is calming work, as it requires all of my attention to not let the knife slip. When I do it, I feel the steady purpose a cat must feel when bathing itself with its coarse tongue. Some of my most peaceful hours have been spent in this way. Outside there could be lightning, wars, or a festival and it would be all the same and nothing to me. At least normally that is the case. That day, Anna's timid boldness had unsettled me. Her remark over breakfast intruded into my thoughts. As I worked, in my mind I saw her holding her spoon. I saw her hesitating. I saw a backgammon chip nearby.

She was going to ask me to stop helping Katharina. To stop associating with her, even. She was afraid, perhaps with good reason, that the shadow and suspicion of the whole affair was falling on herself. As much as I try to keep myself out of society, I can't say I didn't notice the way Katharina and I were looked at that day when we were returning from our conversation with the clerk, Herr Sebelen. And even the clerk himself, who had extended a kindness to Katharina—he had told us to worry. Had he regretted his openness with us? And what had he made of my presence, why had he included me in his concern? I far prefer to be not known than to be known, even benevolently. He had looked at me as if he knew me better than seemed possible, which, now that I turned my mind to it, made me shiver.

I looked down at the hide I had been working on. I saw so many missed spots, bits of hair still there, as if a ten-year-old apprentice had done the work.

I did fear that there was a rumor that my work was suffering. But my work hadn't been suffering, had it? A short time before Katharina left, I had received a cancellation of an order from Stuttgart. The cancellation came in the form of an abruptly worded letter. I couldn't help but think of some vile and untrue rumors about me that had caused my family such difficulties when I was young. I don't want to detail those troubles. Maybe trying to relate the canceled order to the current situation with Katharina was foolish. Could news of what was dire, but also a small-town affair, really have made it all the way to Stuttgart? At the time, I remember, I mentioned the dropped order to Katharina.

"He spent the money on drink," she declared. "That's the most likely story."

"You don't know that," I said.

She shrugged.

I didn't want to push the idea that maybe it was my association with her that had cost me this order of three saddles. That wouldn't be standing by, or seeing through, or seeing no monsters. It also wouldn't be fair. I'm getting older. I imagine there are young saddlers out there, better than I am at advertising their qualities in taverns and inns. Better than I am at going to taverns and inns.

Now of course the situation with Katharina had escalated, but at the time of the dropped order, I was still under the illusion that all would be resolved quietly and reasonably if we simply waited it out. I know what it is to be falsely accused, and for that very reason I dreaded being asked by my beloved Anna to abandon Katharina, who was in just such a position. But how could I disappoint my only child? I had to stand by Anna, too. I would try to reason with Anna. I would point out to her that Katharina was likely already leaving town. That in effect there no longer would be any issue.

Before Anna and I sat down for our evening meal, I put away the backgammon board.

We sat down to a simple dinner of dumplings, Anna and I. She had fashioned the dumplings into fine shapes, so regular and even. We had carrots as well, bright as jewels. When Anna began to speak, in a steady and studied voice,

I found myself holding the leg of the table. I felt my knees trembling. But above the table, I smiled.

She stammered. She said something about how she regretted there wasn't more meat in the dumplings. Then she said: "Papa. About what I had mentioned. About talking to you."

"Yes," I said grimly.

"Well."

"Go on."

"I'd like you to bring me to market on Tuesdays."

"On Tuesdays," I repeated.

"And I'd like to alter Mother's red dress. So that I can wear it as my own."

I didn't say anything, I was so bewildered.

"The dress in the trunk. I looked at it, and it's still in good condition."

I was still quiet. The dress?

"Are you upset about Mother's dress?"

"No," I said. "It's a very nice dress."

She paused. "Yes, a nice fabric."

"So, anything else?"

"Nothing in particular, no."

"The dress is what you wanted to talk to me about?"

"And the Tuesday market," she said.

She was speaking with so much more force and clarity than usual. Her simple requests startled me. They may as well have been spoken by a marmot, that's how unexpected they were. "Yes," I said. "Okay. Very reasonable. Yes."

I looked at that woman who was my daughter. I saw something I hadn't seen before. She was wearing face powder. That was the difference. How could I not have noticed earlier?

Christoph accompanied me. Our journey to Linz was cold and haunted. I saw many light-feathered owls. I didn't see a single mouse. Christoph spoke of his plans to ascend in the town. He had taken on bookkeeping responsibilities for the guild. There was a call to train a local militia—he planned to answer that call. They had threatened to put a lien on Christoph's house to pay the court fees, but I advised him to be as slow with the paperwork as possible, because you don't store sausage in a dog's house. Our journey was a long one, and I thought it would be too boring for Christoph, and for me, if I let myself despair. I remember well when Emperor Matthias kicked the Protestants (including Hans) out of Prague. I said to myself: Here's the end. But I was wrong. It wasn't the end. Hans always manages, I will give him that. He found himself this position in Linz, teaching mathematics at a small school for young men who so far as he tells it are no more gifted in mathematics than I am. Such is the world. And people try to tell you that Emperor Rudolf was the one who was cruel to the Protestants. There is little good to say about Emperor Matthias, a man who put his own brother in prison.

I will not further detail an old woman journeying through frozen mud to Ulm, spending more than a night with donkeys, and taking a long boat trip up the Rhine, with a family of thieves, who were kind enough to share some jam with an old woman and her son. By the time we arrived to the crowd of red roofs that was Linz, I was weak, my traveling costume was torn, I must have looked like an old beggar woman, as my handsome Christoph asked strangers for directions to the professor's home.

And Hans was not in! His sensible second wife, Susanna, greeted us. She was dressed in a dark housedress, with a very clean and starched lace collar, but still she didn't hesitate to embrace us. I had to pull away to blow my nose. Susanna began to cry, but only silently. She wiped away her tears and then it was done with.

Johannes, she said, was away near Bruchhausen. He was on a mapping expedition. This was part of his duties as Imperial Mathematician.

"That sounds like a task for a child," Christoph said.

"He'll be back soon," Susanna said. She brought us small kerchiefs perfumed with rosemary and lavender to wipe our brows, our hands. She brought out tea, and cheese. I felt dizzy. I fell to the floor. I was moved to a simple improvised bed in a room off the kitchen.

HOW MANY DAYS did I lie there, shivering and confused? I didn't make it to church. Christoph headed back to Leonberg. I almost never get sick. I've had lice, but that's different. When I'm sick, I tell myself: Chamomile needs to see my face. I make it down the stairs. I scratch her chin, and also pet her nose. If the size of eyes is indicative of the size of souls as maybe Paracelsus says—someone says it—why isn't there more praise of cows? She likes to lean her head against my neck. I have never wished she could speak, because we understand each other. I mention another thing about cows. They don't cry. They mourn, they make lowing noises, and if they have an infection, then their eyes will water and pus—but they don't put on a show of their emotions, but instead keep them to themselves, to whom they belong.

One morning I went downstairs to attend to Hans's cow, who wasn't Chamomile. (Simon, I can hardly express to you how grateful I was to know that you were attending to Chamomile, that she wouldn't have to leave her familiar home, that she wouldn't have to be attended to by a stranger.) Hans's cow wore a bell and was called LittleHammer. Susanna tells me she found me asleep near LittleHammer. I was breathing heavily but couldn't be woken. She had to go out and get the rope maker from down the street, and he helped her carry me back up the stairs from where the animals were. A mushroom soup was prepared, with dandelion; the apothecary also tried to sell some unicorn horn powder to Susanna. Unicorn horn is the devil's trap and I told her not to take any and that I wouldn't take any, either. I may have been given a local mugwort. The dreams I had were more than the usual set of fears and lizards and underclothes that would not come clean. In one dream my dear and dead father came round knocking, a vagrant, asking for bread, and saying he was from Livonia.

Livonia! That had been another Gertie obsession. Gertie believed the stories of cannibalism in Livonia. She had heard them from an honest blacksmith, she said. A widower, with six red-cheeked children. Six healthy children in Livonia was not a detail I could believe. I know how these stories work. Probably someone had found something valuable in Livonia. Maybe silver. And they had wanted the land for themselves at a good price. So they spread the cannibalism story.

I'm off track. I was still sick and fevered in bed. I heard the chitchat of a young girl. Like birdsong. That cheered me. Probably that was Hans and Susanna's Maruschl. Surely it was. I hadn't yet met the child. Susanna was keeping the girl away from me, which was fair enough; we didn't know how long or dangerous my illness was.

Yet Susanna cared for me. She brought me a hard-boiled egg. She offered to read to me. Hans didn't consider Susanna's literacy a point in her favor. She didn't force it upon his notice, but she wasn't ashamed of her learning. When she had time, she read to me from a story that was familiar in essence, but whose details were strange.

A young man had killed his mother. But this was back-story and somewhat beside the point. The real problem was the young man's pursuit by three furious young women, whose appearance Susanna could tell me little of. She said the story didn't say what the man looked like, either. I asked her why couldn't she tell me anyway. It's not as if she were reading from the Bible, and there was room for her to add to the story from her own experiences.

"I've never had the experience of being a young man pursued by three angry women," she said.

I told her she was being too by-the-book.

She closed the book, and looked set to leave.

I'm capable of saying I'm wrong and apologizing. Susanna's reading was taking my mind away from feeling so unwell; I was enjoying it. I asked her to go on. I did add that I was nearly certain that what no one would say was that the young man had made one or two or three young women quick with child and now had completely abandoned them in their troubles. That was always the story, really. If you cleared the brambles away.

"Okay, but it doesn't say anything like that here," she said.

"Yet we know, don't we? We know how likely that is."

Susanna returned to reading. The three very angry young women nearly killed the young man. The man had a difficult and foreign name that never stuck in my head. The women caught up to him! They were right on the point of tearing him limb from limb. They planned to scatter his body parts and let them be eaten by crows. That was very interesting. Susanna thought so, too. I imagine Gertie would also have been interested.

I said I knew a story where hawks are fed the body of a boy. The stepmother does the feeding. The stepmother then lies to the boy's sister, and says she doesn't know what happened to the boy, he just went missing. But the birds sing the guilt of the stepmother all day and night. It's quite a tale. In the end, the poor murdered boy returns. One of the birds becomes the boy.

"You're feeling better?" she asked.

"No," I said.

"I see. Well. This story is like that story you describe in one way: it also has a happy ending."

The boy in my story had done nothing wrong; the young man in Susanna's story was another case. That said, I never like to think of punishment.

Susanna read on. The young man was saved. A goddess intervenes and saves the young man from being torn limb from limb.

"Ah, this is one of those stories," I said.

"One of what stories?"

"One of those goddess stories."

The goddess intervened to insist that the man should be put on trial first. Depending on how the trial went, maybe he would be torn limb from limb, or maybe he wouldn't be.

I said, "But who would the judges be? That's the thing with a trial."

Susanna left to do some housework. I imagine she had a lot to attend to. I had been wondering who would attend to the cleaning, to the animals, to the little girl, Maruschl.

I let the worry go. It was not my home. People like to be left to their own business. Later, though I wasn't sure how much later, Susanna returned and read more to me.

The verdict was that half the judges said, Yes, kill the man, and half said, No, don't kill him. Perfectly split.

The trial was about whether he was to be punished for killing his mother, but, again, that was somehow not center stage, not in this telling. It was more about the bailiff and the procedure and the arguing back and forth.

"The voting is silly," I said. "You can't discover what's true based on how many people think it's true."

The goddess spoke up, and made the final decision. She said: Free him.

"So the goddess was okay with him killing his mother?"

Susanna said it was a story with many parts. As with the Bible, she often got lost as to which way to feel. But she had trusted those who had recommended the story to her. Johannes, for example, respected this writer. Anyhow, that was nearly the end.

I thanked her for reading to me. I said I thought it was a very funny story.

"Funny?"

"It was meant to be funny, right?"

The three furious young women were renamed: The Kindly Ones.

That part was definitely funny.

Separately, I was feeling dawning health. I observed to Susanna—and this was maybe my first clear thought about my case—that though I was glad courts existed, and I was eager to have my case heard—if it would ever be heard—and to have my name cleared, I also thought that sometimes the courts were there mostly to make money for the court scribe.

"That's too dark a view, Mama Kepler," Susanna said.

I said she should see the view I had, of a spiral staircase inside a new tower added to the Korn family's home in Leonberg. The Korn family worked as scribes.

"Say these things to me but not to other people," she said.

I thanked Susanna and was again asleep. I dreamed that I was well, and that I was seeing my granddaughter, who looked like an adult in proportions, but smaller, the way they paint the infant Jesus as a small man.

Do you understand that any false testimony you knowingly give will provoke God's great anger in your earthly life and will deliver your soul unto Satan upon your death?

I'm not going to swear an oath. She's a powerful woman and God knows I might find myself falling off a bridge if I come out too strongly against her. Oh, sometimes I want to knock her over the head with my rolling pin, I'm so worried, but I don't do it, do I? 'Cause she'd knock me right back and something fierce. No, definitely no. I'm only telling you. You can do with the information as you want.

Please state your name, age, and profession.

I'm forty-one, Rosina Zoft, the wife of the baker.

Tell us what you know of Frau Kepler.

I'm glad she fled town. I feel safer now.

Is that why you only came forward now?

Why didn't I come forward before now? I was very busy. I'm still very busy. I would have told the truth to you if you asked, if you came by to see me.

We want to get back to what you wanted to share about Frau Kepler.

I now see that I always knew. I didn't know I knew. But I knew. You can know and also not know something. I try to be kind, and generous. I do my very best, and some people will see that and think: There's my mark. I'll take advantage of her. I will take everything she has and make her say thank you very much in return. Katharina barely said thank you for the milk I gave her in the darkness of what was a very hungry February. As if she were the only one with a child to feed over the winter. And a grown child, at that! She comes asking me for fresh milk, as if I have a magic cow, different from all the other cows. Then she gave me a look as if what I had given her wasn't enough. This was for her son Heinrich. He was a broad-shouldered soldier, and she was begging round as if he were an invalid. Then she comes back round again, asking to use my oven. You do someone a favor and they hold it against you, saying it wasn't favor enough. As if God gave me life so I could do favors for her.

Now, this is what I wanted to say that is even more than that. This is something I bet you she will not be telling you about. She comes into my bakery, furious, like an aggrieved raven. Paying no attention to who else was there. And she has that strange smell on her, those so-called medicines she makes. She tells a young woman there, with her basket, that she should ask for a thirteenth loaf, tells the girl she's skinny, tells the girl she'll never be overfed buying from me. Then comes up to the counter accusing me of spreading lies. She says I'm lying. In front of everyone. Now, I'll tell you what a lie is—she comes right into my own place and tells people I'm doing something I'm not. She's friends with that pathetic and envious baker Jerg Hundersinger, that's what that was about. He relies on her for money, so he can't be trusted. You absolutely cannot listen to a thing that unfortunate says.

Then Katharina threatens to hit me over the head with a log. She says that's what she'll do if it's true what she hears I'm saying about her, that she's a witch.

A log?

I am certain that is what she said. Over the head with a log. You don't forget that sort of thing. I cried out for my husband. He shooed her out of the bakery with a big loaf of bread and a rolling pin. It sounds ridiculous, it sounds like laughs, sure—but it was scary. I couldn't sleep, not that night, or the next, or the next.

What made you suspect she was a witch?

Okay, yes, I know, you want me to talk about Heinrich, the son? I now see that I had long suspected she was a witch, even before her son called her one. But Heinrich said it to me plain as a cloud. The boy. The man. This was shortly before he died that winter. He said his mother had ridden a goat backward and then she had roasted it. She had done that and then she gave him nothing to eat. Or she gave him a leg, a small amount, the part that was all bones and sinews. Well, who rides a goat backward? I'm a humble woman. But even I know that only witches and sometimes devils do that. Heinrich wasn't well. He frightened me. But I had no reason to think he was lying. Why would he lie?

I don't know if she poisoned Ursula Reinbold or not. That's a rumor that might be true or might not be true. I know Ursula says Katharina gave her a poisoned wine. And I know that Katharina says that she didn't, that maybe the wine had gone sour, but it wasn't poisoned.

If you asked me who I trust more, well, you're not asking me that. But I know the answer. And I'm not going to be pressured by all this fanciness here into saying what will only cause me troubles. Can I leave now? All I have to say, I've said.

I half woke to the sense of a very slight man in the doorway. Who was it? I fell asleep again. By the time I again awoke the figure in the doorway was gone. I put on my housedress and quietly went down the stairs, looking for an intruder in the house, human or animal or spirit. I saw Little-Hammer, their cow. Also several plump brown hens, and two frowning, bored goats. Something was eerie, but what? When I was a little girl, my brother showed me ghoulish, greenish sparks flying off our donkey's fur. I was sure the devil was visiting us. But my brother was laughing. Had he turned to dark spirits? I cried and approached the donkey. The donkey showed his teeth. I ran off. Only days later did my brother reveal to me the trick: he had rubbed sulfur against the lie of our donkey's fur, backward. That was what had made the sparks hop and leap. To this day, when I picture the calm and toothy expression of our donkey amid the green light around him, I think there must be a secret lying in wait there. A secret of real import, I mean. Not a recipe of tricks to perform with sulfur.

I saw no revenant in the house's downstairs barn area. That was disappointing. I'm not afraid of the dead as I used to be as a child. I'm eager to meet and see them. I'd like above all to see my father, to see the young man he was when I was a child. He thought well of me. I've lived so many years, Simon. Maybe you understand this feeling. Being alive at my age is like being woken from a grave and walking the earth to see the alien world of my descendants. I feel more at ease among the animals and, God forgive me,

I don't think it would be a punishment to have been born an animal. But not a horse.

Since I was feeling better, I was already thinking that I would go back home soon. Chamomile would be pleased. She loved me. That morning my illness felt like a rocky valley between my past and present, and the threats I faced back in Leonberg appeared small, or even imaginary. They were a ghost story for children on a winter's night. The accusations that had so terrified my whole family—they would pass. As an illness passes. As a sparking donkey reveals itself to be an ordinary ass.

I went back upstairs . . . and there was my Hans! He was at the kitchen table, going over paperwork with a young man I didn't recognize. His beard had grayed. The gray in his beard annoyed me. Also he looked thin. But his low mumble I recognized. My heart was singing.

Hans then caught sight of me. Before I even spoke, he did something strange. He rose and greeted me, calling me Frau Guldenmann. He said he'd be with me shortly, about the milk. Guldenmann is my maiden name. It took me a moment to recognize it as my own. I stood there startled, unmoving. Hans then took me by the elbow and directed me toward the top floor of the house and repeated that he would be with me shortly.

NOW, THAT WAS not the greeting I expected. An hour or so later, he called me back downstairs, and he wept and embraced me, and it was really a bit much.

"Frau Guldenmann?" I asked.

"I don't involve irrelevant people in family matters," he said.

"I see," I said.

"Thanks to heaven that you're here."

"Who was that young man?"

"It's not important. A student."

"Your beard is gray," I said.

"It isn't gray, Mama."

"I see gray with my own eyes," I said.

"It has some gray in it, but it isn't itself gray. It hasn't grayed." He asked me to sit, encouraged me to have a bite to eat. He had a slice of apple on a tiny fancy spear of some sort.

"What is that toy you're holding?"

"It's a fork. And I know you know it's a fork."

"It looks like the tail of a devil," I said. "Not in a bad way."

"You're going to give me trouble about my fork?"

"When did that happen?"

"The fork?"

"Your gray beard."

"Mama, you are . . . unrelenting."

"That's what Christoph says about you," I said to him. "Respectfully, of course. He says it with respect."

And our arguing could have gone back and forth in that way for a long while, it was making me feel healthy and alive, but then dear Susanna appeared at the door. She said it was time for me to meet little Maruschl. She brought me over to a young and sleeping child. It is a common misconception that all children are beautiful and full of spirit. They aren't. Some are fearful, or aggressive, or aloof, or selfish. Some are wonderful but unreachable and private. I have known and cared for and loved many small people.

I petted the forehead of the sleeping Maruschl. She opened her eyes and looked straight at me. I thought maybe she would be afraid of me. I was a stranger, and I'm no fresh beauty.

She said to me directly, "I was in the woods and I saw a fox."

"You did?" I said.

"It's true. The fox didn't run away. We looked at each other."

And all through that winter, we were together almost all the time. Being in Linz would have been unbearable without her.

I can still hardly believe Hans didn't die as a child. He had the pox before he could even speak. The bumps on his tender skin at the time looked like small, round burns, as if an army of the tiniest creatures had left mines across the landscape of his skin. Hans has remained dreamy and touched ever since, also stubborn and secretive. His illness coincided with his father, Heinrich, leaving Leonberg to seek his fortune as a soldier. Seeing little Hans suffering gave me the strength I might not otherwise have had to leave Hans behind with my in-laws and set off to find Heinrich, and talk him into coming back home. Hans recovered, though he remained too skinny, even as I put bone marrow into his mashes.

Having gotten over my own illness, I was set to go to the well the next morning with Susanna. She shook her head and suggested I stay home to rest another day. I went downstairs to clean out the animal pens. Two of the sheep had a little sneeze, and I set out for a walk with them. When I returned at midday, Susanna was tense, concerned. Maruschl was there at Susanna's skirt, wearing a red dress, and her cheeks also were red, and she smiled. That's what life is: a bunch of thorns, and a berry.

Hans must have heard us speaking and he emerged from his study looking annoyed.

"Mama, I hope you haven't been midwifing around town," he said.

I said I didn't know what he was talking about.

"You can't persist with your little remedies, whatever

they are," he said. "I've done nothing wrong either, but you don't see me trying to convince churchmen of the vision of Copernicus. You have to abide by the most basic precautions."

He went back into his study. He was setting the rules, like with a new dog. I was happy to see he had become more manly. Maruschl looked at me and opened her arms, asking me to pick her up.

BUT OVERALL, IT was a grim winter, Simon. Even a treatise on wine barrel sizes that Hans had written had faced trouble—who had strong opinions about the shapes of wine barrels? Though I have always found the squat ones deceptive. Any sense of Hans living the high life dissipated with proximity. At least when Hans's two older children from his first marriage, Ludva and Suze, came home on a break from their schooling, there was a respite from the household's heavy mood. Ludva and Suze were young and full of laughter. Suze had come across a draft of a letter Hans had written to an old friend, and she found it very funny, though I couldn't understand why. "'Whoever is accusing me of the slightest passion for innovation is not fair to me,'" Ludva would say to Suze, in a fussy voice, quoting the found note. Or, "'I will not take part in the fury of theologians.'" I asked Susanna what the kids were going on about. She said Hans had been petitioning for permission to take Communion at the church in Linz, but despite many efforts, he was still being denied. He had not agreed with a part of the Augsburg Confession—about whether the blood and body of Christ were really present in the sacrament. He was only sixteen or so at the time he was pressed to agree about the sacraments, but that boyish resistance, Susanna said, was also why he wasn't given a position at the University of Tübingen.

Ludva said it couldn't really be about that, it must be about something else, because one of the pastors had two bastard children and that hadn't been an obstacle.

Susanna said none of it really was hers to understand. She said Hans received an offer from the University of Genoa, but she hoped they were going to stay in Linz.

"He's too straightforward and German to live where people have been burned for not believing in eternal damnation," Ludva said.

"People are too stupid," Suze said, which of course was unbecoming, if correct.

Myself, I began to see that, unfortunately, I had in my way made too great an impression on Hans's character. I began to think it was more unwise than he realized for me to be staying with him. This troubled me nights, even with Maruschl there, sleeping alongside me. In March, when Susanna announced she would leave with Maruschl in early April for a visit to her parents', I resolved that it would be the right moment for me to leave as well. Though I confess I felt timid about announcing my intention. I, too, was stubborn and secretive, like my son.

"You're looking at my fork again," Hans said, at the very meal when I resolved to make my announcement. "You think it's an affectation."

"You don't know what I'm thinking," I said.

Outside there were leaves again, a few bold cherry blossoms. Susanna had set out a full and nourishing meal, including a rich butter and two jams, as well as a porridge with cuttings of bacon. I knew very well that it had been more than eighteen months since the Emperor or the Duke had provided Hans with the salary due him. I saw how Susanna opened her pantry fully nonetheless. I would be glad to unburden Hans and her both, though I would miss

Maruschl, who was at the table, playing with a square of cloth. She was laughing and smiling and eyeing me suspiciously and murmuring about a great battle.

Susanna said, "In Prague, lots of people use forks."

"Yes, I remember you told me that," I said. I offered Maruschl a piece of buttery biscuit. She set it in the cloth and wrapped it up. A girl who thought of future hours, I thought. A planner. Myself, I still couldn't manage to announce my own plans. "I heard in a sermon that Martin Luther didn't like forks," I said.

"Enough about the fork," my Hans said.

I said, "I've never understood the complexities of church thinking. They should leave the details to God."

"I'd like to have a more serious discussion," Hans said, and of course I wanted to have a more serious discussion as well. About how much I missed Chamomile, for example.

"I wrote to Besold," Hans said, speaking of his old friend who was a law professor at Tübingen. Besold's response, he said, was not encouraging. Hans said he had also written to the Duke. The Duke had not answered. He had written to the Leonberg Senate. They, too, had yet to answer.

"I've faced worse in my life," I said.

"I don't think you have," he said.

"I have," I said.

"You're so stubborn. You won't be corrected."

"Did you get the wine barrel thing published?" I asked.

"I won't let you change the subject," he said. "And I want you to know that I'm no fool and that I can see very well your extremely misguided intention of going back to Leonberg."

Now that surprised me. He *did* know what I was thinking.

"You should never have filed for slander, Mama. Now the ducal governor fears for his own humiliation. You've cornered a mangy cat. I know this is difficult for you to understand, but when someone is turning against you: You should double your kindness. You should give them a gift. Something valuable."

He paid me no mind, even when I agreed with him. He's a lovely and intelligent boy, but I couldn't be bothered to listen. I was remembering yet another time he was ill as a child. I put crackers in his bed and a red kerchief and also I made a sachet of spearmint and valerian, but I knew I had to leave it to God and the in-laws, as Heinrich had left town in a fury again, and I had to set off after him again. I can still hear Heinrich's mother shouting at me as I left town to seek out her son. I did bring him back a second time. Not that I heard a word of thank-you about it. And the next time Heinrich left, he never returned. It's possible he's still alive after all these years, but wouldn't I know by now? My heart tells me it's not the case. Those Keplers were small-hearted. And they left nothing in their will for the upkeep of their grandchildren. Hans was more of a Guldenmann, more from my side of the family. Perhaps that was why, under stress, he greeted me as a Guldenmann. Hans even looks like me, poor thing. When he was a boy of about five, my father, Melchior, gave him a set of marbles, and I confess I thought he was weak in the mind because he played with those marbles so much longer than other children would—he did not lose interest. It had frightened me somewhat, his focused playing. His indifference to coming out to the fields. His overzealous interest in poetry. He was never of any help with the harvest. Again and again I had expected him to die of one of his many weaknesses or catarrhs or rashes; again and again, I prepared my heart.

I could hear him still talking: "I was thinking to myself: How did this happen? How could this happen to Mama, who works so hard, who is kind even to animals, who never complains, who never uses foul language, who has no troubles with drink? Last time I was in Leonberg, my dear mother had no such troubles. There were no such rumors. Now, Christoph—I could see him getting into a scrape. But how has Mama, who has been a hardworking widow for so many years, who has been so generous to so many—how has she been so viciously turned on? It made no sense to me. It was more perplexing than planets. But living again with you here, I remember. I understand. I'm not surprised."

I was not hurt by his words, Simon. That is the honest truth. He was saying I was a person of substance, which I have always felt. And maybe this is because I had to be a mother and a father both to my children. It was a joy to see my son, however thin or weak. I didn't take him seriously. He's my child. If anything I was cheered by his confident dismissal of me. I felt again like a young mother.

"It is far too dangerous, Mama. Do you hear me? You're in real peril. And so are your children. I know it will be difficult for you while Susanna and Maruschl are away. But under no circumstances can you return to Leonberg. Absolutely not. They even are accusing you of having fled the jurisdiction. Returning would be like a rabbit running to the foxhole."

How happy I was to be back in Leonberg! It was a time of rhubarb and honeysuckle and high feelings. How my heart sang to see Chamomile again. You had been attentive to her, Simon, I could tell. I'm good with cows. Also with calves. I once asked a crowd of noisy swallows to quiet down, as I had a headache, and the swallows did. I have sometimes wondered: Why didn't God leave the world as frank and easy to understand as a cow? Instead, it's all a puzzle, for us to tease out which points of light are planets and which are stars, and who can be trusted and who cannot. No mind: I was happy to be fetching my own water, cleaning my own stalls. Happy to be eating my own pickles, drinking my own wine. Happy to hear Christoph complaining of sausages again, and happy to hear Gertie tell of the finding of the skeletons of unthinkably large beasts. So what if the weeds of a neighbor's garden sometimes breezed into my own? I would see no monsters, Simon. I was resolved. That was how I could stay home.

"Witches aren't even real," Greta's husband, Pastor Binder, said to me. He had just been granted a parish, outside of Stuttgart, and the position seemed even to have increased his height. They had traveled down to Leonberg to visit me, and I served them the best I had to hand. "Now, some old women do believe that they have powers. Yes, they do. But they are to be pitied, not punished. They're deranged, but not powerful."

Greta looked on peacefully. "All will be well, Mama. We have to believe that."

It was a curious idea about belief, but who was I to say?

"And even deranged old ladies are made in the image of God," Binder went on. "God isn't a rabbit, scurrying away to its burrow. God isn't a wolf, waiting to pounce. God is not a beaver, with teeth ever growing. God is not a lynx, nor a woodpecker, nor a fan-tailed grouse."

"He's working on this sermon," Greta said.

"God isn't a pygmy owl."

"I think the suspense is too much," I said to him.

"You're waiting to see where the thought goes, right?" Binder asked.

I CAN MOCK them, but they were more uplifting company than Christoph and Gertie at that time.

"The forester has joined the side of the Reinbolds," Christoph said.

"Which forester?" I asked.

"We were in the forest," little Agnes said.

"The old man Cosmas."

"Cosmas? He talks to squirrels. I never see him in town. He was handsome when he was younger, but odd even then."

Christoph took a cherry sucket from the table, and puckered at the sourness. I had made the candy for Agnes. "Cosmas is saying that you asked to borrow his cart to move hay."

"He's saying I was untoward?"

"He says he didn't loan you his cart."

"He probably didn't."

"He says you were angry about it."

I shrugged. "Something from a long time ago. I don't remember. Simon has been loaning me his cart for the recent harvests."

Gertie chimed in: "He says in revenge you made one of his pigs go wild and die."

It was not the only news they bore. There was a seamstress who wasn't from Leonberg, she had stayed one night with me after offering me minimal help during the day, this was many years ago, and she later told the marksman's wife, whom she briefly worked for after, that I had asked her, the seamstress, at midnight: Didn't she want joy and debauchery beyond measure? The devil could give that to her. That's what was said I told the girl. It wasn't the seamstress who was saying this now—no one knew where the seamstress was—but the marksman's wife was saying the seamstress had told her so. The marksman's wife is generally respected, though she has the overexpressive hands of a busybody, and I've never seen her laugh.

"'Joy and debauchery beyond measure'?" I said.

"What are you talking about?" Agnes said.

Christoph said, "I can picture you wandering around and grousing—that part makes sense."

I said, "I never should have left Leonberg! The whole idea was to cut short the vicious gossip, wasn't it?"

"Yet the gossip is only growing," Christoph said.

"I'm growing," little Agnes said.

Gertie petted her head. "It sounds like the baker's wife isn't your friend, either."

"The other baker likes me. Jerg. He'll speak well of me."

"In better news, the silversmith has ordered a dozen pewter goblets."

"That's not bad."

"I think he's trying to tell me he's on our side."

"Or maybe they like pewter goblets," I said.

AS I WAS returning home that night on the narrow path that runs along the side of the Junker's property, I saw a crowd of young peasant girls, eleven- and twelve-year-olds or so. Maybe one or two younger. The girls were carrying bricks to that kiln run by Lorenz Neher. I wouldn't have thought anything of it, but, for some reason, this day I saw that I was walking to the end of my life, and they were walking into their bloom. They were walking toward the center of their lives, and I was walking toward my own perimeter. I'm not usually detained by fanciful nonsense like that. It was a curious angle of the sun, of late light.

When I was a child, a kiln had exploded in the nearby village of Magstadt. The kilnsman had died, as had his horse. The talk had been of alchemists, also a thin-tailed devil. Our kiln in Leonberg had more down-to-earth problems. It was wood-fired and run by Neher, who is too much taken to drink and also cheap on wood. Or so Christoph says. He dislikes the man for having called Gertie names at the solstice festival—nice names, like lemon cake, and poppy.

The path was narrow and muddy. I could feel the diffuse curiosity and disapproval and fear and interest as I moved among them, like a groundhog among chickens.

That was all that happened.

Then I came to your home.

"It's poor manners to be so gloomy at dinner," your Anna said.

I told her she was right.

She was open and talkative. The girl was changing. She was looking well. She had taken an interest in her appearance—and why not?

Do you understand that any false testimony you knowingly give will provoke God's great anger in your earthly life and will deliver your soul unto Satan upon your death?

Every moment of my life.

What is your name, age, and profession?

Wallpurga Haller. I am forty-one years old. I live outside the walls of Leonberg. My husband is a day laborer.

You were also a witness in the witchcraft case of Helena Frisch?

We all knew she was a witch.

You're an expert.

The evil I have witnessed would be overwhelming if I didn't have my faith in God.

How did you come into the case of Katharina Kepler?

Very miserably.

Please be clear.

My beautiful daughter, the blessing of my life, was on the path near the Junker's fields, bringing bricks to the kiln. She's always been a good girl, helpful to her parents, respectful, obedient. She was with seven other girls when they saw the figure of a woman all in black, muttering to herself. The woman in black was headed in the opposite direction as them. She may have been cursing, my daughter wouldn't have told me that. All of a sudden the evening sun hid behind a cloud. The girls were frightened. Only my daughter had the courage to walk in the front. And as their paths crossed, the woman in black, who was the Kepler woman, struck my girl, roughly. For no reason. This left a witch's mark on my daughter's arm and finger and also caused her terrible pain.

How old is your daughter?
But a child of eleven.

She wasn't alone—why will none of the other girls come forward to speak of what happened?
She was alone in being hurt. [Weeps.] We were singled out by the Kepler woman. I don't know why.

You told us she was with seven other girls. Will none of those girls confirm her story?
My daughter has the rare blessing of courage, sir. One other girl had the decency to speak up, but is afraid to do so under oath. Like I said, only my daughter has the courage.

Yes.
As do I. I also have the courage.

Yes.
If people were punished for lack of courage, perhaps things would be different. Instead, they punish you for laughing too loud after curfew, or holding on to a great-aunt's ring. They put you in jail for working on Sunday.

You say you've had other dealings with Frau Kepler.
My son, Theodor, a gentle boy full of the grace of God, was afflicted. [Weeps.] He had an angry rash that looked like St. Anthony's fire. He suffered terribly. None of the usual remedies helped. We prepared a special bath for him, at no small

expense, and were instructed to keep him out of view for nine days.

The remedy worked?
He was witnessed. That's why the remedy failed. He was supposed to be out of view.

How was he witnessed?
By Frau Kepler, in the form of a blackbird. At first I thought it was only a blackbird.

What kind of a blackbird was it?
A black one, sir.

An ordinary blackbird?
I trust you know a blackbird.

Is the female blackbird not more brown than she is black?
I'm not an expert on birds, sir.

But you know the bird was Frau Kepler?
It was very obvious.

Was it a red-winged blackbird?
I am here to help the court, sir. Not to give a school lesson.

Your husband is currently charged with theft, Frau Haller, is that the case?
Many false charges are made.

Are you in debt to Frau Kepler?
Frau Kepler is a well-known witch. She messed with my daughter and my son both. Who would describe that as me being in debt to her? No, no; she's in debt to me. She owes me. More than anyone has ever owed me. Just thinking

about it gives me a devilish headache. It's not an ordinary headache, but different, like a vinegar.

You receive alms from Ursula Reinbold, is that right?
She's a kind person.

You visit her every day, yes?
She's no stranger.

Did she promise you a measure of Frau Kepler's possessions if she wins her case?
I'm pursuing truth, that's all.

You have filed asking for a thousand thalers from Frau Kepler's estate?
I've followed the advice of the law.

Do you expect this court to reward you the house of Frau Kepler?
I never have any luck. I only ever do the right thing. I tend to my nest and sing my gratefulness to God and I will keep on my good path no matter the difficulties.

* * *

Simon, the way I remember the conversation with Einhorn was as so.

He said: I am given to understand that you were on the path near the Junker's fields.

I said: I often walk that way.

He said: I've received a troubling report, which is why I've called you here again.

I said: When will my slander case move forward? I thought you had called me in to resolve that.

He said: The bricklayer's daughter says you hit the Haller girl on the arm. So does the Haller girl's mother. You know the bricklayer's girl, that's the blond girl with the beauty mark above her eyebrow. So that's two girls who witnessed you—the one you hit, and the one who is too afraid to say she saw you hit her.

I said: What? I've hit no one. Never in my life have I hit anyone. Not on purpose.

He said: I inspected the Haller girl. Her arm hurts her. So does her finger. Her finger especially.

I said: I didn't touch her.

He said: You understand my obligation to take seriously any complaints that are brought to me, Frau Kepler.

I said: What about my complaints?

He said: The Haller girl comes from a questionable family. But the daughter of the bricklayer is said to be a very nice girl, and reliable. She told her parents about the assault.

I said: Sir, I don't want to put her down, but, again, sir, she's a child.

He said: You confirm, then, that you were on the path near the Junker's field?

I said: Sir, if we could proceed with my slander trial, this would all be simplified. I beg of you to give me justice. These other things will then fall away. The right thing is to clear my name first, so that we know who we are dealing with. This nonsense of the bricklayer's daughter and the Haller girl—that's weeds traveled from Ursula Reinbold's accusations. I'm sorry to say, sir, but if we'd had my complaint dealt with in a timely way, as would have happened in Duchess Sybille's time—if we'd had my trial earlier, then this would never—

He said: Each thing in its time—

I said: That's what I mean to say—

He said: I have another question for you, while I have you. Should I put you down as a widow? Or as abandoned by your husband?

I said: What?

He said: You have no confirmation of the death of your husband—is that right? Was the split bitter?

I said: There was no split, sir. And no confirmation, either. This was nearly thirty years ago, and it's very difficult to hear for certain about men who have gone to war—

He said: Do you claim to be a widow, or do you not?

I said: I have two sons still alive who—

He said: Okay, very well, that is the end of our business today, Frau Kepler.

You'll recall that interview, having accompanied me, Simon. You can confirm my memory. It would be a few more days before I understood the catastrophic escalation that had occurred. Over an encounter with a child no more dramatic than wind untidying hair. I believe the Haller girl was pushed to say that she had been injured by me. Her mother, Wallpurga Haller, has been in prison twice. Everyone knows Wallpurga tells fortunes by measuring heads—a superstitious and unlawful practice, which, besides, she is no good at.

Do you understand that any false testimony you knowingly give will provoke God's great anger in your earthly life and will deliver your soul unto Satan upon your death?

I come here with a clear conscience.

State your name and age and your relation to the defendant.

Dorothea Klebl, wife of the marksman. I am forty-three years old. I do not know Katharina personally. She is not a friend; she is not an enemy. I live a small distance outside of the gates. Ursula Reinbold also is not a friend. Also not an enemy. This only came to my attention through my husband, who was at the market stall of Butcher Frick, and I was shy and reluctant to be involved.

Please share any information you have that may be relevant to the case of Frau Kepler.

I know very little. Here it is. I'd say it was about six years ago that a young girl from the Schfitzenbastian family came and worked in my home for a few months, doing housework. Before she came to me, she had worked at the house of Katharina Kepler. She was a quiet girl, very dutiful and nice. Not pretty, but with a good heart. I liked her. She felt comfortable with me and opened up to me. She was very young, even younger than her age, if you know what I mean. And skinny.

The Schfitzenbastian girl told you something about Frau Kepler?

She said that Katharina Kepler wandered around the house very late at night, when other people sleep. The girl—her name was Hildegard—asked Frau Kepler what was distressing her, why was she pacing? Why couldn't she sleep? Frau Kepler asked Hildegard, didn't she like the night? She said a girl could meet a lover at night. The devil could arrange such things. Wouldn't she like a carefree life? One of pleasure and excitement? Those were the questions Frau Kepler asked her.

Hildegard was frightened by the way Katharina was talking. Any good girl would be.

Hildegard told me that she told Katharina she wished to live a life with God and find happiness in heaven.

What Hildegard told me is that Katharina answered her by saying that there is no heaven and no hell. She said that people die no differently than an overworked ox in the road.

Is there anything else the court should know?

I don't think so. Hildegard was a nice girl, but I don't know where she is now. She was one of those who dreams often of love.

In the small realm of my own familial concerns, there was news. More or less happy news. Certainly unexpected. Katharina cared for my Anna in her way, and maybe that is why I write of this here, because it shows something of Katharina's influence on those around her. Perhaps it feels like an intrusion. The sayers will say what they will. Anna had gone first to the pastor and then to the chemist. We went to the tailor that Katharina said had done fairly priced quality work for her in the past, the tailor Schmidt. Schmidt adjusted not only the red dress of Anna's mother, but also another simple but still flattering light blue one. He altered the neckline to make it more fashionable. All in all, he had a good and well-meaning eye, and Anna and I both were pleased with the results. As was Katharina, who offered her opinion, of course.

Then, one afternoon, there was a knock at the door. I'm not used to unexpected knocks. Clients visited on expected days at expected times. Katharina would walk in, or if the door was locked she would call out to me. This knocking—I had no idea who it might be. "Are you the tax collector?" I asked the fellow at my door.

But it was not the tax collector knocking. It was love knocking. A suitor. Not necessarily a suitor that makes a father's heart sing. A rope maker's assistant. With a wide head, though pretty in his way, like a young boy or a woman. Very courteous. I thought at first he was an orphan. He made no mention of his parents. He was not a citizen nor likely to become one. Love is one of the lowliest reasons for courtship. In its best form, a marriage is a contract of guardianship. But no one asked me.

The suitor's name was Alexander.

Anna was visibly pleased to see him.

He brought with him as a gift for Anna a green silk ribbon. Green is normally a color that lifts my spirits, though this was an unappealing hue. But, again, Anna was pleased.

She served tea to this Alexander. She sliced an apple and laid out the slices as if they were the opening petals of a flower.

And as the weeks and months passed, things proceeded pretty much as these things do. With one small irregularity. I came to understand why Alexander made no mention of his parents, or of any of his relations. He was no fool. Though he himself lives outside of Leonberg, he is a nephew of Rosina Zoft, the baker's wife. When I say the baker, I mean the one on River Street. I used to think of the Zoft bakery as the cat bakery, because Rosina had an unusual soft spot for cats, though she would deny that, but cats are often at her windows and doors. She has said they are to keep out rats, but I have seen her more than once making soft mew calls, giving them a tangle of weeds and old rags to play with. But I no longer think of the Zoft bakery as the cat bakery. I think of it instead as the bakery I avoid ever since the conflict with Katharina.

Not the old conflict, about feeding Heinrich when he came back to town to die at home. But the new conflict: the shouting, the threats, the rumors of a vicious deposition, and that capped off with the strained recapitulation of all of that under oath. Alexander was Rosina's nephew, but from the husband's side, may he rest in peace, he was lost in the difficult February.

Alexander and Anna first met, as I should have known,

at the market. He bought her some chestnuts. The girl never ate a chestnut I offered her in her life. But these chestnuts were apparently very fine. He is a very short fellow, some people say, and with hairy arms and a dark and nervous look. But I liked him. I very much did. Anna, for her part, smelled like lavender. She sang songs about birds eating sugar. I felt I had to stand by, and see it through, and see no monsters. Even as I firmly believe that the life of a spinster is often better than that of a married woman. No dying in childbirth. No beast in the house.

OH, I ALMOST forgot to mention. Now I remember perhaps what made me pick up the pen at this miserable time when Katharina is still in the midst of this perilous trial against her. Not long after Alexander's first visit, I received another unexpected knock at my door. That irritated me. What was I, a tavern keeper?

I was not in the mood to see the wide-headed Alexander so soon again. I opened the door with a frown.

It was the red-cheeked pewterer. Katharina's son, Christoph. The man was a busy citizen. I had heard he had answered the call to help with the formation of a militia, he had a busy shop, he was a guild member—what was such a man doing making a call at my home? A hummingbird once rested near my shoulder. It was a very ill omen. For one who isn't a flower.

Christoph walked past me, set down a sweet jam on my table like a man setting down a boot. "Friendship," he said. "I'm not going to put down family. Family is a field of hay, a well of water, whatnot. But friendship is a sausage. Or, no, it's not a sausage. Romance is a sausage. Friendship is a lemon. Do you know what sailors take on their journeys to the here-be-monsters parts of the maps? They take lemons, because lemons are steadfast. I'm training soldiers, as you know. Some of the men have been sailors before being soldiers. They're the ones who tell me the lemon is a forever friend."

I'm not one to interrupt. Also he smelled of drink.

"And you have been that lemon, Simon. If the court saw that only her children were standing by her—how would that look? Of course her children stand by her—"

"Not all children stand by their parents—"

"Even the babes of wolves don't turn against their parents."

I said nothing. If there were a guild of non-sayers, that would be my guild. That's also the guild of standing by.

Christoph then asked me if Tanner Kramer had been by.

"Your neighbor?"

"Yes, exactly the one."

I have at times bought leather from Tanner Kramer, but I wouldn't say we have a close working relationship. That said, I had purchased a skin from him the day prior.

Christoph said, "He's an eavesdropper and a gloater, and he doesn't keep the cleanest of workshops. But I like him okay. I suppose he told you about what Hans wrote in his book."

"Who's Hans?"

"My brother."

"Oh yes, of course, sorry." I had heard nothing about his book, I said. I stood up to offer Christoph some bread, which he refused, and asked instead for some cider, if I had any.

"*Lullaby for the Lepers*," he said. "*Choral for the Crabapples*. That's the title of the book, you see."

I said I couldn't follow the meaning.

"Or *Hassling of the Household*."

I asked what the book was about.

"It's not really a book. It's my brother sewing another layer onto the rear of his pants."

"What's that?"

"Protecting himself from the mule's kick."

I still didn't follow.

"I wouldn't judge Hans for trying to protect himself. I gave the beastly Einhorn the finest almond cake at tax time. I say, How do you do, and, Thanks so much, and if someone gave me shoes to lick, I would lick them, no problem, you won't find me in hell for the sin of pride."

Finally Christoph set down the specimen in question—a fine book. It had Turkish marbled endpapers, like my old copy of *The Golden Ass*. And I'd have thought the Turks were too out of favor for now. The title of Hans's book was *Harmonices Mundi*. I looked it over. It didn't look like a useful or entertaining book. It was in Latin. But very pretty. Drawings of spheres and triangles and elaborate baubles as might decorate a Christmas tree.

"Never mind the schoolboy sketches," Christoph said. He pointed my attention to a passage. It was difficult to read, as Christoph was so red in the face and kept turning the page and redirecting my attention, now to this, now to that. Also my Latin is poor. Hans had written something about knowing a woman who was born under a similar star pattern as himself, but who was fractious and difficult and totally different in nature than he was. Some argument about astrology, it seemed, not my stuff. This fractious woman, it went on, was the author of her own considerable misfortune.

The author of her own considerable misfortune. I thought

that was a nice phrase. And considerable. In its way, it was ennobling.

"You don't understand," Christoph said. He turned a few pages and pointed to another passage of Hans's listing how much more went into one's destiny than the stars. There was the matter of whether you were born rich or poor, a man or a woman—those, too, powerfully affected one's fate and character. Himself, for example, having not been born to land or money, having been slight and inclined toward study, having been a man rather than a woman—those had separated him from others born under similar stars.

On other pages, it was about nature breathing, belching, and other such speculations, and the earth singing mi and fa, for misery and famine.

I poured Christoph another mug of cider.

"Now, what gets me about that is he's not the one here in Leonberg. He's not the one being splashed as the cart drives through the mud, now, is he? I bet he wrote this while Mama was with him in Linz, but—wouldn't you ask your brother first, before writing something like this? Wouldn't you ask your brother, before running a cart through an arsenic- and vermin-filled mud puddle that was directly outside of his home? Wouldn't you ask your brother, maybe, for his opinion, seeing as he would likely know much more than you, however famous you might be, given that the subject was your very own town and people that you saw with your own eyes and ears? Wouldn't that be what you would do, before you would include damning speculations about your very own mother right alongside talking about planets spinning and trees singing and other nonsense?" Christoph had quite a lot to say in this line of thinking. I began to suspect his wife had sent him out of the house, that she had had enough.

I tried to reassure him that the number of people in town interested in reading elaborate books in Latin about stars or whatnot was limited. But also I let him rave. I am not completely unaware of basic human needs. I poured him more cider. He began to cry. This was happening around me altogether too much. I brought over to him the same handkerchief I'd so recently brought over to my dear Anna in an unexpected moment of tears. And I then busied myself rearranging tools on my workbench. The young man's dignity required a measure of privacy.

Eventually he heaved a deep sigh. He shook his head. "Look, a dropped sausage gone to the dogs is gone to the dogs. Hans wrote what he wrote and it can't be changed. I still have hope."

"Because of your mother's innocence," I said.

"Oh no, that's neither here nor there. Rather, it's what I came here to say. I came here to thank you for helping your neighbor. For helping my mother. If it weren't for you, she'd have only her children at her side. And how would that look? It would look terrible. Without you, she'd be halfway to the rack already. Hans thinks it's his special status that protects Mama, Greta thinks it's God that protects her—I think it's you. Well, you and me, too. So, from guildsman to guildsman, I thank you."

I felt very ill at ease and hoped he would leave. Maybe I was hungry.

Christoph stood up. On his way out, he asked me to please not mention to Katharina what Hans had written about her in his book. He said he hoped she wouldn't learn of it.

Then why, I wondered, did he come and tell her neighbor about it?

I resolved to forget about the whole embarrassing encounter. It wasn't that I found his thanks unwelcome. Or that I felt he was pressuring me to stand by Katharina—that was anyway my intention all along.

   ✦ ✦ I repeat that it was an ungodly error. Johannes, Christoph, Greta—I apologize to all of them, as well as to God, to whom I have privately repented. And also to you, Simon.

I was in a terror. When there had been only the one person accusing me of bodily harm, that was not legal grounds for torture. But now there were two—that was grounds for torture to yield a confession. I was told the case against me was "good." I was told it was likely to succeed. One could call into question the accusers—the case would be much stronger if they were men—but those around me began to expect a bad outcome. Even Greta's Pastor Binder had changed his perspective. Who were we to ask the why of suffering? he said. God's wisdom was not a clematis vine that we could draw and dissect. It was not a fence post whose height we could measure. And so on.

Okay, I have stated my apologies.

I will begin this ignominious portion of my story by mentioning some of the silver items that I am aware of in the home of the False Unicorn, also known as Ducal Governor Einhorn. The False Unicorn has a cockerel made of silver, about the size of a baby's head. He has two silver soldiers. One holds a shield bearing a unicorn balanced on its hind feet. The other holds a sword, but no shield. He has a set of simple silver candlesticks, as well as a second set in which a young boy or god holds up a bowl of some sort. He has a silver sculpture of a fishmonger. My sources tell me he has no shortage of silver tea strainers, nor of silver cupholders. He has a silver hare standing on its hind legs that he sets in his window at Eastertime. I learned all of this from reliable sources, including my own eyes. Now I am losing track, there is much more. What I am saying is that the ducal governor Einhorn is a man who has received a lot of silver in his life. I doubt all the silver objects were gifts from his mother.

Many people in this area get their silver from Rammelsberg. My beloved father, however, taught me that the silver from Freiberg and the Black Forest is of a finer quality because the earth gives it up more readily. The miners of Rammelsberg, Saxons of course, are known to be cruel to their horses, and to one another.

I had a goblet of Rammelsberg silver. It had been a gift from my father-in-law, whom I could not love. My father-in-law had given the silver goblet to me on the occasion of Hans's baptism, which Hans's father, Heinrich, did not attend, he was out hunting or something. I hated the goblet, though I understood it was valuable.

I went to the ducal governor's home. I was in the waiting room again. With the stuffed pheasant again. Someone had given the pheasant a dusting. This improvement had drained the bird of its power. Like a moody and terrifying revenant who yet cannot survive the light of day. The pheasant no longer frightened me. The spirit inside it had died. I felt sorry for the small devil. What or who had killed the spirit? I asked myself. I answered myself, Your fears are feeding the beasts, Kath-chen.

That pheasant and I waited quite a while. When I would feel a fire rise within me, I would sing to myself a little song from when I was a child:

Can you count the meadows,
Can you count the stars,
Can you count the fishes and their scales and the dead of wars?

God can count the mountains,
God can count the stars,
God can count the fishes,
God knows where you are.

"Frau Kepler, you're back again," a voice said.

I startled. The voice was from nowhere.

No, it was from behind me.

Turning, I saw the False Unicorn. He was wearing his dark hat, his wool jacket with a collar of fur. He had a handkerchief out; he was sneezing, sniffling.

"Where's your guardian about whom you are so insistent?" he said with a laugh.

I said nothing.

He gestured me into his office.

"I'm sorry to see you suffering," I said. I was referring to his cold, about which I can assure you I knew better than to suggest a remedy.

"Let's be quick about this? I should tell you this is no setting to be putting down the Haller girl, we already spoke of that."

I asked after his beautiful spaniel, who I hadn't seen at our earlier meeting about the stupid Haller girl.

"She died," he said.

I worried he would find me responsible.

He said his princess had been an exemplary dog and it was wrong.

I gave my condolences.

He gathered himself and changed topics. I can't say he wasn't polite, or indeed unctuous: "Frau Kepler, I am aware that your situation is a stressful one. Every effort for a fair inquiry is being made. I can't help but wonder," he said carefully, "if you hadn't pressed this foolish charge, then perhaps there would not now be all these other charges coming against you. I told you at the time: This didn't happen. Not officially. If only you had listened to me."

Be like a deer in the forest, Kath-chen, I said to myself. It is not easy for me to be a deer—if I were an animal, I would more likely be an owl, or a plover. But my situation was that of the hunted deer. I tried to be still and quiet, even as the silver goblet that I held under my shawl seemed almost to be alive, wriggling, growing spiky.

"I've refrained from saying it until now, Frau Kepler, but you didn't think of my position, did you? Your charges, put together in a hasty and sloppy fashion—they put me in a difficult position. Why? Because they were inaccurate. Untrue. Incorrect. Wrong. And so, slanderous. Funny, that, since it was of slander you were accusing others. I'm not going to attribute malice to you. Nor rancor. Nor ill will. But I will say that your charges made it appear that the ducal governor—that is, myself—had violated the law of the Carolina."

The law of the Carolina, as it was explained to me by the children, stipulated that with a charge as serious as witchcraft, I could only be questioned under oath. And only in the presence of a legal guardian. The Carolina also dictated that someone accused of witchcraft could not be tortured without two credible eyewitnesses of sorcery. Or one credible eyewitness plus evidence of a relationship to another proven witch. Hans had told me that some small districts had flouted the Carolina in their trials—but that some of the district officers in question had been punished or dismissed as a result. Some, but not all. When I was in Linz, Hans had been clear on how the law could protect me, but I confess I did not much listen.

The False Unicorn went on: "I would never violate the law." On the contrary, he said, he was a limb of the law.

Didn't I know that? Didn't I see his position? Now here he was, ducal governor in a strange backwater, not among his people, and at risk—and why? "Because I tried to help. Because I was foolish enough to try to make peace among the residents here. If I had turned a blind eye, I would be sleeping easy. Instead, I sleep hardly at all. Also I have the gout."

I had suggestions for that, too. Especially celeriac. But I was not so much the fool as to say them aloud.

It was no mystery that these were troubled times, the False Unicorn said. Grape harvests were failing. A whole mountainside of goats had died of unknown causes. Why did all the blame come to him? And all the begging! One man wanted money to clothe his wife and children. Another kept coming back for more grain from the public stores. A third had a grotesquely enlarged leg, which had gone unconsidered since the death of Duchess Sybille. Leonberg! Why could he not have been placed somewhere more . . . elegant? More civilized. The False Unicorn, I was given to understand, was accustomed to finer things. Leonberg didn't even have chocolate! In Prague, who didn't have chocolate? The False Unicorn sneezed and coughed through all this. I almost shouted out that I had something very fine for him, indeed. "Frau Kepler—in your long life, have you ever witnessed such a persecution as mine? Your son the astrologer has been quite meddlesome, as I'm sure you're aware."

I averted my eyes. I was thinking of the sin I was planning to commit, the fine object it involved.

The False Unicorn began pacing. He began to sermonize about those who took their worldly power too seriously. He said the true realm of power was elsewhere. He said he had heard things about Hans that he wouldn't repeat— who was he to say what had or had not happened in distant lands? But he did know that some considered my son such a heretic as to bar him from taking Communion in the church, that still Hans would not stand down from his unholy positions. Was stubbornness a family trait? Johannes did have worldly power, but his power was like smoke—any strong wind would disperse it. "He implicates me in his hasty, foolish notes to the Duke and others. I don't want to insult your child, who is perhaps ill-informed, and panicked, but I ask you: Isn't it true that I was in no way involved with the accusations made against you? Why, I sat in a chair, petting my dearly departed dog. I may have been present, but I was not an official witness. I was also not an instigator. Far from it. I saved you from mortal threat. Herr Kräutlin was agitated—and I intervened to save you. All I did was help, and that is why I'm punished."

I was sitting in a church pew, and at the pulpit was the devil.

"What I would advise to you, Frau Kepler, is to have faith. Have faith in the truth. It will save you."

How stupid I was not to have walked out. The meeting had gone on too long. The position I was in had been made clear to me. There was nothing more to be done. I couldn't count the stars, and God didn't know where I was.

In a scene I had rehearsed in my imagination, and as if in a trance, I began, as if a stranger within me were speaking: "Are you familiar with the story of the silversmith?" I said the good Pastor Blenem, who had passed four winters ago, had given a sermon on the silversmith.

"I didn't know Blenem, but the pastor I've installed, the yellowy-bearded fellow, has effectively improved attendance. I have a list, you see. Showing attendance at the service, and who has and hasn't taken Communion, and . . ."

I wasn't listening to him, I was rushing heedlessly ahead according to my plan. My father and mother had different stories about the timing of my birth, and I sometimes suspect I am more foolish in character than I like to think—and such a character better matches the birth time argued for by my mother. I said to the False Unicorn: "A man went to see the silversmith, wanting to learn how he did his work. The silversmith told him that one held the silver in the center of the fire, where the flame is hottest and most intense. Not just in any part of the flame." I paused. I was losing faith in my story. I touched the Rammelsberg silver cup I had under my shawl. "The man asked the silversmith, how long did the metal have to stay in the intense heat? To which the silversmith answered that he had to watch it at every moment—"

"Frau Kepler, can we get to the point?"

"The silversmith knows that the moment to take it out is when he sees his own reflection in the metal—"

"Yes, yes," Einhorn said, "and the silversmith is the Lord. Who sees his reflection in us when we are in pain. I get it. I don't need to spend my afternoon listening to children's stories, so if that is all you wanted to say, Frau Kepler—"

I pulled the irksome yet valuable silver goblet from my shawl. Like I was pulling a feral cat from a pocket.

I dropped the silver goblet onto the floor.

The False Unicorn picked it up.

"It's for you," I said. "A gift."

For a moment nothing happened, not anywhere in the world, it seemed. Then a childish grin came over his face. He looked so happy. "How perfectly lovely. Shiny. Beautiful. Funny. Unwise," he said, rotating it. There was a dragon on the stem, with a relaxed expression. If I were a dragon, I might also feel relaxed. If I had talons, the ability to breathe fire. If I no longer existed. Those would be relaxing qualities. The False Unicorn placed the goblet high on a shelf behind him, among candlesticks, a silver dish—

I saw what a fool I had been.

I hadn't asked explicitly that he drop the case against me in exchange for the silver. But I now understand I may as well have. He would in any case say what he liked, and he had the cup as false proof. He was going to keep the goblet as evidence of a bribe, as a confirmation of my wrongdoing. That silver cup would resolve his problems, not mine. "It catches the light very nicely," he said. "Now, please leave, Frau Kepler. I have a great deal to accomplish this afternoon. You people have no idea of the scale of burdens placed upon me."

I went home and sat for many hours next to my cow Chamomile.

Leonberg, January 10, 1617

To the most exalted and kind Duke Frederick of
Württemberg,

Following up, in addition to what she has done to my own
self, she rode a calf backward, to death, and then roasted
it, and for those and the following reasons and more, I
have filed a suit with your magistracy and ask that Frau
Katharina Kepler be held in prison until the time of a trial
to prove that she desired to teach witchcraft to the daughter
of a citizen, and that she told same daughter that if a person
were to die it would be due neither to heaven nor to hell,
but instead would be the same as what befell any dumb
beast; and that is not all, there is more that Frau Kepler has
done; she went and asked the gravedigger for her father's
head so she could use it as a drinking goblet and it was only
when the gravedigger explained he would need to ask for
permission from the authorities that she gave it up; and
there is even more than that: she injured Ziegler's wife's
foot, she also injured the schoolmaster, she also poisoned the
barber's assistant, and also she harmed the butcher when he
was standing outside the town hall. She cursed many cows,
which then ran riot and destroyed fences. She is seen and has
been seen and will continue to be seen, walking about, to
and fro, disturbing everyone. It is clear as day and everyone
knows about it, and also that Frau Kepler uses witchcraft
to confuse witnesses, and this is so well known and

detailed that you don't need my testimony or any further permissions from the Empire or the Kings or the clauses of the Carolinian laws, all those laws so well and benevolently put into place. Nothing more is required in order to act against Frau Kepler, to seize her person and her property, to detain her in the territory of Your Royal Grace, I ask that you renew the mandate for her capture and detention and that she not be released until she is questioned and brought to sweet justice and thoroughly dealt with and this I humbly and pleadingly ask for the sake of God, to Your Royal Grace, so that you, as the highest authority, can exact due punishment on the guilty.

Ursula Reinbold, wife of the glazier

Thank you for coming here today. Do you understand that any false testimony you knowingly give will provoke God's great anger in your earthly life and will deliver your soul unto Satan upon your death?
I've never heard of such a thing.

Do you agree to the proceedings as described?
I don't feel I have much choice, but okay, I'm here.

How old are you and what is your profession?
I'm Daniel Schmidt. I'm forty-six years old. I'm a tailor. There are seven tailors in Leonberg, but my family has been tailors here longer than any of the others. Probably this is why Frau Kepler and her family chose to work with me over the years.

Did Frau Kepler ever behave in a suspicious manner with you?
What do you mean by suspicious? I have no complaints about anyone. I'm here because I was asked to come here, but I have no complaints against anyone.

Can you tell us about what happened when your child was ill?
It wasn't one child. It was two children.

Yes. Can you tell us about that?
The girl suffered even more than the boy.

The names of your children?
Lucia was two and a half. Hans David was not yet two.

And how did you come into relations with Frau Kepler during this time, when your children were ill?
I was doing some work for her in her home. She had a coat that was in need of mending and required a new lining. She also needed her dress to be adjusted, she had grown very thin. It was an extensive job, which I carried out well, and for a fair price.

When was this?
Six or so years ago.

Frau Kepler said something intrusive to you, is that right?
Maybe.

What did she say?
You probably mean that she said that my wife and I were suffering. She said that though we said our blessings in the mornings and in the evenings, still, difficulty met us at every turn. She was speaking of our children's illness. I didn't want to speak about it with her or anyone. She asked after Lucia and Hans David at every opportunity. She would visit us unannounced. Often she brought food. She also encouraged others to visit us. We never knew when she was coming. Or when the others were coming. It was a terrible time. One appreciates that others try to help, but also one wants to be left alone. I remember one difficult day in particular. My wife had taken the girl to the doctor in Stuttgart. It had been a long journey. The man was supposed to be an expert. My wife had put so many hopes in him. She insisted on the pointless trek. She is so easily convinced. I waited for her return with dread, without the smallest bit of hope. Little Hans David was crying the whole day, he wouldn't eat, he wanted his mother and sister round. Before my wife had

even made it back to the house, when she was at the gate, carrying Lucia, Katharina intercepted her. What a cross you bear, with this child, Katharina told her. There's nothing to be done, my wife replied.

Your wife found Katharina suspicious?
My wife was suffering. That is her business. Only God knows.

What else happened at the gate?
Katharina pressed my wife to try another treatment for the child. She told her special words to say. It was a song of sorts. My wife had heard the words before.

It was a devilish incantation? Something superstitious?
I can't say. Katharina told my wife that she had said the same words when her own child was sick. That child of Katharina's had died. Why even recommend the words? But Katharina said the words could do no harm. Maybe God would see to save the child. Katharina told my wife to say the words three times over, at night, under the full moon, in the churchyard.

What happened to Lucia and Hans David?
Both are in heaven.

Do you think the pagan words Katharina encouraged your wife to say harmed them?
I think they're in heaven.

Did Katharina give the children harmful salves or trinkets in the guise of gifts or medicines?
Sir, I have nothing more to say. Only God knows.

You said Katharina sent others to your home to visit when your children were ill?
We did have many visitors. Too many visitors.

Did any of those visitors give you potions, salves, gifts? Or lean over the cribs with curses—
I don't know why my children died. That is for God to know.

Could any of those visits, gifts, salves, potions, or words have led to the death of one or both of your children?
Sir, do you have children? They are in the care of God at all times.

You cannot say that Katharina is definitively innocent of the deaths of your children?
Sir, I am being forced to say the same thing again and again. I feel like a hooked fish waiting to be tossed back into the water. I don't have the answers you want. If someone looked into the situation in detail, maybe they would find something of the nature you are seeking. But me—I can't say.

Do you understand that any false testimony you knowingly give will provoke God's great anger in your earthly life and will deliver your soul unto Satan upon your death?

If you say so, okay.

Your name, age, and profession?

Jerg Hundersinger. I'm thirty-two years old. I work as a baker. Though, as you see, I have this extra thumb, which has brought me bad luck.

What do you know of the character, good or ill, of Frau Kepler?

I have known Frau Kepler for, well, many years. I don't know how many. She was friendly also with my father, God bless his soul, when he was around.

Have I had any reason to doubt Frau Kepler's character? Oh, I don't know. I've been a very unlucky man in my life, that's my feeling. Why have I been so unlucky? I don't know. Could it be that Frau Kepler has been part of this unluckiness? Even the author of this unluckiness? I don't know. What can I say? I mean, if she poisoned someone, that would be terrible. If she did it. Of course that would be terrible. I wouldn't want people to think, simply because I have been friendly with her, that I think it's okay to poison an enemy. I've had enough bad luck, I don't need more.

Do you understand that any false testimony you knowingly give will provoke God's great anger in your earthly life and will deliver your soul unto Satan upon your death?

Yes. That is part of why I am eager to speak here.

State your name and profession and age.

I am Ella Schmidt, I am the tailor's wife, I am thirty-four years old.

We have the testimony of your husband. Is there more you wish to add?

It was stockings that Frau Kepler was inquiring after. My husband misremembers—it wasn't waistbands, as he has sometimes said. Nor was it a mending of a coat, though he has done that work in other times. Frau Kepler was a friend to both of us for many years and that is what I want to say. My husband was very worked up when he gave his testimony. Pity should be taken on him. Frau Kepler did recommend to me a song that I sing with the little angel. I don't think she said to do so under a full moon, as my husband said. I am sure he said it in all honesty, but I believe he misremembers. Katharina meant only to help. I had been told about the song before. It's a grandmother sort of a song, not anything suspicious. Not as far as I know. The song hadn't worked for her baby, who is buried not far from her father. That was my waiting, my hesitation.

Was there more you wished to share about Frau Kepler?
While our children were alive, my husband had nothing bad
to say about Frau Kepler. He never complained of her to me,
not that I can remember. I am so sorry to be troubling the
court with the difficulties of a humble couple such as our-
selves, who have been very blessed in having two beautiful
children. Even if they lived only for a short time, they were
a blessing beyond imagining. Hans David was a very bright
and cheerful boy and smiled more often and more brightly
than I have ever seen since. Lucia would laugh when she felt
wind blowing, and often hid under a blanket. My husband
can say what he wants, but I am a very fortunate woman to
have known my children. Thank you for listening to me. I
was crying last night worried about poor Katharina, I had to
say what was in my heart, which is knowledge.

Simon, you will remember already I was no longer allowed to collect earnings from my land, all my holdings were under the control of the ducal governor's office. The Hallers alone were asking for a thousand thalers in damages, more than triple the price of my home. The Werewolf and her clan likely expected more, though on different days I heard different numbers. She liked to go around saying she didn't care about money, only about her health and safety. The inspectors, in their blue uniforms, came and paced around the home I inherited from my dear father. They measured the windows. They wrote down in their ledgers every spoon and mouse as best as I could tell. I'll forever be grateful to you, Simon, for keeping me company in that low moment. I don't even remember if I won or lost those rounds we played. You have always been reserved, and I have respected that, and for that reason all the more I was gratified to hear you rage against how I was treated, against the destructive power of rumor, against how again and again you saw people ready to see monsters, not ready to stand by, not ready to see somebody through. Your rage brought you to a state that was almost a trance, or fever. You knocked over the backgammon board, and I can still hear the clatter of the stones on the ground. I had not seen that side of you before. I confess it calmed me.

Perhaps that's why I recall what a perfectly magnificent October day it was. The sky was bright, the air smelled of wood. I had one small silver spoon, and a small collection of lace and ribbons that I had been meaning for some time to bring as a gift to Agnes, so I felt I was in the right to have removed it from my home in order to bring it to her. I headed across town to their home. It was on the day of the slaughtering of the pigs. As I walked through the town square, I saw the rope maker's children playing with a pig's inflated bladder. In front of the scribe's house, a wooden frame had been set up with a swine corpse tied to it in elegant splay. The pig's hind feet were nearer to the sky, and the front feet toward the ground. A young man was on the ground, holding a pan to collect the last bits of blood draining. The splayed legs made it look like a headless near-human figure. The kidneys were still attached, looking like decorative flourishes on a fine dress. Where was the head of this pig? Maybe already in a pot somewhere.

I passed by and went to visit the six-fingered baker, Jerg. If he couldn't pay me, he would at least give me some rolls. He looked alarmed when I entered. He said, "Frau Kepler, it's been a terrible time." The bakery smelled of apple strudel, of cinnamon. "I never said anything bad about you." He took his gloves off, and had one of his apprentices take his place at the counter. He led me to a space near the back. He nearly whispered: "I had two batches of butter go sour. My pheasant began molting, he had to be killed, but the meat couldn't be trusted. A complete waste. My nephew, in Esslingen, has leprosy now, and can no longer help my sister, he can't even play among the other children. I'm trying to help her as best I can. She has given me a fair price for her harvest even in years when she could have squeezed me. I was so unkind to her when I was young—why?"

He offered me some beer, he said he would pull out his one stool for me.

I told him no thank you.

The route I took to Christoph's passed by an unholy spot.

There it was: the third-rate glazier's house. The residence of Ursula Reinbold. I saw the curtain of the upstairs window closed against the cold. What a frippery, that curtain. As if she weren't shouting herself all over town, now pretending to want privacy. I don't know how fully to account for it, I am not quick to say the name of the devil, but a greenish light surrounded her building. Then the curtain was parted. Ursula leaned out the window, she had a pan of pig's blood, she tipped the pan and the blood poured on my head, spoiling all my clothes. Then she held a baby at the window there, and dropped the baby as well, one baby after another, it was only for me to catch them. I was trying but it was an awful and terrifying and confusing rain of bodies. A crowd of onlookers gathered, some laughing at me, others shouting at me, telling me it was wrong how I was hurting the babies. Small blankets also were falling, as well as mittens, bonnets. I called out to defend myself, and in the distraction I missed a child.

But that didn't happen: I was standing still on the street, in the clean cold.

I had faced real difficulties in my life. I had cared for my dying father. I had brought back my husband, Heinrich, from war. I had watched my own infants die; I had watched as the infants of neighbors died. I saw the peach trees fruit too early and freeze and give no fruit. I knew a forester who could no longer speak after being hit on the head with a falling branch. I had seen my husband squander our money. I'd seen him set off one last time, an old soldier at forty, sure to die. Why had Einhorn asked me again if he was dead? Maybe he isn't. I'd managed births and baptisms almost entirely on my own. I'd managed the fields without a cart or horse or even a donkey. I had offered help to others when I could, and even when I couldn't. I had felt the terrible pride that the good that had come to me through my children was a reward for my own labors. Though I had often contemplated how and when I would die, I had been certain my death would be a happy one. I had not always felt so open to death, but once I had seen each of the children stepping into their adult lives, married, working, I sometimes pictured death as a package that would be left at my doorstep, that I would step into the gift box and that would be my gentle end.

I hurried on to bring the gift to little quiet Agnes. It began to snow, lightly. I arrived to Christoph's home, the pewter baubles in the windowpane. A little parade of cubes and bears and bunnies. I opened the door. It was so warm inside.

Gertie hurried across the room to me. Her stays were not neatly tied—that was strange. What was on her mind? A rash of horse deaths? A story of a Jewish clockmaker roasting a baby on the site of an unfinished church? I wouldn't let her gruesome broadsheet tales further agitate me. But I was wrong to judge Gertie. "Mama Kepler," she said. "Christoph is out looking for you."

"Is Agnes sleeping?" I handed the gift to Gertie, who set it down without even looking at it.

"There are armed men at your home now," she said. "Others are headed to your fields. They'll take you to prison. Everyone is saying it." She took away my shawl. She wrapped me in an old woolen blanket. I was made to look like a beggar. She said that Agnes was with the tanner's family nearby and knew nothing of the plan. What plan? She said she was taking me to meet someone.

I have asked myself many times since if I made a mistake on that day. I never told this to Katharina, I didn't want to add to her worries. Christoph came by my house. Presumably after going by Katharina's house. He was sweating, despite the cold. He had only one of his gloves on. He held a pipe with no tobacco in it.

"Can you come up with me now? To make a statement attesting to Mama's good character?"

It seemed a poorly thought-out and impulsive plan. Come up where? Make a statement to whom? "It doesn't work that way," I said. "I haven't been called up. I wouldn't know where to begin."

"It's very simple. We tell the clerk, whatever his name is—"

"Sebald Sebelen," I said. "He's been unwell—" He had in fact not passed, as Katharina had worried. His recovery was thorough.

"We tell whoever's there that you have a statement to contribute—"

"Better to lie low in these situations. I really think—"

"So you've also turned against her."

"I'm her legal guardian. I was and am. How can I be her guardian and also turn against her? But I see no need to beat a drum—"

"You're afraid," he said. He picked up one of my dull scratching awls and thrummed it on the table. "Or maybe you think it's bad for your business."

"I stand by people," I said. "That's who I am."

"It's been bad for *my* business," he said. "I'm at risk of losing everything. They have so much *energy*, Ursula's people. It's like going up against a thunderstorm. I have work to do, I have other obligations, whereas *they*—*this* is their work. They're the guild of rumormongers. The society of theft-by-accusation. People are stupid, sure, they're ignorant, yes, they're greedy, okay—but these people are fine with basically murdering her if it suits them. Why did they choose my mother? I sometimes wonder if it's because her children have come up in the world. Is it my fault, Simon?"

I have asked myself whether there was something more I could have done for Katharina. Something I could have said. Or not said. Someone I could have appealed to, or unmasked. After considerable reflection, I decided: If the rumor of my moral record were more clear, then perhaps I could have been of better, or at least more vigorous, help to Katharina. What this rumor is or was is of no consequence now. The truth of who I am and what I have done is one thing. The rumor quite another. I wonder who I am writing to at this moment. Maybe a foolish part of me believes that God might concern himself with a flea such as myself. It is my place to concern myself with God, not the reverse— that is my view. What I am saying is I had more than the usual reasons to worry that the accusing crowd that had turned on Katharina would soon turn on me, especially as word of Katharina's case was now reaching beyond the boundaries of Leonberg.

I came to Leonberg from a small town, about a day's walking distance from Stuttgart. It doesn't matter what the town is called, and I prefer not to name it. Maybe not naming it is foolish superstition on my part. When I was young, there were more monasteries than there are today, and of course they were Catholic monasteries. My family were followers of Martin Luther—my father especially, he had a copy of the Luther Bible, and even of some of his sermons, his letter against Henry VIII—and it was never on the horizon that I myself might become a monk. Still, I had a boyish interest in the small monastery at the edge of town. I was a child. I liked the cassocks. I thought of the men there as knights, or even as soldiers. I did some work in the garden there at the monastery. One of the monks gave me as a gift a precious book whose margins he had decorated with rabbits. It was a magnificent, small book. I wish I had it now. I did a strange and regrettable thing with it, hiding it in a furnace. But it was too extravagant a present.

Next thing I knew, and while I was still early in learning my trade, before I had been accepted to the guild, rumors had spread about me and my connection to the monastery. Rumors that said more about the back rooms and dreams of the rumormongers than about me. After that, my father insisted I marry, though I didn't yet have the money to start my own household. There was a great deal of stress and tears and expense but, in part through my father's great efforts, and with some luck, I achieved stability.

I've said more than I meant to. I thought I had left that all more than behind me. On another planet, you see. On a distant star.

Then in the town hall on the day of Katharina's questioning about the Haller girl, the ducal governor Einhorn, on exiting, paused near my seat. He bent down to pick up some small scrap of paper. He handed it to me. I uncrumpled it. It read, simply, in tiniest script: "I know about you."

Probably an idle threat that would work against pretty much anyone with a conscience.

Though I didn't take or have the time to explain that to

Christoph that day, still, I feel confident, it did not affect my decisions in any way. If there was something I could do to help Katharina, I had done it. And would continue to do it. I am, anyway, of the rare opinion that there are no such things as witches at all. Even Christoph seems to believe in that nonsense. Perhaps even Hans.

The man that Gertie introduced me to at the edge of the woods—on a path that leads out of the bitter orange garden, not far from the sheep's meadow—was a curious fellow. I won't tell you his name.

He was a Jewish man, or at least he was wearing the clothing of one. He had a cart filled with all manner of goods, and also two geese. "I apologize for having no horse," he said cheerfully. He didn't look like he'd ever had a horse. Or even had a close friend who had had a horse. He had no teeth at all. He had what looked like a burn mark on his left cheek. That reminded me of my lost Heinrich, who had a similar marking. This man, whom I nicknamed Yellow Gill on account of how he reminded me of that old story about the fish on the plate who starts speaking, had a funny kind of gallantness. He almost knelt before me when helping me onto his cart, offering his hands as a step up. I wasn't ungrateful.

In his goods' cart, I was hidden like so much market fare. But only a curtain separated the cart's contents from the driver, from Yellow Gill. He had put hay inside to make me comfortable, as if I were a cow. Which I didn't mind, I admire cows, as you know.

It was a long journey. The fellow seemed to feel obliged to entertain me. Or maybe to entertain himself. Did he know my predicament? He didn't mention it or ask about it, though he seemed to know to keep me hidden, and along the way we slept far from other travelers. Yellow Gill was a real talker. He spoke in the morning, he spoke in the evening.

He spoke when we stopped to gather water. When we set up camp for an evening, he spoke even more. "I always carry a bit of vinegar," he said. "I haven't yet found something to eat or drink that doesn't taste better with vinegar. Not always easy to come by vinegar." He talked about whatever. "When I have a cut or a scrape, I don't cover it. I leave it to the fresh air as much as modesty allows. If I come across a bay leaf, I'll touch the wound gently with the leaf, then put that into a tea." I didn't agree with all or even many of his medicinal remedies, but he knew more than most apothecaries, that is my opinion. I will only say that he was perhaps overenthusiastic about jasmine, using it for pain, for trouble sleeping, for heart flutterings.

I know there are those who believe that there has never been a Jew who would not be better off burned. You once told me, Simon, that Martin Luther praised the Jews for resisting the Catholic Church but then could not stomach their stubbornness in not becoming his followers. You told me that he advocated that their houses of worship be burned down and that, when possible, sulfur and pitch be added to the bonfire. I only mention it.

Or rather I mention it because it sounds like something in this spirit was carried out in my chatty guide's childhood village. He told me this on the third night of travel.

"Was your father a peddler, too?" I asked.

"So you think I'm a peddler?"

"You know all the back paths," I said.

"I do," he said.

"You have lots of wares," I said.

"I do," he said.

On the third night, he told me that when he was twelve, a group of soldiers arrived in his neighborhood on horses.

"These weren't cart horses," he said. "They were dark, almost blue." The soldiers set about stabling the noble creatures. Yellow Gill was sent to get feed for the horses. "They were the most beautiful horses I'd ever seen. Still to this day. I brought those horses a mix of nettles and grasses." When he returned, he smelled meat, boiling, roasting. It seemed almost as if a festive meal were soon to be served. Near the bonfire was a pile of scrap metal. He saw his own family's samovar in the pile.

I can't share what else he told me, save to say that it would be of interest to Gertie and that it made the burning of witches, in sum, seem an orderly and civilized affair. At least it involved the theatrics of a trial, the shape of an inquiry.

"Though I was twelve years old, I was very small, and could easily have been mistaken for eight or nine. That saved me, I think. My smallness." He saw the strongest man in his village with a rag in his mouth and dirty water poured over him. He saw no women, save a maidservant who was hiding near the stabled horses. Though she could hardly walk, she handed him a jar of honey and told him to run away. She said to wait until at least two full moons had passed before speaking to a single soul, that everyone I saw would be a devil's servant or a ghost, that I could trust no one. Now, I'd never say that to a child. But she meant the best for me. Now I'll tell you the strangest and maybe the worst part."

"What is it?" I asked.

"I'm a happy man. That's the strange part. I think it's the way that I'm made."

Next he told me a more cheerful story, about a simple-minded woman who thinks she is having an affair with an angel of God. It doesn't go well. The next was a story about a good shepherd who tricks a dishonest king into kissing the ass of a donkey; he also succeeds in marrying the king's daughter. Another story was about a land that had everything except for salt. They had brandy, bread, dumplings, cream, honey, almonds, chicken, radishes. But no salt. When mealtime came, the parents would abuse one another, or sometimes hit the children, until someone provided the tears. To salt everything up.

Finally we had reached our destination. Until that moment, we had eddied out of the world of ordinary days and people and might have been in that forest indefinitely. As our path reached the woods' edge, my friend hid his cart in a grove and suggested we walk the last stretch of the path backward. "It keeps the dark spirits from following you into town," he said. I did walk backward. But not from superstition. I walked backward to be a good companion. And to delay the end of our journey. I was sad to part ways.

WORD HAD BEEN put out that I had planned to move to Greta's in Heumaden this whole time. In truth, I was back in Linz, with Hans and his family. I don't countenance lying— but I didn't tell those lies. There were arrangements: My land was leased to Christoph. A few goods were borrowed from my home. If this meant that they were not included in the assessment of my possessions, I can't be blamed, for I was mysteriously left out of the process of discovering what I owned. Most of the items of value, in any case, belonged not to me, but to Hans. I was only the keeper. In Linz, best as we could tell, no one knew of my trials in Leonberg, even still. And though I had been uncomfortable with the idea of saying I was with Greta, I saw its wisdom. No one has anything negative to say about Greta. How could they? She has been nothing but kind, humble, virtuous, and quiet her whole life, and of course I worry she will one day suffer for that, or has already.

Do you understand that any false testimony you knowingly give will provoke God's great anger in your earthly life and will deliver your soul unto Satan upon your death?

I do.

Your name and age and relation to the defendant.

I'm fifty-one years old. I live in Eltingen. I have six hectares. It's only more recently that the cheeseworks has been in operation. I am Katharina Kepler's sister-in-law, Regina Guldenmann. I've known her for thirty years.

What do you know of the case of Ursula Reinbold?

I have never met the Reinbold woman and so cannot speak to her character, save for what I've heard from others, and that would be hearsay.

Do you have insight into Frau Kepler driving away her husband?

I have no reason to believe that she drove her husband, Heinrich, away. Who says that?

Didn't the couple argue?

He was a handsome man, and difficult, and very good at hunting, and very bad at business, I am sorry to say.

So she did drive him away?

Let me tell you about that man. Katharina admired him very much, too much, I'd say. He'd never been made to work properly in his life, that's my opinion. He expected to move up in the world and wear a fur trim without doing anything. Anyone can run an inn. It takes no gift at all. His parents helped him buy that inn, The Sun, and who did all the work? They had to sell the inn and they moved in with his parents. Heinrich made Katharina cry nearly every day. Eventually all those tears changed her. I haven't seen her cry for many years.

Don't interrupt me, when you asked me this question. Heinrich left town for the last time when their youngest, Christoph, was barely walking. But who says Katharina drove him away? If anyone drove Heinrich away, it was his parents. The father was stern and snobbish. The mother had one skill, which was criticizing. Heinrich left to be a soldier because he found that sort of thing very glamorous. I'm sure he didn't care one way or another, he would have fought on any side of any battle, so long as the uniform was handsome.

Did he fear his wife?
He was a large-handed man who loved guns. Why would he fear her?

Wouldn't you be afraid to live with a witch?
Sure I would.

He didn't fear she was a witch?
I heard more details about that marriage than any woman should have to hear about another marriage, and I never heard that.

Isn't it true that she had a relative, an aunt, also named Katharina, who was burned as a witch?
And the sky is royal purple, and rabbits write songs.

Please remember that you're speaking under oath. It has been testified that she had an aunt, also named

Katharina, who was burned as a witch. That this runs in the family.

You want me to sit here and be afraid of you and listen to you tell me that you know about an aunt of my own husband, an aunt I've never heard about, and—

It would be understandable if your husband's family kept quiet about something shameful—

Katharina is a woman of good character. She comes from a family of good character. I've always been able to see good character. Even in animals. I can pick a donkey from a crowd. I'm a woman of good character, too. I hope God is listening to you. I hope you're afraid.

⁺ ⁺ I am old but not useless. Simon, I want you to know, as my friend, that my next months were joyful, bright, busy. I was a great help with Hans and Susanna's little Maruschl, who showed an especial liking for pine cones, sugar plate, and a spinning top that Christoph had made for her. Maruschl was four then, or was she already five or even six? If there was one person in the world who thought highly of me at that time, it was Maruschl. There was a special connection between us. She came with me mornings to bring water from the well; she sat next to me evenings when I did spinning and weaving. When Maruschl was near me, I felt as if I were wearing an emerald; at times I was anxious that my good fortune was so visible outside of the home. When Maruschl developed a small limp, I thought, Okay, maybe it will help to ward off the evil eye.

"It was a spider," Maruschl said to me.

"What was a spider?"

"My foot killed a spider," she said. "That's why it's not working now."

We went into the woodland to find the glossy leaves of the wild ginger to feed to the cow, LittleHammer. I missed Chamomile, but I felt she was well. The wild ginger for Little-Hammer was not easy to find, hidden as it was under leaves, but we had some success. The cow had been thin in her milk, but also I thought that a milk nourished on these leaves might help with Maruschl's foot. I also gathered any bitters I came across, in case there was something to the spider story. I tried to get Maruschl to take them, dipped in honey.

Hans of course was still worrying and letter-writing and one afternoon he spoke very directly of my troubles in front of Maruschl, after we had received a letter from Christoph. The mail service was so poor in Linz at that time that the bad news from Leonberg felt both urgent and imaginary.

Maruschl had trouble falling asleep that evening. Could she really understand commissions and witnesses and oaths? She sat on my lap in front of the hearth and asked for a story. I told her the story of the band of animal musicians—a story my father had told me when I was a child. An old donkey overheard he was going to be killed, I explained. And who was going to kill that donkey? His own family! He had carried their firewood and their sacks of grain, he had given them rides when needed, he had enjoyed their tender pets on his nose. But now he was weak, and he was of no use to them, and they were going to shoot him at dawn.

"Donkeys are half dog and half horse," Maruschl said.

I told her I didn't know that but it made sense. I said that the donkey decided to set off to become a musician. He had a great hee-haw. Musical and sweet and it made you want to tap your foot. He was practicing his hee-haw, quietly, as he wandered down the road. Then the donkey came upon an old rooster who was facing the same sad problem.

"What problem?"

"That he was going to be killed, silly."

"Because of his crowing?"

Because they wanted to eat him for a Sunday supper. So the rooster joined the donkey and also ran away. The rooster had a cock-a-doodle-doo to add to the donkey's hee-haw. They were joined by an old dog with a bow-wow. An old cow with a moo-moo. They were a band.

Maruschl laughed at all the sounds the different members of the animal band could make. All children do. My own dead father was there in the room with that story, it seemed. Both the old man whom I had nursed for so many years, and the young father who had yelled at me for stealing a ribbon. He had told me the story, of course. A better story than the trial story Susanna had read to me from that book. Before I reached the next part of the story, where the animal band scares away the thieves at a banquet, Maruschl was asleep on my lap. The turn to dreams is so fast. I thought it would not be so bad, to be dead, and with my family. Do you ever feel that way, Simon?

Do you understand that any false testimony you knowingly give will provoke God's great anger in your earthly life and will deliver your soul unto Satan upon your death?
Absolutely.

Name and age.
Michael Stahl. Thirty-two.

In what way has Frau Kepler caused you suffering?
It is my cow that became ill. The cow recovered. But the cow really was very ill, sir. This is no idle complaint. The cow was sitting down, and even losing some of her hair from the side she was leaning against, and she had this heavy breathing. She went from looking young and fine like a heifer to looking like a wobbly old lady.

What led you to suspect Frau Kepler?
Frau Kepler walked by the cow's shed every day. Every single day. Sundays. Market days. You could count on her passing by as regular as a cock's crow.

The defendant's son claims that his mother was storing grain in your shed, and that was why she saw your cow every day.
That's true, to a point. On those days, when she came to get the grain, or add to the grain—fair enough. But she came much more often than that. Widows generally keep to themselves and don't go here and there all over town like a whirligig. Frau Kepler has been more like a man in her

out-and-aboutness. Maybe because she is a widow. Still, I wouldn't have been surprised to see her come mix it up at the tavern, not in a friendly way, but with one business or another.

Do you have knowledge of the poisoning of Ursula Reinbold?
I have no knowledge of the Reinbold case. I can't speak to that. Though I do remember they used to be friendly, so Katharina would have had a means of giving her a poisoned drink.

Why are you only coming forward now about your cow?
I'm coming forward about the cow now because I heard there was suspicion. I wanted to do my part. If there are people who say I'm prone to storytelling and exaggeration, I would say it's those people who are prone to exaggeration. I'm no more a storyteller than the next man. Much less.

Anyone who takes gentle care of a cow is someone I trust. It's a more telling characteristic of a person than taking Communion. Certainly more telling than good teeth. Every cow has a secret name that you can discover if you spend enough time with the creature, if you present yourself as open to learning the secret name. There are a number of methods. The one I use I came across by chance as a child, when I was regularly the first person to the animals in the morning, bringing them branches and feed.

The way I learned our cow's true name as a child was this: I used to sing to our cow the names of all the babies and children who had passed on. When I say "our cow" I mean not Chamomile, and also not the one I had been kicked by as a child, and who died of a milk fever. But another cow our family got later. It may sound like a sad practice to sing ghost names, but I did it cheerfully. It was a private thing. I had loved babies as a child, more than most people do, even. I loved their small fingernails. I loved the way they seemed to arrive older than their parents. I loved the courage they had to sleep as if there were no wolves, no soldiers. For those babies who had died before being baptized, I had a special verse I would sing just for them.

I asked a learned man about this practice, and he said there was nothing wrong or pagan in it. The songs were my attempt to protect the babies, I think. When I was a young girl, I imagined the Lord as someone before whom I was making an argument or pleading my position or, occasionally, who I was serving at my father's inn, where he stayed in the guise of a stranger. In my young mind's eye, the Lord had a soft boyish face, and a head shape that made him look like an owl.

Anyhow, I was singing this little song, and petting our cow—whose name in our household was Monday—and as I came to the chorus, the cow began to cry. The name Apollonia was making her cry. Say what you want. It was recognition. It was her true name. Now, I want to be clear—I don't think that the baby had become the cow. I'm only saying that Apollonia was the cow's true name.

When I married Heinrich, that cow, Apollonia, came with me from Eltingen to Leonberg. She gave little milk by then, but it was an easier time.

I SHARE THIS, as, when I was in Linz that second time, I came to know Susanna and Hans's cow LittleHammer very well, a dun cow with a wry temperament who had a habit of taking a few steps backward when a person entered the barn. It's rare for a cow to step backward. Most cows don't give credence to what is behind them, only to what is in front. Some fear a backward-walking animal—I myself have done so in the past—but I do my best to avoid superstition, which can be difficult to separate from the quiet knowledge with which we are born and that sometimes reminds itself to us.

Susanna was far along with child, and needed extra care while Johannes was again away in Prague. So it was a good thing that I was there. I repeat that I wasn't useless or a burden—and that made me so happy. Susanna had lost three children in a row, each before seeing five weeks of life. Unlike my last visit to Linz, this time around I was allowed to be of service. In the evenings, Maruschl would hand me the

wool and I would spin. She was very good about not putting her finger in the spokes of the wheel, much better
than other children. She could sense a consequence earlier than others her age.

For Susanna, I made sure that she had at least some pig's
fat in every meal. When I prepared beans, I made certain
that no sand or soil persisted in the mix. How a pregnancy
proceeds is up to God and not us. But God doesn't frown on
those who take care of themselves. Susanna had her own
ideas for not losing children as well. Perhaps discredited.
I can admit, in this setting, speaking to posterity, that I've
also had my moments of trying anything to keep a baby
alive. I've tried songs about sunshine, also prayers, I've tried
every kind of blessing. They tried to twist the tailor into
saying I'd advised his wife to use devilish incantations, but
what kind of monster would see it that way? Sorry, Simon,
sometimes I see monsters. Everyone who has been around
babies has done these things that I have done, and more.
I've rhymed nonsense words to the tunes of musicians who
pass through town. And of course I have tried keeping the
window closed, and keeping a candle near the child's bed,
and putting crackers inside the cradle. I've even cursed and
begged. Again, who hasn't?

Maruschl and I, when we went to the well, we'd often cross paths with the goldsmith's wife, Regina Short.
Regina Short is fat, cheerful, and has eight children, each
one healthier than the last. I don't trust her. Maruschl still
had the limp, which Regina commented on each time, sug-
gesting a cane. "You should try a honeysuckle salve for
Susanna," she said, unasked. "I've always relied on a honeysuckle salve."

"Moths love honeysuckle," I said.

Regina Short shrugged, smiled, and made off, with one

of her oldest children helping her with the water. That oldest girl tripped on an oak root, hardly paused to stand up, returned with a smile to refill her pail, and then left again.

In my heart, I was arguing, and arguing strongly, against the honeysuckle. Why? Maybe she knew something. I had not even succeeded in helping my own Greta. Maruschl and I went to the winding creek and gathered some honeysuckle after all. But only because I needed a counter-scent to the hay of the house, which despite my efforts wasn't staying fresh.

When we arrived home, there was a well-dressed man there, a stranger, speaking with Hans. Maruschl wanted to run over to her father. I said we should wait in the kitchen, he was busy with a meeting. This time around I was perfectly happy to be a Frau Guldenmann, and remain at the side, and not be properly introduced.

The atmosphere in the other room was tense. The man was saying that he had made every effort, but no response had arrived. And that they could in no way be assured of permission to use the Dane's observations. Hans was saying that it was a constellation of calamities, and that if he weren't struck by lightning before the day's end he would be surprised. It's not in Hans's nature to share his troubles or be melodramatic. The visitor said it wasn't in his power to remedy the situation, and that many promises were falling to the side in these difficult times.

Hans then said he had gone to bring copies of his book for a ship set for Frankfurt, but the copies were rained on overnight, then he waited three days to see that they dried properly, and he caught a case of lice in the waiting. Now he was having to convince booksellers, especially the Italians, that his book put them in no danger, that it could be sold in good faith. Meanwhile, he had no choice but to spend his time on mule calculations, and, what with no pay, he could not afford an assistant, and now here he was in the position of having to journey all the way to Prague to beg for the pay due him, and surely soon, as things were developing, his family would be pressured to leave Linz. The flower of astronomy was more to him than anything, but he had no means to pursue it. He said what was more was that he was irregular and even lazy, and that infuriated him, too, that he was part a greyhound lapdog, he knew that of himself.

What he was saying about being a greyhound was correct in some ways. But greyhounds aren't merely lying around, they are gathering speed in their apparent idleness. But I did not interrupt the men with my desire to embrace and encourage and praise my son.

I notice that I'm speaking little of my own trials, the case in Leonberg, the Werewolf Ursula, her horrible forest administrator brother the Cabbage, the dog-killing False Unicorn ducal governor—perhaps I really did feel far from it all. Let them gather their poisonous roots. I did other things.

There have been some further questions since our first deposition, so we are hoping we can go over everything again from the beginning.

I don't know if I have the strength to go over everything from the beginning again.

I'll be as clear and quick as possible.

I'm not a strong badger.

We're asking your help in pursuit of the highest of high ideals, of truth, and will respect your age and health. Now, do you understand that any false testimony you knowingly give will provoke God's great anger in your earthly life and will deliver your soul unto Satan upon your death?

I understand.

And your name and age and profession?

What I said before, I stand by all of it. Hans Beitelspacher. I'm so weak. I may meet death tomorrow. I may meet him before sundown.

Let me try to focus on the points of contention.

I stand by everything that I said before. Nothing has changed. Save my getting weaker and older. I stand by.

You said you were a schoolmaster—

I am.

You also work in the vineyard, yes?

Schoolmaster is my main work.

At a school for little girls?

There is a range of ages—

You believe Katharina is the cause your lameness?

More than that, sir. Also the cause of my wife's illness and death. She was here like a flower before. I repeat: Katharina, with her brews, was also the death of our friend Margretta Meyer, whose daughter Barbara Meyer should also be called to speak to the court. Why has no one called Barbara Meyer? A triple curse. And it's more vicious than you can imagine, sir. Because I, and my wife, and Margretta Meyer—we drank with Katharina as friends. As friends, sir. I trusted her, she was like another mother to me, I went to school with her son, you see—

Couldn't your lameness have been a result of, say, your hard labor in the vineyard?

No, sir.

Why do you say no?

Because I say no.

Lots of people who work many years in the vineyard injure themselves, many walk with sticks—

I'm a schoolmaster. That's my main profession.

You said earlier that Katharina came by to have you write her a letter. But her son has filed a statement that Katharina says that you had borrowed grain from her and that she had come to be repaid.

I don't remember exactly. I don't remember what happened on what day.

But you remember the wine, and you are sure it was poisoned.

Yes, that was clear.

If it was so clear, why are the circumstances difficult to recall?

I did borrow grain from her now and again. More often I wrote letters for her. I was speaking generally.

In your original testimony, you said you were doing her a favor, but her son alleges that she was doing you a favor—

I've done enough to protect the Keplers.

Excuse me?

You're talking to me as if I'm a liar. You're trying to humiliate me. But the truth is that the only thing I've left out of my earlier testimony was in an effort to be kind to the Keplers.

Please, sir, we were talking about the emendations from the earlier testimony, about—

Don't bully me or shame me when I've been more than noble. I didn't want to hurt my old school friend. But it was Hans.

What was Hans?

It was from Hans that I first learned that his mother was a witch. From Hans and not from the poisoned wine, which was later.

Obviously Herr Kepler is arguing in his filings to the court that his mother is not a witch.

But even when he was young, he wrote something, you know, about visiting other planets. Haven't you ever wondered how a humble man, no different than myself really, became the Imperial Mathematician? I'll remind you that we were in school together. Well, he wrote about this, about his mother's demonic connections, while in school. I mean, this was in the schooling that followed the one we shared.

But I heard word of it. From the barber, for example. As a young man, Hans wrote a story about how his mother sold herb packets, to sailors but also to demons. And so she had these connections, to demons, that later came in useful, when he was older. That's what I am given to understand. At a later time, one of those demons took Hans and his mother to the moon, and it was from that special trip to the moon that he learned so much. So much but also no more than a schoolgirl would learn if she also were on the moon. Please don't interrupt me. I'm an old and tired man now and I won't be interrupted when I have energy. Hans, yes, I'm sure he regrets having ever told this story, but he was young and boastful and always seeking after reputation however he could. He was not so special as a student. It was only that he walked about *as if* he were something special. I'm sure if you took me to the moon, I also would be able to tell you some interesting information. Same for you, sir. I also would be sought-after by the Emperor—

Where is this alleged writing?
He wrote a pamphlet about it. Or a thesis. Some such thing. Some thirty or forty years ago.

Do you have a copy?
He never saw fit to give me a copy.

So where did you read it?
Though I had done so much for his family, I have never been given a copy of any of his works. No, I don't have a copy. But ask the barber. Ask the hatter. Ask the rope maker. It's widely known. It has been widely known for a long time. Everybody knows that Hans's mother is a witch, and every-one has known for a long time, and if only we had taken that more seriously, I suppose we thought it was games

and tales. I thought it was schoolboy talk. I thought people were telling stories when they were telling the truth. Now I tell the truth and get accused of telling stories. If only I had understood earlier what was really true. It can be so difficult to tell, the way people talk. But now I'm older and wiser—I know what's real. I have nothing to gain from this testimony. Nothing. It only brings me trouble. As you say, Katharina used to lend me grain, when I needed it. Who will help me now?

* *   Hans was in Prague again. Though he wrote to us often, and Susanna would read the letters out to me. Especially the parts about his plans and concerns and strategies. How bizarre it all sounded. More ludicrous than the book she had read from to keep me company when I was sick in bed that first time in Linz. Something had changed in me since then. I heard Hans's reports like they were scary stories told to children, or reports from the moon, told by liars. A law professor friend had suggested this. The tailor's wife had said that. A gravedigger had been contacted, we would need a list of all the times and places when I had seen a skull coated in silver. Who could attest that I had not run my husband out of town? The death of a pig twenty-five years ago had been attributed to Katharina Kepler, too. That poor woman from Leonberg—I felt bad for her, but I didn't think she was me.

Reality was closer at hand. I remember well a fasting day, a Tuesday, when Susanna, now full along in her pregnancy, was churning butter. I was mending. On the floor next to us Maruschl was playing with a wooden turtle, also shelling peas inefficiently. She had a weak cough and was thin, though still magnificent. She was so pale she seemed illuminated from the inside. I could hear her speaking for the turtle, or the peas. There was a battle, or a gathering. She noticed my paying attention. "No looking or hearing!" she shouted. Her play was private. That moved me. I can still see her now, with her real peas and that toy turtle.

Susanna went to lie down.

Maruschl came to my side.

We went downstairs to visit LittleHammer. Maruschl looked worried, or sad.

"I know this cow's secret name," I told her.

"Her name is LittleHammer," Maruschl said.

"That's the name we call her, sure. But she also has a special name, too, her true name."

Maruschl said I was wrong. "Cows don't want special names. They are already lonely enough."

I said the secret name I had discovered was Rosemary.

Maruschl repeated with some annoyance that the name was LittleHammer.

Either way, we fluffed the hay near LittleHammer-Rosemary. We pitched out to a manure pile what belonged in the manure pile. "Look at her eyes," Maruschl said.

The creature's eyes were wet, it was true. She was a beautiful cow, expressive and lowing. She had long lashes. She made a purring sound like a cat, but had none of the stored viciousness of cats.

"She's okay," I said, petting LittleHammer's neck. "That's how her eyes are meant to look."

Maruschl shook her head.

EARLY THE NEXT morning I went down to the animals alone. Rosemary was panting, like a dog back from a chase. But all she was doing was standing there. One of her eyes was bloodshot and oozing a sticky liquid. She shook her head as if afflicted by flies.

I heard Maruschl on the steps, coming down to greet LittleHammer.

I called out that she should stay up above, that Little-Hammer wasn't feeling well. "I'm coming," she shouted. "You can't stop me." At the bottom of the stairs, when she saw LittleHammer closer up, she cried. I hurried over and took her hand and said we should go for a walk.

"She'll be fine," I said. "She's very strong."

The world outside was in its glory. As healthful and bright as LittleHammer was unwell. We passed by rapeseed fields, yellow and bright as lemon, and then we passed fallow fields crowded with cabbage butterflies, the murmur of grasshoppers. Spring was with us. Maruschl was quick, even with her small legs and limp. I decided the girl was in better health than I had ever credited her. Hans, too, as a small boy, had been one illness after another, I reminded myself. Again I remembered my Heinrich's mother shouting at me that she would not have Hans's death on her hands, when I left Hans with her to fetch my husband back from his love of uniforms and glory. Nonetheless, Hans took root and grew hardy, and weathered trouble, and offered shelter to his siblings, and has shown strong heart—let him have forty forks if it pleases him, let him have the stars bow down to him like haystacks. Maruschl would take root like her father: late but strong. We gathered some of the rapeseed, which I thought would be strengthening food for LittleHammer, whose lowing I kept thinking I was hearing in every breeze, like the way every sound for a time resembles the cry of one's baby: creaking timber, a night owl, a drunk past curfew.

"Have you ever seen a wolpertinger?" Maruschl asked me.

"Not alive," I said.

"Are they real?"

"My neighbor had a stuffed wolpertinger," I said. "A bunny face, antlers, and pheasant wings."

"Papa drew me one," she said.

"Your Papa knows about a lot of strange things. Did you know that when he was your age, I took him to see a comet?"

"What's a comet?"

"One day you'll see one."

"Wolpertingers eat the blood of dead soldiers," Maruschl said.

"The blood of dead soldiers is eaten by crows," I said.

"I don't care," Maruschl said. "The soldiers are already dead."

"The crows who feast in that way are punished by God," I said. "They can't find their nests. You see them wandering the roadsides, usually in pairs, they don't know how to get home."

"Are dead soldiers real?"

When I was not much older than her, I saw three dead soldiers by the river. I wasn't going to tell anyone about it.

That night, LittleHammer was hot. I hung some leathery moonwort fronds at the stable's window and hoped for the best. I also set sage leaves there at the sill. I can hardly think of a more capable plant than the sage. It can steady a hand, it can counter a fever, it helps with a palsy, it is worth a try with a paralysis. Some say it can make you blond, but I have never witnessed such a thing. We should never forget to honor sage. Even when it fails us.

SUSANNA, EVER GOOD-NATURED, was too unwell the next morning to attend to the household. She thought she might be in labor, or that it might be a false labor, like she had experienced before. I didn't want to give her milk from an unwell cow. With some anxiety, I went next door, with Maruschl at my side, to ask at the neighbor's home for some milk. I knew the neighbor only by sight. She was an older woman, a shoemaker's widow, who still kept up the trade. We knocked.

I had a bitter memory of going to Rosina Zoft to ask for milk for Heinrich that miserable winter.

"Maybe we shouldn't ask?" I said to Maruschl.

"I'm hungry," she answered.

"Tell me the honest truth, Maruschl. Is she a mean old woman?"

Maruschl said she didn't know. She said the shoemaker's widow smelled like tar. Also, she had seen her feeding birds. She said she had never taken a cookie from her.

"But she offered?" I asked.

Maruschl said now she couldn't remember. She said once the woman had kissed her cheek, and it had been wet. "Let's hurry," she said.

I knocked again. I immediately regretted knocking. I started to step back. I wouldn't make the same mistake again.

But the shoemaker's widow had already answered the door and Maruschl had followed her in. So I followed, too. The widow was wearing a pinkish scarf wrapped tightly at her neck. Her hands were stained with dyes. She wore a frayed lace kerchief over her thin gray hair. Was this what I looked like to others? So old and undecorative and with frowning lips. On her table was a large cleaver, scraps of leather. I held Maruschl's hand. The widow led us to her barn and gave us not only milk but also honey.

Do you understand that any false testimony you knowingly give will provoke God's great anger in your earthly life and will deliver your soul unto Satan upon your death?

I agree with that.

State your name, age, and profession, please.

Topher Frick. I am fifty-two years old. I was with Jacob Stocklin and Simon Bernhart, it was on a Saturday morning, I was inspecting meat for the holiday evening. It's strange, I can't now remember which holiday. Was it the feast of Saint Barnabus? It was May or June, I remember by the weather. When it's hot you have to be a hawk of meat inspection; you have to see detail in what is darkness. Even a well-meaning and honest butcher can make mistakes. I had a friend, very honorable guy, very kind and gracious and serious; he was put in the stockades for selling rancid meat. It was in the weeks after his child had died.

Share with us what happened with Frau Kepler.

This day with Katharina—the sun was very bright. I remember squinting. Katharina passed by, dressed all in dark colors. She glanced at me. At exactly that moment, a pain shot through my leg. It was like a stabbing with a long skinny knife, snaking down past the back of my knee, and the pain was as if hooked at the end, catching on something, forcing me to bend my leg. I was like an animal being clumsily and unmercifully bled, slaughtered. I felt as if my heart were in my knee. I couldn't straighten my leg, I could barely walk. My friends tell me I was shouting like a woman in childbirth. I suspect my pain in that moment was worse than childbirth. I probably looked like a madman.

Frau Kepler had cursed you?
I was preoccupied with the pain. I felt I was being thrown to the ground.

Did your friends think it was Frau Kepler?
They were taking care of me. Simon Bernhart lived right there. I washed the afflicted leg.

Then what happened?
It got better. But I was worried about the pain returning. And it did return, but more mild. It was when I discussed the pain in reflection, with my friends, after it had subsided— that was when we had the insight about Frau Kepler. I'd been told that for this kind of affliction, you have to ask the perpetrator of the pain for help three times. Simon told me that. Simon knew what he was talking about. He had had a blurred vision problem when he was a young man and it had passed. When I saw Katharina again I whispered and begged her three times: Katharina, help me; Katharina, help me; Katharina, help me.

How did she respond?
We have had trouble getting along of late.

Did you get better?
I did.

So we see that she was responsible.
I can only say that I got better. I had also followed the recommendation of my mother-in-law that I wash my leg with a cloth damp with my own urine. It's difficult to describe what

it feels like to be attacked by pain as if out of nowhere. One moment you are living your life, the next moment you're pork in a hot pan. You think it will be that way forever. I can't, under oath, say for certain that it was Katharina. I still don't understand why I was hit with so cruel a pain. It was like a fog came before my eyes that day in the market. Was it the fog itself, or was it Katharina behind the fog, or was it something else?

But you believed it likely enough that it was Katharina that you asked for her help?
Yes.

I don't put much faith in horoscopes myself. So much ill fortune follows from eating strawberries, which grow so close to the ground, where the vapors are stale. But who warns us about strawberries? Only the people no one listens to. People prefer starry explanations. It makes them feel big, their breasts puffed out like grouse. If instead of asking about Saturn's rising, people looked at their own wheat fields. If they stopped digging up the white asparagus too early. If they knew better how to clean mushrooms. I have so many corrections for the thinking of others, but I know better than to offer them. I mention the horoscopes only because of course I had no way of knowing what was going to happen. Christoph once read out to me a horoscope Hans had done for me—this was when he was young and more foolish. It made no predictions, only said that I was querulous and had secrets.

Simon, I don't know how well you remember the birth of your little Anna. I am unusual in this, I know, but I pity men that they will never suffer and nearly curse God and then see the beautiful child who will have that wandering misaligned eye of a newborn, still looking for where she comes from. For a moment the child is the newest person in the world. Only we women ever see that. Susanna had the baby. Hans is not like his father, and he helped with the lying in and the hosting of visitors and the whole familiar drama. He had returned from Prague with three nice heavy copies of yet another book, but he put them on a high shelf and said nothing of them. He still had not secured the salary promised him.

Hans and Susanna together chose to name the baby Katharina.

I thought that was a poor decision. But again, no one asks me. Still, baby Katharina was perfect, as all babies are. Even the ones with dark stains on their faces or weak cries or an irritable yellow pallor. She had a full head of dark hair and a weak appetite and her feet and hands had the slippery texture of water lilies. After the first month, she spent a good deal of time looking at the sunlight reflecting off the copper cauldron.

LittleHammer's health had improved, too. She was eating butterblume, and she gave a creamy milk that tasted of grass. Maruschl hugged and kissed LittleHammer when she fed her, and whispered encouragements in the cow's ear.

THEN, ABRUPTLY, MARUSCHL was unwell. She was confused, slept most days, came to me crying in the night of itches and scratches, then would fall asleep again. I dug up a ginger root after midnight and made a gingerbread with it, I had the pastor come by three times, and I changed all the bedding. I brought her drinks with ginseng and mint. She looked fragile and was rarely hungry. I began to plead with God, to offer those bargains that so far as I know are never taken up. I prayed for God to blow health into the girl. I said I could promise not to come asking again for myself. I offered to die on any day. I offered to embrace my enemies in Leonberg and face torture with a smile and a sense of peace if Maruschl could be allowed to come through her illness.

"Bring me baby Katharina," she whispered hoarsely, between coughs. "I want to hold Katharina."

Soon, we said. Susanna and I had left baby Katharina wrapped up in linens and in her crib in a far corner of the living room, to keep her safe.

"I want to see LittleHammer," Maruschl whispered. "Please."

We said later.

That night I woke worried and Maruschl was not in her bed. I thought of terrible shadowy creatures, of slobbering large frogs. I thought of earthworms and of cold toes. But I could sense Maruschl nearby. I begged of my heart not to panic, and not to have reason to panic. I found her sleeping near LittleHammer, just as I had done when I had been sick. She seemed in her sleep to be smiling.

"Can I hold baby Katharina?" she asked again in a whisper the next morning. We couldn't bear to turn her down again. We brought her the baby. I also sang a prayer from my childhood every night. I have used this prayer with all of my children, and grandchildren, and sometimes with the children of others, too. This prayer came to be of issue later, as you know, Simon, and it was suggested to be soothsaying or, worse, a devil's incantation. I spoke with Johannes as well as Pastor Binder, my daughter's husband, and they said there was nothing wrong with the prayer I spoke, though Pastor Binder said it was more like a song than a prayer, and that it predated the Reformation, best as he could tell, but he also reminded me that Martin Luther said that those who do not love music deserve to hear nothing but the grunting of hogs and the braying of asses.

The prayer or song was one that I would set down with no shame whatsoever:

> *Welcome me, dear God,*
> *On Sundays and sunny days,*
> *You come riding,*
> *And there we are. Hear our prayer,*
> *God, Father, Son, and Holy Ghost*

And the Holy Trinity.
Give us strength and life
And good health, too.

I was reminded of Pastor Binder saying that old ladies only think they're witches, only think that they can do harm, when really they are powerless. Old ladies may have viciousness in their hearts. They can wish ill upon others. But God decides. It would be wrong to believe that a witch could overrule the plan of God.

Perhaps the same is said of prayer?

I don't think so. I can tell you that there have been times when I have said this prayer and the outcome was good, and times when I have said this prayer and death came none-theless.

I am astonished at all the expense and effort given to the useless work of books. Each party forbids the books of the other party. It's a vanity. Hans tells me his books can be bought even in Rome, he says it proudly, and, sure, I see that. He also says the bookseller has to hide the books under the counter and offer them only to those who know to ask—the books are mistresses. The men brag about them. Another realm for snobbery. And recklessness. I suspect the only thing I would be interested in reading would be a history. But I'm told histories are hated, which is not surprising. People prefer to make it up themselves.

I sat by Maruschl's bed for days and told her stories.

"My eyes hurt," she whimpered.

I tried to squeeze her hands, to soothe her, and so she wouldn't use them to rub her eyes. I started telling the story of the crow who wanted to be king of the birds. That crow! He was just a crow. There was going to be a contest, and the most magnificent bird was going to be named king, and the crow thought he had a chance. And maybe he did. A date had been set for the judging. The crow gathered together a collection of magnificent feathers that had fallen from other birds brighter and more beautiful than himself.

When the time came for judging, he looked magnificent. He was going to win the contest.

The other birds stole back their feathers. They called him a cheat and a liar and a plain old crow.

"They're mean," she said. "So mean."

It was a stupid story, I realized, and I regretted having

begun it. It had simply been the first thing that came to mind. I'd forgotten where it led. I dislike stories that end in failure or punishment. I should have changed the ending.

Maruschl napped and sweated and then woke again. "Tell me a story. Tell me one with scary things." I told her one my grandmother used to tell me. About an orphan boy who'd been taken in and was like a brother to the little girl in the house. The father of the house was a woodsman and out most of the day working. There was no mother. So the cook was in charge of the kids. The cook had a plan to eat the adopted boy. Or so she told the girl. She told her she was going to put the boy in a soup.

"Papa's always saying he's going to eat me in soup," Maruschl said with a tired smile. "With salt and pepper."

The girl took action. She went to her adopted brother and said: Do you promise to never leave me? And the boy said, Yes. And the girl said: If you never leave me, then I'll never leave you.

"That's not nice. To only save her brother if he obeys her. I would never do that to baby Katharina."

"I bet she'd save him no matter how he answered the question," I said.

"She's only going to help if it suits her," she said. Her eyes were watering.

I tried to reassure Maruschl that it would be okay. I told her how three times the girl and boy escaped the cook. They escaped the cook by transforming themselves. The boy became a tree and the girl became an apple on that tree. But the cook found them. The next time the boy became a church tower and the girl became the bell in that church tower. But the cook found them. Then the boy became a mountain lake and the girl became a duck swimming in that mountain lake.

"Yes," said Maruschl. "And?"

I had again run into the problem of starting the story without remembering where it was heading. In that last iteration, the girl who had become a duck pulled the old cook into the lake, and the cook was drowned. I don't like those sorts of endings. But I couldn't think of anything better.

"A duck can't be that strong," Maruschl said.

"But the duck was really the little girl," I said.

"She still wouldn't be strong enough."

I shrugged. "Magic?"

Maruschl shook her head, said it was a bad answer.

I said maybe the cook just fell into the water and drowned. Maybe she was at the edge of the lake, drinking, and the duck conked her on the head, and then she fell in and drowned. "One way or another, she drowns. The girl and boy are free."

"The cook was *joking* about putting him in a soup," Maruschl said. She began crying again. "She was making a joke. It's very sad!"

I was certain she would recover. She had so much strength in her, and spirit. I started making some pickles; I was thinking that many months ahead. The cucumbers were so green and compelling, and I carefully cut away bruises. But Maruschl was gone before the next Tuesday. The baby Katharina died as well within the month. To hear Susanna weeping in an unspeakable misery saying, My baby, my baby, was worse than my own losses. I was willing to give everything and anything to bring the children back. As we waited for Hans to return, there was a part of me that held out the hope that when he returned, so they would, too. I dreamed of walking hand in hand with Maruschl. I dreamed even of us arguing, of her growing angry with me, or disappointed, I wanted that for her much more than I wanted to live. I also felt that I had failed Hans in failing to save his child. Poor Susanna, in that house with me, but really alone. She mended every garment in the home, even those of the children. LittleHammer survived. But she had become cold and aloof. I understood her—to love others is to suffer.

✦ ✦ I don't know how I felt, Simon. I am very old. Probably
I have been on the earth too long. Days, maybe weeks, were
happening. Hans did return. He did not say much. He tried
to eat some of my pickles, but they were not even half sour
and I could see he did not want to eat but did so out of duty
and misplaced determination. The fork Hans ate with was
so small, like for a child. I remember some instances of Hans
telling me over a meal that there was "good news."

What good news?

He had found a source in Ursula Reinbold's hometown,
attesting to her past affair with the apothecary, and his pre-
scribing to her of strong herbs, and her suffering ever since.

I didn't care. I even pitied Ursula, who had never had a
child, maybe for that very reason.

Another day Hans informed me that he had made prog-
ress against the allegation that I had an aunt, also named
Katharina, who had been convicted and burned as a witch.
This was a particularly bad accusation—offering grounds
for torturing for a confession. It was so threatening, to the
entire family, the children included. But Hans had obtained
an attestation from the recordkeeper that there was no record of such a relative, or such a burning. It had not been easy
to get the attestation, but he had done it. Hans was working
so hard. He did not let even the worst of hardships deter him
from his pursuits.

But again, I really didn't care.

He repeated how imperative it was that I stay in Linz
with him, that this time I not run off as before. They will

arrest you if they can find you in the whole duchy of Württemberg. Better to stay in Linz, in another jurisdiction.

I didn't say anything.

Don't be superstitious, Mama.

Superstitious about what?

Our misfortune now is not an omen of our misfortune later.

I said I wished it was.

Mama, don't go back to Leonberg again, impulsively, as last time.

He never spoke of his own work. I know he thought it wasn't for feminine minds. That bothered his first wife, who knew Latin, and spoke with his many visitors, and who came from a family accustomed to important guests. Susanna seemed more okay with not being a hostess to great minds. She was well brought up, and humbly. And of course, myself, I didn't care. Though I had in the past. I did take Hans as a boy to see a comet: Hadn't I helped him? Wasn't he my likeness? I had once brought up the comet—okay, maybe more than once—and he said his eyes already were so weak that he couldn't see it well in the first place. For him it was just a tiring hike up a hill and pretending to see what he couldn't. He said he relies on the observations of others and does the math, and the dreaming, and has no need to be watching all the while. I admire Hans's strategy now. I also now have no interest in close observation of the world as it is around me.

Even you, Simon, you were kind enough to write and tell me that Chamomile was well, and that you had weeded my garden. I really didn't care.

I was of no help anymore. Two of Hans's older children, Ludva and Suze, returned again from their schooling. Beautiful, handsome children. But I am sad to say I did not care much about their arrival. Hans had a letter set on the wall in a frame, and I asked the children, what did it say? It was from the Italian Galileo Galilei, Ludva said, telling me that the Italian was a very important man, and that the letter was from when Hans sent him his first book. The bit I remember is that the Italian said, "But this is not the place to mourn about the misery of our century, but to rejoice with you about such beautiful ideas proving the truth." What a schoolboy, my Hans. So full of hopes and ambitions. Susanna told me she had the good fortune of another pregnancy already. And even that I did not care about. I felt the family would do well to be rid of me. I don't mean to be superstitious, but wasn't I the unlucky charm? Hadn't that been made clear to me by God? I wanted to leave my family a note, before I left under cover of night, against their best judgments. They should not have to wonder at my disappearing. But who would write the note for me?

I went to the shoemaker's widow next door. I would ask her. Yet she wasn't there when I knocked.

In the end, I drew a picture, hoping they would understand my walking away had been a choice, not a black magic or a disappearance. The drawing looked crude and mysterious, but what could I do? There was a small regret in my heart, remembering Hans's father walking away, too, leaving the children behind without a word. The younger Heinrich left soon after that. Maybe he thought he would find his father, though I didn't think of it that way until now.

With Katharina out of town, and for so long, my obligations to her increased rather than decreased. Her son Hans sent me many missives. I was kept busy bringing this, then that, to the clerk at the town hall. In that way, my alliance with Katharina was much more visible than before. I was determined to stand by her. But I had much preferred when that standing by was a personal resolve, a private matter.

I was not turning on Katharina. I absolutely was not. I need very little, and certainly I don't need the nodding approval of the crowd. But I had my own troubles. Or, rather, I had Anna's troubles. I wouldn't have cared if it were only my own troubles. I mean: It was not without some bitterness that I was thinking how I would put together at least the midday shadow of a dowry. But it was much worse when a contrary bitterness intruded.

I first registered the change in Anna when her dress looked too loose on her. She was pale and thin.

She was avoiding even the Saturday market, making do from our larder. We ate the same porridge for eleven days straight.

"What's going on, my Anna?" I asked.

"He thinks low of me," she said quietly.

"Who?"

"You know who, Papa."

"I'm sure he doesn't think low of you. Someone doesn't show up with a green ribbon one day, and turn stranger the next. When someone loves you, they stand by." But why did I say that, when I knew that wasn't true? Hearts and alliances shift all the time, for reasons no better than the weather.

"He thinks poorly of me, he does, for certain."

"I think more poorly of him," I said.

I was in a cross mood after that. I went later to tend again to Chamomile. Also to Katharina's garden, which I had been too busy of late to care for properly. The edges of her radish patch were crowded with milk thistle. A note had been nailed to her door, complaining of the weeds traveling. Everyone thinks himself a Luther. The note was unsigned. But the handwriting communicated impatience, intemperance, some violence.

I plucked the flowers from the thistle, so no more could go to seed, at least not that week, then went to tend to Chamomile in her stall.

When I got back home, I found myself annoyed looking over the orders that had come in, that I was working to fulfill. So many requests for stirrups, a trend I didn't esteem. What was it, everyone asking for stirrups? When earlier in the year there had been a call for more patrolmen for the Leonberg town wall, for a more strictly enforced curfew—I had paid little mind. The anxieties of young people, that was my feeling. Jerg Hundersinger had taken up the work, for extra cash, but I had not had to. I heard people curse Emperor Ferdinand one to the other, and I thought of it as simply the next fashionable phrase, an affectation—these people weren't courtiers, did they really think such matters were about, or affected, them?

As has often been the case with me, I was wrong. Thinking about those stirrup orders now—that is my first recollection of understanding that this catastrophic war had really begun, was expanding, was not like the others.

* * * Hans is against baths and thinks they breed disease. He's bothered by water generally. It opens the pores, that's how the illness gets in—that is his thinking. But when I headed out before sunrise on a Wednesday morning, I found my feet did not take me to Leonberg, and they did not take me to Greta's home in Heumaden, either. They took me to the baths at Ulm. It was Yellow Gill who had told me of a certain Dr. Pferinger there, at those baths. I was told he could tell a woman—a woman who asked, and who paid—if indeed she was a witch. That wasn't the main of what was offered at the baths, but it was a service that could be obtained.

When I reached the baths, I was surprised to see so many young women. Either they wore no clothing at all, or they sat not far from the water, wrapped in a simple undyed linen cloth. Crowded round the water, they looked like so many badgers and otters. When I was a child there had been a hot spring I sometimes visited with my stepmother, but I had otherwise not been to a bath of this kind before—outdoors, largely in its natural setting, with a few simple benches nearby.

"Have you got apple biscuits?" a woman asked me.

I pulled back the hood of my traveling cloak.

She stepped back, a startled fawn.

"I'm looking for Dr. Pferinger?"

"Oh, your cloak confused me, I thought you were the woman who sells the snacks. I don't know where the doctor is."

I should explain that these baths were not in a town, they

were outside of the town, up a hillside, and so essentially hidden. A fairly basic stonework had been set around to expand what was a natural spring. Yet, within the humble buildings nearby I saw fine red scarfs, elegant shoes with silver buttons. I couldn't find the memory or knowledge to make sense of what I saw. I couldn't even tell from what kinds of families these women came. Without their clothing, each one was Eve.

Yellow Gill had described Dr. Pferinger as an old friend of his. I didn't really think I was a witch. But I have never been one to be afraid of increasing my knowledge. I couldn't trust anyone in Leonberg, or in Eltingen or even in Stuttgart, or Linz. But here at the baths, it was something else.

I eventually made my way to a stone cottage and was given a space to wait on a bench behind a curtain. My mind was crowded with a vision of Maruschl, playing on the floor near me, but I could not reach her and she could not hear me. Eventually a small, clean, beardless man arrived. He wore silk hose and a dark cotton jerkin. This was Dr. Pferinger.

After a short conversation, he said, "Show me your feet."

No one wants to see the feet of an old woman. I made no move.

He asked again.

Still I didn't move.

"You're afraid of something."

More correct would be to say I was having second thoughts. A young woman appeared from behind the curtain. She brought in a single acorn set upon a fancy pillow of red and white taffeta, and then exited silently. Pferinger brought the pillow to me. "One feature seen in witches is a hole in the foot. Not a tiny cavity. A hole about the size of an acorn."

Was he a doctor or a squirrel? "I've no holes in my feet," I said. "I can promise you that."

"I could leave you in privacy if you want. It's no matter to me if you're a witch or not. I report to no one. That's not my business."

I didn't take the acorn.

He set aside the pillow, but held on to the acorn as if it were a rosary.

"Why aren't you afraid of me?" I asked.

"Why should I be afraid of you?"

"Or, if not of me, of the others here who come to you with their questions."

"I'm afraid of spiders. I'm afraid of weapons. Of thunderstorms. Of the quest for glory that's overtaken all three of my sons. But women, no. I'm not afraid of women."

"You think witches aren't real," I said.

"They're real. Sure they are. But what can they do, really? Not much, is what I have observed. You're the astrologer's mother, aren't you?" I had mentioned Yellow Gill as our mutual friend, and now regretted that. "That interests me. A horoscope could be fun. I'd love to have one. All the fancy people do it, right? Anyhow, do you want the witch exam or not? No judgment. But let's have a decision. And you have to pay either way; you've asked for my time, you know?"

I noticed he wore several bright rings. "I don't want to be disrespectful, Doctor. But suddenly I'm not sure why I'm here. What do you do for women? What do you know or have to offer?"

"Do you think you could get me a horoscope? Would you ask your son to make one for me?"

"I could ask. If you give me the date of your birth. But: Who are you?"

He paused before he spoke. He seemed to be thinking something through, but what? "I spent seven years of my life as an assistant to an executioner," he said. "Women walked in and showed me bruises at their pudenda. They showed me the thickness or thinness of their vulva. I see that you're bothered by my language. But I ask you to consider that I mean no disrespect. I was asked to inspect scratches, moles. I was asked once to look at an extra nipple. There was no way to verify if it was or wasn't used to suckle a devil. When someone tells you that their splinter is from the cross of Jesus, well, maybe it is or maybe it isn't, right? If someone says that these are the silver coins that Judas took to deceive the Lord, well, the coins can't speak, can they? What can a nipple say? I looked these women in the eye, and told them what I saw in them. I have a strong sense of people. Of their true selves. That's all I have to offer. But it's something. What are you worried about? What do you want to ask me? I'll tell no one. What's your secret?"

"I have malice in my heart," I said.

"Yes, of course you do."

"At times I've wished that a wolf would leap into my accuser's window and eat her throat."

"Yes," he said. "That makes sense."

"I've wished she'd die of smallpox."

"Not surprising," he said.

"And that it would be very disfiguring and painful, before ultimately killing her."

"You wish she came to you begging for a cure?" he asked.

"I dream of the whole town clamoring for her death," I said. "The baker tells me that she soured his cream, and the tailor that her face had made his wife go lame, and that the bricklayer would simply weep when he saw her . . . and that I would be the only one who said: Enough, we should take pity on her. I see no monster."

He nodded.

"I'd save her life. And then, a few days later, once the

news had got around of my good deed, she'd die naturally. A stone would fall on her, while she was out walking. It would take days to find her body. A woodsman would come across a wolf with a human hand in its mouth. It would be seen to be God's will." I paused. "Does that make me a witch?"

Pferinger set down his acorn, and his measuring forceps. "I said I was an assistant to an executioner. That was true, but not truthful. The executioner was my dad. I was feared when I bought a muffin. If I was seen spinning a top, other children stopped spinning their tops. I could have whined. Or cried in a wood. I did whine. I did cry in a wood. But I became superior to where I came from. I recognized that I had a special knowledge. An executioner, if he pays attention, knows despondency, dejection, and death. An executioner makes money. I made my own way, doing a job no one else thought a good one, and then I took my experience and knowledge and made myself a new job altogether, and I'm not ashamed."

I asked him for his birthday, to show sincerely that I would ask after the horoscope—though when would I next see Hans? Or any of my family?

He said he may as well read tea leaves or slaughter a goat, it was all garbage.

Oh, I said.

And that was that. I trusted him, because he told me that the seeds of the butterblume delphinium are the swiftest cure for lice, even as the same seeds fermented in honey water can be a poison if used too often on the gums, or for epilepsy. He saw delphinium as I saw delphinium. As a plant capable of good and evil both. As a plant that required the knowledge and good intentions of man.

Finally, Simon, I really did move in with Greta in Heumaden. Exactly as was said in the false rumors we spread when I went to Linz. The lie revealed itself as a prophecy.

Greta wept when I showed up at her door. "How could you leave without telling anyone, Mama? And after all that Hans and Susanna had suffered already?"

She was right to point that out.

She was still crying. She said all was well now. That was why she was crying. She had lost faith, but she had been wrong to lose faith.

"Are you expecting a baby yet?"

She shook her head. Her tears lessened. I still maintain that this was the fault of Binder, and not of Greta. I had prepared a drink of nettle, hyssop, and fennel for him in the past, but he had chosen not to be dedicated in taking it. Children bring joy. Even in my misery Maruschl was still bringing me joy. I wanted Greta to have that feeling. You will laugh at me, an old woman, talking so much of babies and kids. But it's wise to have a large family. Because one loses so much and so many.

THAT VERY EVENING Greta explained to me that her husband meant me no harm. I hadn't seen Binder yet, though I'd heard his pacing in the study. I wondered what sermon he was preparing now. What animal was God not like now?

"Of course he means me no harm," I said.

"And he bears you no ill will."

"I'm glad of it," I said.

"He wrote letters to the Duke, advocating on your behalf," she said. "Very strong letters."

"I'm grateful," I said.

"He uses your recipe for his gall. Remember the one? Though he adds honey to it. He loves you sincerely."

"What is it, Greta?"

Binder's parish in Heumaden was a small one, she said. He had only held the position for a few years. He was, unfortunately, still quite vulnerable. The congregants were already trembling with fear. There was an eleven-year-old girl who had visions of imperial soldiers with fire coming from their mouths and she warned of destruction if the villagers did not purify their souls. The girl was saying the rot must be kept out, and she had a great deal of power over people's feelings.

"He's asking that I not attend his services?"

"I'm so grateful for your understanding, Mama. I told him that all would be well, one way or another."

"Am I supposed to not attend church at all?" I didn't say to her that I had hardly been to church for many months—where was I welcome? The pastor at Maruschl's burial had given me Communion, that was the last service I had attended. Now that I was denied church, however, I felt an overwhelming need to attend.

"He is asking only that you not attend *his* church." Binder's church was the nearest to their home, and he arranged no donkey or other means of transport for me to reach a different service, but no matter. I know they were squeezed already, the childless couple. Though of course not as squeezed as me.

"I see," I said.

"There are places a bit farther off," she said. "Very nice

congregations. Where you wouldn't draw attention to yourself," she said. "You could feel more free."

"I understand," I said.

"You were forced to clean yourself on a sooty kettle," she said. "He is trying to avoid the soot. I'm not sure he has a choice, Mama. It's different for me than for him. He's a public figure. I'm your own flesh and blood. Oh, it's been very trying for all of us, Mama. It's a fire in the field, and we need to contain it. I will write to Christoph and Hans right away. They will be so relieved to know you are here with me."

Leonberg, November 9, 1619

To the honorable and just Duke Frederick of Württemberg,

I write to you on behalf of my good and virtuous and beloved wife, Ursula.

Firstly, it is true that one is not allowed to punish another unless it is just to do so.

Secondly, it is true that Katharina Kepler is responsible for our terrible misfortune and crippling legal expenses.

Thirdly, it is true that Katharina harmed the innocent lamb Ursula, my dear and tender and beloved wife, and that this was unjust.

Fourthly, it is true that in 1613 Katharina lured my dear and tender and beloved wife into her home and gave her a drink.

Fifthly that my dear and tender and beloved wife then became immediately ill.

Sixthly that my dear and tender and beloved wife then suffered unspeakable pain.

Seventhly that this pain was such that all the usual remedies—each of them tried, often at great expense—failed.

And it is true, eighthly, that there are others who verify
that Katharina gave Ursula a drink.

And it is true, ninthly, that there was a conflict and
Katharina, wishing harm, gave the drink to my dear
and beloved wife with the intention to harm.

And it is true, tenthly, that Ursula can claim in good
conscience that it is specifically the drink from Katharina
that has caused her suffering beyond words.

And it is true, eleventhly, that Katharina has relatives
in Weil der Stadt, where an aunt of hers was burned as
a witch, and it is generally known that witches run in
families.

And, twelfthly, as we are thinking of families, it is true
that Katharina was a much too meddlesome mother to her
daughter, Greta, letting the girl go nowhere unaccompanied
until an unreasonably late age, and bragging all around
town in an unseemly way about her match.

And, thirteenthly, it is true that Katharina's own son
Heinrich said that Katharina rode a calf to death and then
roasted it, a common practice of witches.

And, fourteenthly, it is true that Katharina's own son
Heinrich called his mother a witch.

And it is true, fifteenthly, that Katharina encouraged
the young daughter of Schfitzenbastian, who was
helping Katharina with her housework, to take on a demon
lover.

And that yes it is true, sixteenthly, that she told the same young woman the ungodly thing that if she were to die it would be due neither to heaven nor hell, it would be the same as a dumb beast dying in the road.

And it is true, seventeenthly, that Katharina told this young woman that it would be useful to be a witch, it would give one powers, one wouldn't burn a hand on a hot pan, and so forth.

And it is true, eighteenthly, that Katharina asked the gravedigger to dig up her father's skull to make a drinking goblet of it cast in silver—a known witchy tool.

And, nineteenthly, that Katharina harmed Ziegler's wife's foot.

And, twentiethly, that she harmed the schoolmaster Hans Beitelspacher's leg.

And, twenty-firstly, that she harmed Meyer via drink.

And, twenty-secondly, that she killed a young calf.

And, twenty-thirdly, that she rode Michael Stahl's cow at midnight, hit the cow, and that the cow died.

And, twenty-fourthly, that she injured the butcher Topher Frick's leg.

And, twenty-fifthly, that she later healed Topher Frick's leg, proving it was her witchcraft that caused the injury in the first place, since she otherwise would not be able to reverse it.

And, twenty-sixthly, that she fed a cow of the Warners something that made it fall over.

And, twenty-seventhly, that the cow then suffered.

And, twenty-eighthly, that she assaulted two pigs that belonged to the elder Ziegler, and that the pigs then died.

And, twenty-ninthly, that she gave a witch's grip to the Haller girl, causing her terrible suffering.

And, thirtiethly, that the Haller girl reported this to the church warden.

And, thirty-firstly, that the church warden listened and did not see fit to pardon Katharina.

And, thirty-secondly, that furthermore the church warden deemed it so serious as to need to report it to the highest authorities—that the church warden deemed this, and not me.

And, thirty-thirdly, that the noble church warden begged the ducal governor Einhorn that Katharina be severely punished for the sake of sweet justice.

And, thirty-fourthly, that Katharina offered the ducal governor Einhorn a silver cup to turn his head away from sweet justice.

And, thirty-fifthly, that the ducal governor Einhorn refused the tainted silver cup and wrote to an even higher authority.

And, thirty-sixthly, that Katharina then fled sweet justice, leaving town with no announcement even as proceedings were in motion against her.

And, thirty-seventhly, that Katharina has lied to her own children about her many witchy doings, convincing them that she has been wronged and in this way pushing them to obstruct sweet justice as well, compounding her own crimes.

And, thirty-eighthly, that having been advised by her pagan idols and indulging in Marianism she fled the duchy.

And, thirty-ninthly, although it is true that we are so relieved that Katharina is no longer here in Leonberg to torment us and others, still, she should bear responsibility for what she has done and submit to sweet justice.

And it is also true, fortiethly, that her very fleeing demonstrates her guilt.

And also true, forty-firstly, that we heard that in her fleeing, on the path, she hurt a girl from Gebersheim who suffered greatly from having seen her.

And it is true, forty-secondly, that Katharina knew many pagan stories and stories of demons.

And it is true, forty-thirdly, that she chased her husband from the home many times, surely with her witchcraft, and that he then died in the war, thus killed by Katharina.

And forty-fourthly that she is responsible for the death
of the tailor's two children, and pushed a superstitious
practice upon the wife.

And forty-fifthly that it is not only myself and my beloved
who know what Katharina has done, but that the whole
town is aware, and lives in fear.

And lastly, forty-sixthly true, that my beloved wife
would joyfully give up a thousand thalers, the amount
requested from Katharina, if it would relieve her pain
beyond words, and that this case is in no way primarily
about compensation, though compensation is just, but that
the case is primarily about truth and about the safety of
Leonbergers, and that any and all allegations of money
being used to motivate testimonies or depositions is but
more vile calumny of the kind we unfortunately have
come to expect from Frau Kepler and now even from her
children.

Your humble servant,
Jacob Reinbold, Glazier

Do you understand that any false testimony you knowingly give will provoke God's great anger in your earthly life and will deliver your soul unto Satan upon your death?

I did then, and I do now. I am the butcher Topher Frick.

As you know, further questions have arisen and there have been complaints of some contradictions.

I want to say that I really know very little. I know so little, I sometimes ask my wife at dinner about what happened the day or week before. I give my testimony with a pure heart and an uncertain mind. I'm not feebleminded. My memory isn't poor. Kidneys are good for memory. But this is different than memory. It's that I focus on my work day to day. That is where my mind lives.

Did you have a conflict with Frau Kepler after your last testimony?

I do know she came to my butcher stand and was shouting at me. She belittled me. She spoke as no woman should speak to a man. I never called you a witch, I said to her. She called me an old fool. I called her an older fool. I'm not proud of that behavior. I don't believe in fighting with women, or with children.

Did she abuse you?

She said nothing could be expected of a man like me, who cut down saplings. What was that about? As if she's never cut down a tree. Or eaten a young animal. I know, you called me here to ask me if I was put under pressure by Katharina to change my testimony. I was not. She shouted at me. Sure she did. And I have also been asked if my testimony was under pressure from Wallpurga Haller or from Ursula Reinbold or Jacob Reinbold. Again, the answer is no. I do not bend to pressures anyhow. I drain blood and I sever muscle and I make a fine soup of marrowbone and I am very orderly in my preparations and I did receive a mysterious affliction that mysteriously lifted. But I did not waver. If there are inconsistencies or confusions, they are only my human errors, not malice or sin or viciousness or greed.

Do you understand that any false testimony you knowingly give will provoke God's great anger in your earthly life and will deliver your soul unto Satan upon your death?

Look, even if Angel Mountain were turned to gold and given to me as payment, I wouldn't tell a lie. That's the kind of person I am.

Please state if you agree.

I agree.

Your name and age, please.

Donatus Gültlinger. Fifty-seven.

You can confirm Ursula Reinbold's account of having been poisoned by Frau Kepler?

Yes, that's correct.

Please explain.

Frau Kepler often bought cheeses from me at the market. She's a talkative one. Not like some widows who you think have themselves died. You hardly see them anymore. Maybe they have someone who goes to market for them. Maybe they have no appetite. But not Katharina. No, no, no. She didn't wither on the vine. Out and about. Tailing her Greta around until she had that pretty late marriage. Hawking her little herbal remedy packages. Asking around for favors. Yes, out and about like a man of twenty. That said, since I had come out of the hospital, I hadn't seen Katharina.

Please explain how you heard about Ursula being poisoned.

I didn't much like talking to Ursula. I don't like people who get in each other's business. People should keep to themselves. But Ursula was in the hospital at the same time as me. I couldn't very well avoid associating with her, given that I was stuck in the hospital. Very chatty for the ill, she was. Chatty and competitive. I was getting better and she wasn't. She was asking me and asking me, how did I get well? I thought it was a ridiculous question. I didn't know how I got well. I just tried to get well and I did. That's the kind of man I am.

We're here because you said Ursula Reinbold told you something at this time. What was it?

She told me about being sick. She had pains and they were worse when the moon changed. We all knew about it. She said she was given a drink by Frau Kepler, she took a sip and immediately spat it out. Ursula told me she shouted, "What have you given me, it's as bitter as gall!" That's what she said. But I don't get involved. You have to stay out of other people's business. She should have known what kind of woman Katharina is and never had dealings with her in the first place. But again I didn't say anything. Sometimes you pay the price whether you speak or don't speak.

But you can confirm that Ursula was poisoned then?

You try to stay out of other people's business, and then you still find you're in the middle of it.

What do you mean?

Katharina sent someone to harass me at my own market stall. Accused me of saying bad things about her. I told her not to bother me with nonsense. I thought that would be the end of it. I shooed her away like a fly.

**If you knew Katharina had poisoned Ursula, why didn't
you come to the magistrate?**

What did I know? All I knew was what Ursula told me. Like
I said, I try not to get involved. Maybe I made a mistake.
But even when I try to stay out of things, I find I'm stuck
in the tar. After I shooed her away, Frau Kepler came and
harassed me again. You see she's not like other widows. She
came right up to me at the market, this time with her son
the pewterer in tow, and asked me very loudly if I was still
speaking lies about her. Lies! This was about a year ago and I
can still hear it in my ears this moment. Right there in front
of other people. I told her to tend to her own garden. I told
her I had said nothing except for what Ursula Reinbold had
said to me.

Then she turned a corner to sweetness, you see. All
abrupt. She touched my hand. She pleaded. She said that
yes she had given Ursula a drink, but from the goodness of
her heart. She said it was all a simple mix-up. She told me
she had two jugs at her windowsill. One of them had gone
off, she hadn't realized. It was simply a matter of the wrong
jug. Ursula had only taken the smallest sip and then spat it
out. She was sure it wasn't causing her any pain, it couldn't
be. It was only vinegar! Katharina's hand was trembling as
she spoke to me. I felt sorry for her. That's how they get you,
they make you feel sorry for them.

Though Greta read out to me letters from Christoph and from Hans about the trial, its shifting dates, their speculations about adversaries, about friends—I did not pay much attention. Waiting is a difficult sport. I listened only to the letters from you, Simon, and even then only to the parts pertaining to Chamomile. Also to the state of my ginger plants. That you have taken time from your obligations to visit here in Heumaden, to help me note down what has happened to me and to clarify my thoughts before I testify—again, I am so grateful.

I found I learned a lot attending services at the church of Pastor Jüngel at Sillenbuch.

Pastor Jüngel was a short grim man with a narrow beard and unusually large ears. He wore a fitted doublet, and an unusually large cross, one that seemed almost to be a weapon. His voice was small and weak. I watched him from my seat in the third pew, at the edge, near some knitting shepherdesses.

"That our world is in decline is not a hidden truth," Jüngel squeaked. "We have never had so few fish. Both stones and iron have grown less solid. Trees are shorter. The sky is less blue. Instead of blue, its color drifts toward that of a donkey's belly. The blood of our young men runs in the rivers. The popish Antichrist seeks us. Our women are . . ."

Jüngel had an hourglass at his pulpit, but opinions likely differed as to whether it was to make sure he didn't go on too long, or to make sure he went on long enough.

"Yet the evil of man is ever growing. Man has made earth a foul and muddy prison . . ."

Out the window of the church was a magnolia tree in bloom, as well as a field of rapeseed.

"Omens of ill are increasing, coming in many forms. If we fail to recognize them, we will suffer. If we do not clean out our own communities from evil, we will attract more evil." When he got to talking about the comets—we had already had three that year—he had my attention. The comets did not bode well, he said. He spoke of an English king whom he called peaceful Edgar. Or maybe peaceful Edward. A comet of the past had signaled the death of peaceful Ed-whoever-he-was. Pastor Jüngel then spoke of the year 1000, and a comet of that time, that was harbinger of an invasion and the loss of harvests.

I looked at Jüngel's hourglass and wondered how he would get from hundreds of years ago and back to today with only that number of sand grains remaining. Maybe he wouldn't! I watched the race against the sands.

Comets were nearly as common as apples, it turns out. One brought on an earthquake. One preceded volcanoes. Another heralded the killing of Caesar. I don't know—Jüngel could have been making it all up, and what would we have known? Hans once told me comets breathed out their own tails. He so rarely spoke to me of his work, he was so guarded about it all, that I hesitated to break the moment with a question. I didn't understand what he could mean.

I will say of Jüngel that he was one of those who seemed to believe what he said. If he was lying, it was not deliberate. He eventually got round to talking about the comets we had seen in our own lifetimes. What did they mean?

But I had nodded off and woke again only when a congregant next to me tapped my knee and indicated Communion.

How empty my life had become. I didn't know even why I was trying to hold on to it.

A hay maker was kind enough to give me a ride on his cart back to Heumaden.

I set up a small place for me to spin and eat downstairs with the animals, to stay out of Pastor Binder's way. I was tending the animals, yes. I also didn't want to appear for the meal that would be served upstairs. Greta brought me down a soup of carrots and onions, which we shared together, among the animals.

"I'm so happy you're here with me, Mama," she said bravely. "Things will turn for the better soon," she said. "We've had three bad winters in a row. That means we've served our term. God won't give us another season like that."

"Is that how that works? I hadn't heard that," I said.

"I love a soup, whether it's winter or spring, I always en-joy it," she said.

"It's very nice," I said. I wanted to say I was grateful, but I couldn't. Not at that moment. "What do you make of this threesome of comets?"

She drank some more soup before answering. "Luther said that even if the earth were to end tomorrow, he would still plant his tree. I've been thinking about that."

"Where do you get your brightness from?" I asked her.

She said she got it from me.

I thought about that one for a while. Sadly, I did soon come to think how happy I should have been, and now was, for that luxury of a meal in the stable. What I remember was that then Pastor Binder called down at us from the top of the stairs. He told me not to have fear, because if I was inno-cent, then an execution would allow me to escape swiftly to a better world. We can't be assured of justice in this world, he said, but in the next one we can. Then he said, Greta, it's not only your mother. If she is executed, she will be with God, at least, but what about us?

It was around that time that I tried to resign from my position. I was being misunderstood as Katharina's representative. Almost as her lawyer. I was never that. I was simply a neighbor who knew how to read and write. And I was no longer even her neighbor. I paid her one extended visit early in her stay in Heumaden with Greta, as any good friend would, and it was at that time that we put together her pages. She had been out of town a long time now. I helped with errands as directed by her children. I sent her letters updating her. That was a courtesy due to anyone. One must stand by everyone, not only the saints.

It might appear that it was events with Anna and her suitor that made me want to cut visible ties with Katharina. It might also appear that I was cutting ties at Katharina's most vulnerable moment, or one of her most vulnerable moments. Appearances are misleading. The real reason was simple. I was old. I'm still old. And each day older. And each day more tired. Katharina wasn't alone. She had not one child to look after her, but three. She was thrice blessed. What did she need from me?

So on a day when, by chance, I received another cancel of a saddle order, I decided to undertake to walk to Greta's home. I hadn't seen or heard from Katharina for a while. I wanted to say hello. I wanted to see how she was doing. And also I wanted to announce and explain my decision.

Since I would be out all day, maybe two days, I didn't want Anna to worry.

"I'm in need of a long walk," I said. "I might sleep out tonight."

Anna was doing the washing in a splashy, scrubby manner but I believe she heard me. I left a note asking her to attend to Chamomile, please, even if by dark of night.

NEEDING A LOAF of bread for the journey, I stopped by the most convenient bakery. Which, by chance, happened to be the Zoft bakery. I didn't go there to see Rosina Zoft, the aunt of the troublesome Alexander. It was a coincidence, not a providence. I hardly noticed Rosina. My thoughts were elsewhere. I was standing in line reading a letter Alexander had sent Anna. I had picked up the letter by accident, thinking it was a receipt or order. Young people are so stupid. I tried not to read the letter in its entirety. But it was curiously gripping. As bad decisions always are. Suddenly I was at the counter in the bakery, but still consumed by the stupid letter from Alexander. Without looking up, I asked for a spelt loaf. I held out the coins without making eye contact. I mention eye contact because it was my eyes that were spoken of at that moment.

"Very red eyes, Simon."

There was Rosina Zoft.

I folded up the letter and tried my best at a lighthearted laugh.

"I hope you haven't been taking bad medicine," she said.

She had still not given me the spelt loaf, though she'd taken my coins.

"You know, from your neighbor," she said.

"My neighbor?" I said. I acted as if she might mean any one of my various neighbors—and why not?

"I feel bad for you," she said.

I said I hadn't seen Katharina in a long while. Which was true. Depending on what you mean by "long."

"You shouldn't be afraid, Simon," she said.

My cheeks flushed, like a child's. "My daughter, Anna— do you know her, Rosina?"

Rosina said nothing.

"She is so fond of, you know, she very much adores, and values and thinks so highly of your—your apple tarts. Do you think you'll have those soon? Will the tarts be returning?"

Rosina pushed the spelt loaf over the counter. "I expect they'll return, Simon. I think there's a good chance. If you come back again."

A young man in tights was asking me to hurry up already, and I left.

I was trembling as I proceeded across the bright summer day north to Greta's home. I stopped to speak with no one who crossed my path. I gave no more than a distracted nod. Men go on walks all the time to locations of which others are unaware. The chestnut trees were in bloom, their catkins looking like sentries, but what did I care? Poor Anna. What a sad and dim-witted and weakhearted letter she had received from Alexander. All I had done was be an undemanding neighbor, and father, and friend. I was no judge. I was no pastor. Why was Alexander judging others as if he were one? Why did women want to marry at all? I could provide for Anna. The first seven points of order in the last guild meeting I had attended were asking different members to beat their wives less, or spend less money on drink. My legs felt as though they were made of whey. I tossed the spelt bread from Rosina Zoft's bakery to the side of the path, for rabbits and mice to feast upon.

The rabbits and mice that would then in turn be tastier for wolves and lynx and owls to feast upon. Anna had a very easy smile as a young girl. Unguarded as a sunflower. I do so much wrong by doing pretty much nothing at all.

The path grew muddier. I passed meadows and spotted horses and honey-colored cows and brooks and orderly hoed rows of wheat and the overwhelming tidiness of man's petty rebuke to forests. I walked past elderberries and gooseberries and red currants. Would Katharina call me a traitor? A coward? Would she say nothing and turn away? Maybe she would laugh and understand.

When by late afternoon I had arrived at the home of Pastor Binder and Greta, I hesitated. I was nervous all over again. A new kind of nervous. Something struck me as incorrect. A holly bush was surrounded by many of its own leaves, still green and waxy. A chicken feather was among the branches. I heard no voices, no movement. I stepped closer to the modest yellow house. The front door was partially open.

Inside the home looked fresh and abandoned. A jar of jam was knocked over. A confusion of dirty boot prints went this way and that. There was a torn lace shawl on the floor. Two pink bowls on the floor by the window were broken. It was as if the home had been gone over by bears, or soldiers, or both.

"Hello?"

My boot steps in the house felt loud. I tried to look around more lightly.

"Quite a cock's crow that was," said a voice.

Naturally I startled.

The voice came from outside the house, not from within. Turning around, I saw a small but clean man. He looked about fifty. He was wearing simple workman's pants and an altered soldier's jacket. He held a goose under one arm, and a cap in his other hand.

"Are you a friend of the young ones or the old one?"

"Who are you?"

"I wasn't doing anything wrong," he said. "Nothing, nothing. I was out early bringing my geese through to market. Two of them got scared away on account of all the hubbub. I spent most of the day out looking for them again. But I suppose when people ask if anyone saw it, that'll be me—I saw it. Not something you see every day. It was wrong that they took the old woman out naked as a newborn, you know. They didn't have to do that."

"I don't know what's happened," I admitted plainly.

It was then that I learned of the events that had overtaken my small, ugly plans. The goose man seemed more than pleased to be the bearer of a story: "There was a fancy fellow, wearing a fur collar and a green cape—he was the head of it all. Not a fellow I recognized. He sat peaceful as anything on the porch, eating an apple. It was quite rude and unfeeling to be eating at a moment like that, if you ask me. Given all the womanly weeping and crying going on. Meanwhile, he's crunching away, then spitting out the seeds. He has some six or so big guys with him. I didn't know what was going on, but I was curious, naturally, as any human would be, right? With all the shouting, I thought it was soldiers, but I didn't understand why they hadn't gone to one of the finer homes if they were seizing provisions. All the talk about Wallenstein's men, I start thinking I'm about to see them everywhere. But it wasn't soldiers. They were looking for the mother, you see, that's what it was. The mother of the pastor's wife. Rumor had it that she was a witch. Though it's very hard to tell with these things."

"Did they find her?" I asked.

"I told you already, they carried her out naked as the day of being born. It was right at sunup, you see. Someone told me she was hiding in a trunk full of linens. They carried her out like she was a caught turkey. Witch or no witch, I thought it was a sad thing, I admit, but don't quote me. I thought of my own dear mother. Though the big guys, they were laughing and smiling. I suppose it's an adventure for the young men. A special case, you see. I can see their side, too."

"And the pastor?" I asked. "Wasn't he any help?"

"Ah, he fled to the church like a coward," he said. "Couldn't stand to the left or the right. Wouldn't help, nope. But wouldn't *not* help, you see? Didn't intervene, but couldn't accuse him of not intervening, either. Watched his own rump, that was my impression."

The man was a bumpkin who understood nothing. He scratched his head. He took a couple of small biscuits from his bag and offered me one. He said I looked tired.

I didn't want the biscuit.

"The biggest shame falls on the pastor, that's how I see it."

He thought himself quite the philosopher, there with that goose under his arm. "What do you suppose the pastor should have done?"

"The way I see it, the man should have shown his wife that he stood with her. Or shown the fellow in the fur collar that he stood with him—if that was what was right. You have to take a side. That's what I say."

What the goose man would have done was nibble on a biscuit and yabber on about it to whoever crossed his path, that was my sense. "What about Greta?" I asked.

"Who?"

"The young one. I'm sure she had a plan."

"You're a relation of the pastor's wife?"

"Not exactly," I said.

"You're a friend of the family?"

"I wouldn't say friend," I said.

"A man of mystery, then," he said with a laugh. "So maybe a debt collector."

"Where are they now? The mother and the daughter?" I felt weak and jangly.

"If you ask me where a sheep is, my guess is the meadow. The fish is in the stream, if it's not on someone's plate."

"Do you know where they are, or don't you?"

"Calm down, old man. I'm sure the young woman is at the prison trying to work out the situation of her mother," he said. "That would be my reckoning. That would be common sense."

Leonberg, November 5, 1620

Illustrious, highborn, and merciful Prince and Lord, Duke of Württemberg,

I humbly lay my service before Your Princely Grace.

Merciful Prince and Lord, I wouldn't want to disturb Your Princely Grace any further, yet the wrongdoing suffered by my imprisoned mother and her three children, all dutiful subjects to Your Princely Grace, has become so great that we fear she'll soon perish before our eyes. By no means do we suppose Your Princely Grace takes pleasure in this calamity, but rather, as a true father to his subjects, we trust that you will see us through it.

My mother, in her seventy-four years, has never run afoul of the law, and yet she's spent these last four months in prison, broken in body and spirit, enduring torment without a legal conviction. All the while, her pain is made greater by the fact that her alleged misdeeds haven't been properly examined, and she hasn't committed even the slightest offense.

And yet more imperiling are the two keepers charged with guarding our mother. These men, deeply in debt, scheme only to extend their contracts as long as possible, and by

the lowest means. They interpret the cast-off utterances
of an old woman discouraged by her many troubles as
something vile, so that she'll be under more suspicion than
ever before.

Meanwhile, these wasteful and unnecessary guards burn
wood instead of sleeping by the oven, costing my mother
so much that in just a few weeks' time, nothing will remain
of her wealth. Already, in order to raise funds to sustain
her, the authorities in Leonberg have seized her lands
and sold them off, causing an untimely dispute among
us siblings. My brother holds me responsible, as if my
arrival is the only reason behind such lengthy deferrals
and steep expenses, which may soon leave him completely
impoverished, too.

I myself have appealed to God in heaven, since I've
had to leave my poor wife behind, near Regensburg,
without means to carry on, caring for her stepchildren,
and heavy with child. Having no credit in this country,
I'll soon have to return empty-handed, shamed, and
heartbroken.

But, merciful Prince and Lord, in carefully reading the
opening acts of the trial and learning about the royal
counsel prosecuting my mother, I did not shy away
except at the considerable costs involved in a legal
proceeding. Indeed, I deferred to Your Princely Grace
as to whether or not our dogged adversary was acting
wickedly and unlawfully by misapplying God's Mercy
in merciless persecution of our mother, out of desire for
her ruin.

My mother feels that the proceedings will be concluded in due time. She expects to be released from her imprisonment to carry on as a citizen of Leonberg, just as before this dreadful trial stripped away her rights. She believes our good name will be restored. To this end, I've not been alone in humble prayer, and in beseeching Your Princely Grace, inborn prince and steward of the land, whom I praise for his manifold graciousness, and whose mercifulness is extraordinary within and without the empire.

Yet if my mother's accuser should continue in her thirst for blood and property, then in submission to Your Princely Grace, I merely plead that my mother be spared these unjust expenses and provided with a warm and suitable room, in view of her unswerving innocence.

Finally, in case these recommendations may be in vain (although I've prayed many times for God's favor) and mother and children must do without an exemption in awaiting a lengthy trial that will surely end in our financial ruin, without hope of an appeal for innocence, then we humbly request once more that Your Princely Grace condescend to intercede by dismissing the two guards, to be replaced by just one upright and kindhearted citizen or peasant.

Such would ensure that punishment is neither out of proportion nor shouldered by the innocent children, for whom these unnecessary and inordinate costs mean ruinous harm.

My imperiled mother and her children humbly and meekly request Your Princely Grace's merciful intercession.

Subserviently and Obediently,
Johannes Kepler

Greta, I became so accustomed to Simon. Maybe because he isn't a family member. But of course it isn't easy for him to come to visit me here in the prison. Does he look older? Send him my wishes when you see him, please. And ask for news of how Chamomile is holding up. The way it started with Simon was that when he visited Heumaden last year, he helped me write down what has happened already. I wanted to have written up a truer record than the court. I wanted to not be confused or unprepared when I finally have an opportunity to give my testimony. Also, I was thinking of you and your brothers. If I'm convicted, shouldn't you have some record to show that the contrary of what was determined to be true is what is really true? Simon has those papers. I asked him to keep them in Leonberg. Maybe I'm dreaming, and the papers of an old woman won't be able to help you when I'm gone. I also wanted to write down something of the spirit of Maruschl. If you have a child, Greta, you should consider the name Maruschl. Thank you, Greta, for writing these words down for me.

I stay out of your brother's scientific inquiries, but I did get Susanna to explain to me something of what he is doing. The movement of the planets across the sky—which to us here on earth appears chaotic—Hans believes they move according to a profound order. That sounds like a peasant girl's dream of marrying a prince. Though bees know how to make honey, which is unfathomable enough. I believe he will be vindicated, and I believe I will be vindicated.

Let me give a try here with you, Greta, since events are

not yet at their end and should still be accounted for, even if what is written up proves to document a loan that will never be repaid. I don't want to make you sad. I see no point in making you cry, so let's not speak too much of the prison. Some eggs, some celery—if you can manage to continue to get some decent food to me. And ginger, please. Greta, you have very beautiful handwriting. I was told many times what a good student you were. And that you were very pretty, and kind. I didn't share that with you because I didn't want you to be distracted by your capacities. I have always put you down a little bit. I like to think that has helped you.

I am glad to hear that Christoph is still helping to train the Leonberg militia, as I think it will move him forward in the town, even if everyone says his mother is a witch. The town needs him now. Though it sounds like a job herding chickens, and I wouldn't want to see any of those men with muskets. Most of those men couldn't shoot a dead pheasant. I hope the council pays Christoph appropriately for his work. If he weren't stained by my reputation, I believe he could become a councilman. Maybe he still can.

As you know, I was first held in the Stuttgart thieves' tower, to which, under those terrible circumstances, you accompanied me. I understand why you and Christoph pleaded with the Leonberg court to transfer me here, to the prison at Güglingen. It must have sounded awful, for your mother to be held with thieves. Here in Güglingen I am held alone. That they've put me in this irregular and makeshift spot, outside of the warden's quarters, has caused its own problems. I don't want to be ungrateful for all the work you put in for the transfer. I still don't understand, Greta, why I was arrested before the trial ended. I know there had been some clamoring for my arrest ever since I crossed paths with the Haller girl, but I was told the earlier decree to arrest me had been lifted, and that the promise was that it would stay lifted until there was a verdict. Is the date of my testimony set yet? Do you think they will stand by the date, or again push it back?

Let me tell you about someone I shared a cell with in the Stuttgart thieves' tower. She was half my age. She had worked at a hospital for fifteen years. She was in prison for stealing from the hospital. She had taken: an old copper pan, a no-longer-used pair of children's wool socks, some clothing pegs, and three tall, chipped glasses. She had hoped to make a dowry of these sundry. As part of being given the work as a caretaker at the hospital, she had been asked to pledge never to marry. She had made the pledge. Then she met a journeyman carpenter. He told her stories of the northern Italians and their oils and the ease of their fast days—they could still eat butter. The journeyman brought her an embroidered handkerchief. He had a large scar on his left cheek and back to his ear. This woman believed the scar had been God's way of saving the man for her. Instead, she found herself in prison for the humble dowry she'd assembled from junk.

Another woman was the wife of a salt officer. At her husband's direction, she had exchanged salt for lard. This wasn't allowed, but also it was the only way her family could survive. She said if she could change anything, she would still have traded salt for lard, but would have traded only with Gypsies, who knew how not to get caught for these things, and who never gave up your name to an officer, who were too smart for that. Say what you will about Gypsies, she said, but she, for one, thought them highly capable. The salt officer's wife told me that she had been blessed with nine children, she knew God would take pity on her. I liked at least half the women I met in the thieves' tower. Did you write that down? Even an old woman is still learning about the world.

I know you have to travel farther now, to visit me here in Güglingen instead of Stuttgart. I pity you the long journey. Don't come too often. Your brother Heinrich's children are with you now? I can't imagine their home near Prague being so bloodied as you say. I thought the stories were fanciful exaggerations when I heard them. Like those drawings boys make of little soldiers spearing one another, blood coming out in almost happy arcs. The salt officer's wife told me about the men in Prague being pushed out the window, but she said they dusted themselves off and walked away, and what was the problem with that? What that young girl in your husband's parish doesn't know, is too young to know, is that blood and famine are silver birches, and they grow wherever there's water.

Here I was at first kept in a space outside of the main officer's residence, but the officer complained, saying it was unsuitable, as he had children, and they were afraid of me. That's why I was then moved to this location, but the guarding expenses here are higher. And because there's no cell to contain me, you find me in this state, chained to the wall. The ankle brace isn't what's heavy, it's the anchor chain that's a burden. It's on account of the chain that the brace has worn through my stocking.

I don't cast aspersions on gerbils or bats. The guards are what they are. Do you hear the two of them bickering and having a soup in the next room over? They're pleased to have the easy work. But also bored by it. The boredom makes them schemers. They'd be better people if they were loading and unloading carts. I'm always polite to them, Greta. You're right that we have to see the good in people, at least in people who have power over us and who will be angry if we see them in another way.

Hogg is the one who is young and thin and stupid.

Lorenz is the one who is fat and older and, in his way, clever.

"Don't try any of your tricks on me," said Lorenz when we first met. "I'm like a rabbit, only half of myself is asleep at any time. I'm like a rabbit but also like a wolf, and if you attack me you'll learn the length of my fangs." Lorenz is a chest-thumping dolt who quivers with fear of a skinny old woman, is what I'm saying. But a chest-thumping dolt who I have to rely on to bring me crackers.

Hogg said, "I've got you covered, Lorenz. I'm here with you. You're not alone." Also very chicken-livered.

Really these guards are too stupid to fear.

If you can bring them jam, a hard-boiled egg, something, when you come—then they will be more likely to let you bring something for me. They won't even let me have a small, dull knife, something to help cut my food. I know Einhorn has ordered the sale of my fields and house to cover the expenses. Those things will take time. Greta, it's sad, but I'm not going to cry about it—just make sure Chamomile is in good hands.

Do you understand that any false testimony you knowingly give will provoke God's great anger in your earthly life and will deliver your soul unto Satan upon your death?

That sounds good and right to me, sir, yes, and I am accustomed to the seriousness of locales such as this one.

Your name and profession and age.

Lorenz Bausch, fifty-one. I've held many positions. I am currently employed as a guard at Güglingen prison. I have made every effort and many a big sacrifice to be on time and present and do my duty to the perfect-most in serving as a guard. I asked for some of your time, which I know is so valuable, and I am very grateful and view you with the tip-top of reverence and everything. Yes, I'll get on with it. The defendant is much more dangerous than you might be guessing based on her appearance. Even with two of us, it calls on all my courage, even with my having served nobly in various battles including among the Turks and having been considered really a hero among the other men—this has been a difficult but also gratifying job. What I'm saying is, she may appear weak, but she's all bite, you know what I mean?

In what ways has Frau Kepler been a difficult prisoner?

Yes, I can give you some examples. She was there pleading and begging, saying she needed a knife for her food, saying she was just a little old lady and weak and limited and chained, the whole pitiful kitten-mewing thing. I myself have been imprisoned as a soldier and I never complained, not once, and I can assure you the conditions were not so luxurious. She was begging me for the knife, saying that without it she couldn't cut her food into smaller pieces, that it was difficult for her to chew—that it wasn't working. I was sympathetic, but I wasn't going to give her a knife. I'm not the town fool. This is the point I wanted to get to: Then I stepped out briefly, for a meeting with the supervisor, and I came back in and there she was, eating her meal with a knife! I can assure you with my dignity and honor as an experienced guard on the line that she did not have the knife before. So that is the kind of dark magic that we as guards were facing. And continue to face.

Does she still have the knife?
We took the knife from her. She demeaned us with names that I won't mention. Of course my wife worries about me in this line of work.

There have been complaints about how much wood you and your partner are burning.
What is said about the burning of the wood being excessive, I swear to you on all that is good and correct, it is not true. It is a vicious and unfounded rumor. It has been cold and it will be getting colder. We have been very parsimonious with the wood. The absolute minimum. Now, whether or not the cost of adequate guarding services is or isn't within the means of the prisoner—these are things for a judge or counsel to work out, that is my humble understanding. It is not our fault if Frau Kepler has not made sufficient provisions for her old age.

Is there more you wish to share with the court?
Yes, there was one more aspect of the prisoner and the difficulty of the job that I did humbly want to bring to the

attention of sirs such as yourself and whomever else might be interested. The prisoner—she says many ungodly things. She speaks of living no differently than a beast, or worse than a beast. Says that she cares not whether she lives or dies, and such sort. It is very dispiriting, I can tell you. It's an extra weight I carry, hearing the ungodly things that she says.

Thank you for your time and service.

Oh, and I did think that there would be additional pay. For bearing the burdens I bear. And communicating the very useful information that I communicate. Very peculiar not to be rewarded.

Leonberg, December 15, 1620

To the esteemed ducal governor Lukas Einhorn as well
as to his valued assistants and also to whosoever shall be
designated to decide matters regarding the good and proper
incarceration of the dangerous and wicked Frau Kepler.

I write to you first to thank you for your dutiful and
righteous and valorous work in protecting the public good
and safety and especially protecting children by effecting
the sequestration of a dangerous woman.

I do beg of you now a variation in the conditions of her
detention.

The costs of Katharina Kepler's imprisonment are being
paid out of the proceeds from the sale of her assets.
This is just and good, and we praise the wise handling
of putting her in prison wherever you so deem best. We
write only because we wish to bring to your attention
what you already know, which is that compensation for
the victims of this dangerous woman is payable from
these same finite proceeds from the sale of her assets.
Currently there are two guards keeping watch over
Katharina at all times, and she is furthermore chained by
her ankle to the wall, and although we agree and assert
that she is a danger, we argue that to pay two guards
night and day is not only superfluous but also will empty

the coffers, making appropriate compensation of the victims impossible.

These guards are furthermore incurring expenses heedlessly by purchasing and burning an enormous amount of wood. The bills are beyond anything we have ever heard of or seen, even in the worst of winters. Maybe the two guards provoke each other to more and more burning. Maybe they take a cut of the expenses. We don't know. But if they are allowed to continue spending in this manner, there will be nothing left. In the interest of sweet justice, and for that reason above all, we humbly ask that this draining of funds more properly destined to victims be halted. Frau Kepler is an old and weak woman. One guard will suffice. The one guard can be provided a horse blanket. He can be given secondary duties as well, since, again, Frau Kepler is secured to the wall. Even the Kepler family, with whom we continue to have great conflict—they are in agreement with us on these points.

Your grateful and humble servants who implore you, Ursula and Jacob Reinbold, citizens of Leonberg

Greta, I don't know what day of the week it was. I had lost track. But whatever day of the week it was, Lorenz arrived in a low mood. "That glazier's wife has the brains of a pigeon, the heart of a prickle bush. She has the greedy eyes of a lame fox. She can't hunt on her own. She's content to take the earnings of others. She's a horsefly."

Hogg asked what was the concern.

Lorenz read out a letter, including words from a petition she had sent, asking that, for the sake of God's mercifulness, the witch's funds be reserved.

"Well, I don't see what's wrong with God's mercifulness," Hogg said.

"You fat-kidneyed loggerhead. The Reinbold woman proposes to steal from us."

"By Christ's fingernails, if you ask me."

They went back and forth for a while, confused as any pantomime. That's how I learned that even the Werewolf is working to cut short my imprisonment. Strange alliances form. That really does feel like a sign of end-times.

"Are they saying the job is up? Or are they saying someone else is paying our salary?"

"Or are they saying, simply, to be a wee bit more temperate with the firewood?"

"They can't get rid of us—"

"Yes, look at her, she's terrifying—"

That sort of chitchat really didn't bother me. Feeling weak bothered me. Seeing the Reinbold attorney come speak with them bothered me. But this, no. The situation recalled to me that in one view, these two were my employees.

"Please unchain me," I asked quietly. I showed them the sores on my ankle.

They ignored me.

"Where would I go?" I said quietly. "The doors are locked. I can't run."

Lorenz gave a grouchy laugh. "We're trying to keep our job, not lose it."

"I would pay you," I said. I promised them a hundred thalers.

"Show it to us," Hogg said. "You haven't got it."

"I would get it to you," I said.

They were silent a moment. I had them thinking.

Then Lorenz said: "Old lady, I'd do it for you, I really would. Out of the kindness of my heart more than anything else. But I've no faith in women's words. And I've learned that through a great deal of experience in the matter."

The crooked hand of justice acts more swiftly than the straight one. Somebody somewhere said that. I had a prison fever and when next I woke, neither guard was there. The fire was burning low. Then I did begin to wonder if I had died. If I had joined the other women in my situation. But then I started to think of a cooked egg. A dead person would in no way think of a cooked egg, that was my feeling. A dead person, on the contrary, would have cooked eggs aplenty. I was dreaming especially of an egg boiled with onion skins, the shell stained with that toasted color. I could feel the shell of the egg under my fingers. Within the shell I pulled away at that thin, papery part between the shell and the meat of the egg. I pulled the egg apart and the yolk was pink inside. Then I opened another egg. The yolk was an inky dark blue. Another was the color of the sky. Another was a marigold. Those were my egg dreams.

Also I dreamed of strawberries. Of the seeds on the outside. I had always been skeptical of strawberries, growing so close to the ground. But in that prison, I dreamed of the strawberry as a noble fruit, and plentiful. The strawberry sets its seeds on the outside, for all to see. A strawberry has nothing to hide.

Then you were here, Greta. You thought I spent all my time counting my enemies and feeling sorry for myself, didn't you? I do spend time doing that, too. Especially counting enemies.

You say that Heinrich's two boys fight with each other, but with you are kind. Ask them to fight only outside. Their wanting to avoid the cold might be enough to mitigate the violence. It disturbs me greatly what you say of Hans's letter to the Duke going unanswered. You say it's five weeks now and still no response. I know the Duke is in love with his war, or afraid of it. But no response for five weeks makes me worry that Hans's status in the world has fallen, and perilously. What does Pastor Binder think? Hans came to interview me to prepare the defense. He interviewed me so patiently, as if my recipe for wormwood, blessed thistle, and ginger wine were a great matter. He took seriously the songs I sang for children, and asked me if I could remember where I had seen skulls coated in silver. That was, of course, when I visited him in Prague, years back. He looks thin and spent, Greta. You are well to be living outside of Leonberg. I want you to think of things and people other than your mother.

A slim, small person moved into Katharina's house. Someone about the same size as Katharina. With dark clothes. A man, it appeared. Had they already sold the house? I had thought not. I caught sight of the man's animal pacings. By this time, the city gates were shut by nine, the curfew was in place—how had a stranger been allowed in town? Yet there was something familiar in the new neighbor's nightly walks. Almost supernaturally familiar. The mysterious figure began to hold sway over my emotions, as if I were a puppet and someone was stepping on my strings. Katharina, my friend, was in her home again—that was the feeling. It wasn't true, yet felt so true. She was back! Yet she wasn't coming to speak with me. And I wasn't going to speak with her. The coldness was terrible. I tried to put it out of my mind. It was in error, I told myself. I'm an old man, I said. And getting older.

After Anna was asleep, I drank some ginger wine, hoping it would clear the fog in my head. It was a new-moon night. Feeling too much like the criminal that I wasn't, I crossed over, to see who was haunting Katharina's home.

I would like to take a brief moment to say, of this man who I am told is extraordinary, that he was rabbit-like, and small. He was handsome and guarded. I expected to have the door closed in my face, and he embraced me. He seemed only to know me as a man highly regarded by his mother. He called me a great backgammon player. He thanked me for the letters of his that I had read out, for the errands I had run. In my heart I had come over as if with

ax in hand, and he set out a poppy-seed cake, to receive me
as an old friend. He said he was so glad to see me. He said
he felt as if he'd been going mad.

We spoke for what felt like hours.

"Can I ask a favor of you?" he then asked.

I almost answered that I would lay down my life for
him. I think it was the ginger wine. Or the poppy seeds.

The great man said he wanted me to listen to the defense he was preparing.

I asked him, wouldn't he rather share it with Christoph
and Gertie? With Greta and Pastor Binder?

"Passions are too high," he said.

"I do have a gift for steadiness," I said. "But I know
nothing of the law."

"It's about telling a credible story, that's the main
thing."

"Well, I can sit here quietly and listen," I offered. I told
him about how I had been in a school play once, in which I
had played the role of Mary Magdalene. I added with some
pride that the other kids said that my watching them was
very helpful.

"I played Mary Magdalene as a schoolboy, too," Hans
said.

I mention these minor affinities to say how well dis-
posed I was to Hans. When he began to read out loud to me
his defense, I had every inclination to be impressed by it.
Reassured by it. To have faith in it. I was terrified for Katharina, though I tried not to be, since worry doesn't move
even a brick. And I had never blamed Hans for his slip of
fidelity in his book—was it really a slip of fidelity? Christoph had been too hot-tempered about it, I thought.

But Hans's defense was very lengthy. It took so long
for him to read it out. It was a carefully drafted, detailed

story of a town populated with liars and fools, with self-ishness and stupidity. This one had always been envious; that one had always been willing to lie for personal gain. This one had denied his mother Communion. That one was known to be violent. Another was crazy and had a low moral reputation. One had said the left hoof of the pig in one account, and the right foot in another. Another had said fourteen years ago, then corrected to nine, or maybe seven. It was yea in one testimony, and nay in another. Fools, braggarts, and purse-grabbers had caused his mother's misery. Corruption, laziness, and malice.

His defense poured over me like used cooking grease. He saw in Leonberg a horrible place.

That was my encounter with the author of *The Harmony of the World*.

"Is the argument clear? Is it compelling?"

"Well," I said, "it reminds me of church."

"What do you mean?"

I said that I meant that, for example, as a sermon, I thought it would go over very well. The audience would like it.

"Ah, I see."

All the ginger wine had worn off. He was disappointed in me.

"You're my mother's friend," he asserted. "She's a suspicious woman. She's an odd woman, I know. I shouldn't be surprised that her friend is an odd man." He didn't chastise me for having stepped down quietly from my duties as a legal guardian. I returned home.

I don't trust the way they will have written it down, Greta. They see me as a monster. You know my feelings about the scribes and how well they're paid. Meanwhile, my home is being sold to pay the legal and prison expenses, at rates as if I'm staying at a fine inn, eating a beef stew. Of course, once I was called up, they spoke straight off of handing my soul over to Satan.

I'm getting ahead of myself.

"Please, Mama, can you pull your hair back more tidily?" your brother Christoph said. "Gertie, you must have a nice kerchief somewhere." I was a roast pig being prepared for presentation at the table.

"People are more sympathetic toward a tidy and attractive person," Hans said. "Christoph is right. Try not to chew on your lips when you're there. Or to pull on your ears. Try not to sigh, or laugh, or look disdainful. Don't roll your eyes, or harrumph, or show anger, or worry. If you can find within you a gentle and shy smile, try to show it to the judges. When sad moments are discussed, especially the pain of others, see if you can let a small tear show. I know it's difficult—"

I didn't think they were wrong, Greta. "Where's Simon?" I asked.

"He's not well, Mama," Hans said.

"That's not something to worry about," Christoph said.

"We're all here," you said.

"I wanted to ask him about Chamomile," I said.

"It's all been taken care of," Hans said.

But in what way? Was Anna taking care of Chamomile? Where was she being kept?

"I saw Chamomile this morning, Mama," Hans said.

"But you're no good with animals—"

"It's not the time to be worrying about parsley for sausages," Christoph said.

This was the day that I was to give my testimony.

I RECOGNIZED THE clerk at the courtroom. It was Sebald Sebelen. So he had not died of the plague. Though he looked more unwell than ever. He must only have been near dying.

I asked him, from my heart, how was he doing?

"Ah, Frau Kepler, absolutely tip-top here."

"I see that," I said.

He wiped his brow. "You'll find the earlier cases are still being heard. I hope we won't have troubled you for nothing." He directed us to a bench beneath a stuffed ram's head that was mounted at the back of the hearing room. I sat, as still as possible, as several cases were seen ahead of ours. I saw Hans making notes about God knows what. Christoph grew impatient and stepped outside several times with his pipe. Gertie sometimes listened closely, sometimes read. Greta, you kept on a smile, and patted my knee every now and again, though I could see your hand was trembling.

The first case was about a hawker who spent all the family money on drink and failed to clothe his children properly. The next was that of a pie seller who had overslept the morning that he was to report to prison for three days for public fighting; he had not overslept today. He now owed seven days of prison. A third was a case of a yeoman of whom it was alleged he beat his wife too often, and too hard. He was instructed to do less beating in the future.

Only one case was a woman. She was accused of being a cutpurse at the Wednesday market.

And then they got to me. The way I recall it was like this.

AS A YOUNG girl, I was once swimming in the River Glems with friends. We were in an eddy, and then, without my knowing when it had happened, I was in a current, coursing forward, out of sight of everyone. The landscape was changing, rocks were passing by, at times I felt that I could see dragonflies hovering near me, though how could that be—I was moving so quickly. I tried to keep my feet ahead of me, in case of rocks or branches. I was waiting for shore or still waters to find me. I felt I would never die.

In the courtroom, the counsel asked me if I knew that any false testimony would provoke God's great anger and I found myself saying that I was hopeful that was the case, of course, since so many had spoken falsely against me. I had spent so much time thinking what I would say, and there I went saying something provocative right off the top for no reason, like a child who doesn't understand the intersection of tactics and truth. I could feel in the room that crackling before a storm in response to my words. That stoked my vanity.

I felt only more querulous as the questioning moved forward. Of the butcher Topher Frick, who was struck with pain in his thigh, I told the counsel that it was well known that Frick cut down saplings, that it was wrong to cut down a tree when its trunk was still green, and though I could not say, perhaps the pain he received suited the pain he gave. Of the schoolmaster Beitelspacher I could say that his father had been a gentle man and that it was not known to me when envy and delusions had made their way to the son, who I had known since he was a small boy, and no good at sports. The Werewolf Ursula's reputation was well known and that she had won over the pastor with her false-faced flattery and manipulation was something that I was helpless to counter. I didn't think I was saying anything that wasn't clear to anyone with eyes to see or ears to hear, but also it was as if I were no longer in that room. When I looked at those seated in the courtroom, I had visions. I saw a young boy I had been friends with as a child and who had died after being bitten by a dog. He had loved marbles. Two old aunts who had often told me stories, often of clever beasts in the woods who deceived children, and who had died within a week of each other—they also were seated in the courtroom, smiling, pleased with my performance, it seemed. My cow Mare was there! In the aisle. Maruschl was near her, smiling. That was when I understood that likely my dreaming had grown almost too powerful. Yet it gave me strength. I saw a young man I had loved who had died of a fever, having looked well only two weeks before. I saw several dogs that had belonged to the blacksmith. A friend of mine with shiny dark hair who died giving birth to her second child. Finally, I saw my parents, of course, on opposite sides of Mare and each with a Heinrich on their lap.

"Why do you have no pity?" I heard the counsel asking me.

"I do have pity," I said.

One of the judges, whom I had known since I was a young bride, said, "Please, Kath-chen. Can't you show us a little heart? Haven't you any tears to show?"

You were crying, Greta. I could see you. And so were your brothers. But I have cried so much in my life that there are no tears left in me. That was my testimony.

When it ended, I was told the trial papers would be sent to the chancellery, that we would wait to hear back before moving forward, and that until we heard back—and it has been five weeks already—I would continue to be held in Güglingen.

Do you understand that any false testimony you knowingly give will provoke God's great anger in your earthly life and will deliver your soul unto Satan upon your death?

Of course I understand that. I am one of the few who understands that.

And you are not permitted to speculate or act on simple rumor.

I never gossip. It doesn't interest me.

Name and age.

Barbara Meyer. Twenty-seven.

You sound emotional.

My mother, who was a generous woman always ready to care for others and easy with laughter and also very honorable, was sick with consumption in the last year of her life. She saw ghosts often in the evening, who let her know she would be dying soon. They invited her over often. When she died it was very sad, but she was honored and even celebrated. Then, a full ten years after her death, the rumor begins that she died from a witch's brew given to her by Frau Kepler. My mother would never fall for such a thing! Nor would she associate with a witch. She was a great judge of character. Frau Kepler was her friend. She knew a crow from a raven.

How did this rumor begin, then?

You rarely see a spider spinning a web, you more often see webs already spun. But I believe the schoolmaster

Beitelspacher was central, with his whining and going on. It wasn't enough to blame others for his lameness, he had to bring shame on my mother, too.

Were you approached by the Reinbold family or legal team?
My brother was approached.

To what end?
They said they wanted me to formally confirm my mother's early death. Okay, that is a true thing. But I said her death was not a fact that needed confirming by me. Go visit her grave, I said. My brother has always been trouble. Always a schemer, not a worker.

But you did agree to testify.
I did. They insisted that I say a witches' brew from Katharina had killed my mother. Again: My mother would never fall for that. Never. It's completely wrong. They pushed me to say it, but I will not say it. The church warden Johan Bernhardt Buck used my brother to coerce. A man of the church. He told my brother: Why would I not say that the Kepler woman had come to me at night encouraging me to take a demon lover? I was very offended.

Why would he push for such a statement? There must have been a reason for his suspicion.
The church warden Buck is new to Leonberg. I don't know him. I don't know his family.

How did he know your brother?
I don't know what dealings he has with my brother. My brother's life is his life.

You're saying they pushed you to say something untrue?
They tell me I will face terrible consequences, including prison. But I fear eternal damnation more than I fear the evils of men.

You believe that Frau Kepler is innocent of your mother's death?
My mother liked Frau Kepler. I don't know Frau Kepler well, but when I was a child, she brought apple cakes to our home. Another time breads and even cheeses. As a child I wasn't schooled in saying thank you or recognizing generosity. I even feared Frau Kepler. I found the faces and teeth of adults strange and wrong and not pretty. I was only a child. I was also timid with Herr Beitelspacher. His voice reminded me of an animal, and he was often congested, and that disgusted me—but that was wrong of me. What I am getting around to saying is that my mother was sick. We all knew she was sick. She spent the last months of her life bravely facing her death, visiting friends, having a drink with one, a meal with another. That was her way of saying goodbye. She was a good and brave woman. And not a fool.

Do you understand that any false testimony you knowingly give will provoke God's great anger in your earthly life and will deliver your soul unto Satan upon your death?

Yes, I very much do.

Please state your name, age, and business.

My name is Helena Frisch. I am fifty-five years old. My husband was an assistant to a blacksmith. He died seventeen years ago following an accident.

Can you share with the court your involvement in the Kepler case?

Yes, I was accused of being a witch. I was tortured for a confession. A convicted witch in Tübingen was said to be my cousin. She wasn't my cousin. That was the grounds for my being tortured. Also my daughter, who had frenzy and leprosy, told authorities that I had devilish salves and the devil as a lover. My daughter has many troubles, and has not had an easy life. She is not well. She also told authorities that I had attended witches' Sabbaths. I believe my daughter misunderstood the wedding feasts of her own siblings.

I am sorry for your troubles. Can you explain your purpose in being here today, in relation to the trial of Katharina Kepler?

I was found innocent. This was in January, after uncountable difficulties. I had been tortured, but I had nothing to confess. Even after the charges against me were dismissed, I was still held in prison another three weeks. The why of that was not explained to me. At that point, I thought I would never be released.

You have still not made clear your connection to the Kepler case.

I'm getting there. It was during those weeks when I was still in prison, and did not understand why I was still in prison—it was during that time that the first fellow came. He wore a green cape. Tell us about the work you did with Frau Kepler, the fellow in the green cape said.

I said I didn't know any Frau Kepler.

You don't know about the mother of the Imperial Mathematician? he said.

He was trying to make me feel ashamed. I knew her by name, because of the accomplishments of her son. But I did not know her. I had been stretched. I had suffered thumbscrews. I wasn't thinking about imperial mathematicians. I'm still not thinking about imperial mathematicians.

And then what happened?

He said to me, We all know she's a witch. We've always known. The matter of how we came to know is simple—we already knew. I only ask you to show your gratitude and say what you know to be true.

You see, his case against her would be very much strengthened if he could say others had named her as a witch. Especially another suspected witch. Sadly, I came to know all the intricacies of the law of the Carolina as it pertained to charges against witches. Sadly, I am like a scholar on it.

What did you tell him about Frau Kepler?

I disappointed him. He then came back a second time, with another fellow, dressed in black and white, who looked like a goat. Now it was two of them: asking me what works had I done with Frau Kepler. That was the word he used—he said "works." I said I had done no works at all with Frau Kepler, who I didn't know. I began to feel very sorry for this Frau Kepler, who, again, I didn't know. Who I still do not know.

Do you understand that any false testimony you knowingly give will provoke God's great anger in your earthly life and will deliver your soul unto Satan upon your death?

To be questioned under oath about the Frau Kepler case and the ludicrous and offensive and malicious suggestion that as an officer of the law I have done anything other than follow procedure and assist in gathering of information and do my duty to the best of my abilities—no. I will not have the tables turned. You don't get all your pips in place and then say now we switch colors. I'm the church warden, not the other way around. Johan Bernhardt Buck is no one's fool.

Can you swear that you did not pressure Barbara Meyer?

The Kepler crowd has put that idea into the head of the young woman. Ridiculous. The only defense available to them is lies, lies, lies. I do not blame Barbara Meyer directly, I blame the Keplers. She has had the fear of the devil put into her by Kepler and her kin. I would not go after Barbara Meyer. But the rest of them need to be cleaned up. They say I have a reputation for violence. You may as well shout at God for lighting fires in Hell. The world has a proper order. I'm not a source of violence, I'm an attendant of God.

Do you understand that any false testimony you knowingly give will provoke God's great anger in your earthly life and will deliver your soul unto Satan upon your death?

Yes. And let me go ahead and say, my name is Christof Georg Auf Dem Sand. I am thirty years old. I work as a barber surgeon, both here and in the surrounding areas. For the past two years I've served the soldiers of the Holy Roman Emperor.

No need for questions, I know what you want to know.

Yes, I examined the Haller girl after the incident on the path near the kiln.

I applied a salve to the girl's hand, and the girl reported that her pain was relieved.

I didn't think much of the case at the time.

Pain caused by witchcraft is known to be the worst at the beginning and then to ease off.

That the Haller girl's pain is reported to have increased again, after the salve had apparently relieved it—it's a curious case.

But I didn't personally have a second opportunity to examine the injured finger. So I can't speak to the progression.

I can't make it to another hearing. I can sign this deposition, and attach a copy of the visit as noted in my patient log. I came home to see my ill mother. I'm obliged to return to the battalion I serve in two days' time.

As the head of the prosecution, I will now offer my closing statement.

Let us take a moment to think on what the other side is telling you.

The defendant and her astrologer son tell you that the Reinbolds are too low to be trusted. Trust our word over hers, they say. She is of the rabble, they say. Why they say this when she is a respected citizen of our community, I do not know, but that is what they say. Our side says something different. Our side says each human is a reflection of God, and deserves justice.

The defendant and her astrologer son tell you to disregard Ursula Reinbold because she had no children, while Katharina Kepler raised four children to adulthood, including her much-discussed astrologer son. They say this as if it is unique to have family. We say something different. We say that Ursula is a child of God, deserving of our compassion.

The defendant and her astrologer son tell you that the testimony of women and children needs to be discounted. They tell you that women and children are too suggestible, too superstitious, too fragile, too easily deceived. There is something in what they say. But who is doing the deceiving? Do Frau Kepler and Herr Kepler really believe that a woman or child cannot speak reliably even of their own pain?

The defendant and her astrologer son tell you that disease and death happen every day. Can we cry witch every time a man coughs? they suggest. But Frau Kepler has been accused not once, but many times. She has been accused of having killed a pig with a touch, ridden to death a goat, and made two cows and one horse ill. She has brought on dangerous storms. She has injured the leg of the butcher. She has offered false and dangerous remedies. She tried to dig up her father's skull as a weapon of sorcery. She has killed by poison a mother of three. She made lame a schoolmaster. She likely contributed to the deaths of the tailor's two small children. She has menaced her guards. This is without even speaking of Ursula's pains, or of the witch's grip found on the arm of the young Haller girl. Is every evil to be written off as one more trial of our world? As something to be expected? Or is there room for us as men to say: *This* evil we can prevent. *This* evil we can head off. *This* child we can protect. *This* village we can make safe. Beyond our walls, war may rage. But we still have faith that there is that which is within our power, which we can make right.

The defendant and her astrologer son laugh at this court. They attack the court's impartiality. They blame it for delays of their own making. They belittle the citizens of Leonberg. They call this one scurrilous, that one an exaggerator, a third a rumor-monger, another a liar, another a fool. No one can be trusted, they imply, except for them. The defendant and her astrologer son must consider themselves made of a different stuff. Stardust? Frau Kepler laughs at serious questioning; Herr Kepler taps his foot impatiently. The pewterer can show only a red face. His wife sits reading lurid pamphlets. Only the daughter, Greta, shows good faith.

Amid their derision, they want to impress upon you their connections to the late Duchess Sybille, even to the Emperor.

They are right that we are different from them. We respect the court. We know that God dwells in each human being. We—

Counsel, it's been a long day, after many long days. May we ask that, if at all possible, you advance succinctly to your conclusion?

Yes, of course.

Let me say: Perhaps we could have acted otherwise than to convict if we saw some humanity in the defendant. If it were simply that she had strayed, but wanted to return to our loving fold. If she showed some penance. Some emotion. Some consideration. Have we seen a single tear from Frau Kepler? We have not. We say to her, Kath-chen—for some of us have known her since she was a girl—can't you show us something of your heart? Show us your remorse? Children have fallen ill. Animals that families depend on have been afflicted. The will of God is being obscured by the devil. Your own children are here watching you. Give us some sign of your true heart. Weep for us. Shed a tear. And what does she say? "I have cried so many tears in my life, sir, that there are none left." We must call a witch a witch.

It's simple. If an army climbed over our walls, we would pick up arms and fight. We would do so without hesitation. Shadowy troops hide among us. I advise torture in order to get a full confession from the defendant, and then to punish her unto death.

Some dozen or so years had passed since poor Katharina's ordeal. And of all things, I found myself in Frankfurt. The mood at the book fair—that was why I had traveled—was like what you might find at a family wedding where both sides feel it's a bad match. A grim, determined festivity. There were still hundreds of us there, I presume thousands. But business, and spirit, and funds, and good health, and a good grape harvest, and all number of other good things— that had drifted to the Leipzig Book Fair. A decade or so of war does that, I suppose. The Swedes were occupying the city, but best as I could tell the place was overrun by Dutchmen. A gingerbread seller told me his native village, but a day's walk from Frankfurt, had been almost entirely murdered by the plague. He used that term: "murdered." I hadn't thought of the plague that way, but the language was clear enough. He himself hadn't been to his village to witness the destruction—he had read about it in a pamphlet. He related the story cheerfully. Even with some pride. Some people are like that.

"It's better than death by marauding soldiers, is the way I see it," he said.

I bought some of his gingerbread. Ginger protects from consumptive diseases, I believe.

"I count myself blessed," he said. "The wars will end one day—"

"God willing—"

"—and then how will the young men find employment?"

I didn't know what to say.

"You hadn't thought of that, had you? They can't all be night watchmen." He made his cheery way onward.

I liked the gingerbread, even if it left my throat feeling itchy.

I hadn't mustered the business courage to inhabit my stall yet. It was okay. I was told tomorrow was the bigger day. Even in my old, old age I still find myself to be a hesitater, an avoider, a doubter. It can be made clear as the starriest night what my proper role is—still I won't assume it. Foolish un-principled resistance. When I was younger, I thought maybe I had been given the horoscope for the wrong birth date, or rather that God had received the wrong instructions in relation to me; everything was incorrect. All my feelings. All my instincts. I was a dog who chewed leaves instead of bones. A cat who liked being in water.

I was assigned to stall one hundred and seventy-one. How empty it looked. The wooden bench was water-damaged and splintered.

I decided to walk the aisles to see what the other stalls were doing before setting up my own.

One man was hawking a play about a man who falls in love with his sister.

Another was selling a treatise on how to redress the abuses in the weights and measures used in markets.

I came across *Selected Disputations with Aristotle.* And: *The Feminine Monarchy: A History of Bees.* The next aisle had more than the usual number of Christian treatises on one or another way of living. *Munition Against Man's Misery and Mortality* caught my attention. I turned a few pages. It was the usual, usual. I was handed a free advertorial page for *The Jew of Malta.* Another advertisement for a book about a one-hundred-and-forty-year-old Scotsman still fathering children. A tale of harrowing journeys to Siam was illustrated with etchings of a delicate butterfly. I bought only one thing: a compendium of dirty jokes, nonsense jokes, rhyming verse, retorts, and charming tales.

I had failed to notice the people running the stalls. Though watching them had been the original motivation for the walk. I set off for another turn. Some paced in front of their tables. Some had the smile of fruit-sellers. Some sat quietly, as if it didn't matter to them whether one came by their stall or not. Then I turned a corner and recognized someone. Or I thought I did. Where had I last seen that face? She was a modest-looking woman, maybe forty years old, maybe more. She was in widow's clothing. She sat there quietly, at stall two hundred and eleven. Set out in front of her was a small pewter bowl filled with purple snap candies. A number of well-dressed men took a candy as they passed by. She looked out at the crowd, offering a timid smile now and again. No one stopped to speak to her.

She was situated between a stall decorated in red that was hawking an edition of Luther's pamphlets, and another stall that sold yet another edition of *Death and the Ploughman*. So the stalls on each side of her both sold books from a century ago. Why no interest in the awful and dramatic present?

"You're Katharina's friend!" the woman called out to me.

I suppose I must have been staring. "Friend?"

"Yes!"

"Katharina. Which Katharina?"

"Katharina Kepler," she said. "You were her friend."

Startled: "I tried to be."

The woman stood up, she even embraced me.

It was the astrologer's widow, Susanna. Now I recognized her. I had only met her when she had visited

Heumaden at the same time as myself, but that visit had been memorable, and intense, as I already knew so much of her troubles from Katharina's telling. And now I had heard the sad news of Hans's passing. Why did I hesitate to offer my condolences? I don't know. But the moment passed.

"Anna is very well," I said. I wanted to make a dowry for her. She was engaged to a widower as old as myself. She had in the end married Alexander, but he had died of the plague.

"Anna?"

"Oh, that's right, you probably never met my daughter."

We had a little laugh.

Susanna was here at the book fair hoping to sell some of Hans's juvenilia, it turned out. Something he had composed as a student, his dissertation, she explained. Then she blushed. Which seemed odd to me. "It's written as a dream that he had. An imaginary dream. About a boy who travels to the moon. And sees the earth from there, and the other planets. There's a strange bit about the mother of the boy that you might find, well, curious. Yes, strange and curious." She blushed again. Susanna's shawl was worn. She wore gloves with mendings. I suspected she was in difficulty.

"That sounds familiar," I said. "I could never keep up with your husband's accomplishments."

"It's a beautiful book. It's like a story."

"Very nice."

Susanna asked me what had brought *me* to the fair.

At that very moment, a well-dressed Frenchman approached Susanna's table. Wearing ludicrous red silk hose.

I hastily suggested we meet up later and she agreed. I walked away quickly, then glanced back and saw her speaking hopefully, somewhat pathetically, to the peacock in the red hose.

I wondered briefly what might be "strange and curious" about Hans's childish writings. Then I put the mystery out of mind.

I WAS READY now to give stall number one hundred and seventy-one a try. I had traveled this distance to Frankfurt. I wouldn't let my aversion to action rule me. I had an important manuscript to sell.

At first I spoke to interested gentlepersons of the terrifying and moving tale of a devout Christian woman, a good woman, a hardworking widow, exemplary, facing the worst calumny, with dignity and—

No one had much interest in that.

"Is it the tale of a virtuous woman whose head is turned?"

I hesitated. "Not really."

The stranger walked away.

Next I tried: A tale of the viciousness that lurks in village life! Liars, scoundrels, purse-grabbers! Malice, greed, revenge, ignorance—

I grew tired. Tired of pretending to be something that I wasn't.

In the neighboring booth was an Englishman selling the story of a young woman set to marry a much older man. "A real old piece of horseflesh. Hair in the ears. The whole December if you follow, right down to the kisser. Meanwhile, she's the prettiest pink in the garden, full of bloom, in love with a nice young fellow."

"So she marries the young man in the end?"

"No, she marries the old man."

The Englishman was getting a lot of chitchat and interest from passersby.

In a quiet moment, the Englishman said to me, "If you don't mind a bit of advice: People don't like an old lady story, you know? I wouldn't lead with that part." What would he lead with? He said he wasn't sure, he would give it a think. He went on: "Even Shakespeare, very popular on all topics as he is, sticks to daughters and wives. An occasional mother. But not front and center, you know? You don't want an old lady front and center. Honestly never heard of such a thing."

Who was Shakespeare? I knew asking would only extend the conversation, so I didn't ask.

I MET UP with gentle Susanna in the very crowded tavern of the modest inn where she was lodging. Why did I not call her the widow Kepler? It was too unsettling to do so. For me the widow Kepler could only be Katharina. Poor Katharina. She was a better backgammon player than she would admit. Or I would admit. She was a frighteningly intelligent woman—also a fool.

Susanna told me that evening the story of the so-called juvenilia she was there with at the fair. I hadn't asked about it. She must have really needed to hear herself explaining her position. I dimly remembered hearing of it being spoken of in the testimony of that poor weak-minded schoolmaster who had been so envious of Hans. It had not come up in the later stages of the trial, I was told, but I didn't know why. "Hans emended it in detail," she said. "Of course he did. He cared so much. He didn't want there to be room for anyone to misunderstand. None." She showed me a copy of the book, with all its emendations. The book was still quite slim, closer to a pamphlet.

My eyesight was too poor for the smaller print. But the main text was laid out handsomely. "You can have this copy," Susanna said.

I should have turned down her generosity. It was too much. But again I missed the moment. She wanted to lead me through the pages. I let her.

The story starts with Hans himself, falling asleep while reading a book. He has a dream. In the dream there is a mother and son, living in Iceland. The mother, Fioxhilde, sells packets of magical herbs to sailors. Her son, still a young boy, accidentally ruins one of the packets. Fioxhilde impulsively sells the boy to a sailing captain as punishment. The captain is pretty nice. He drops the boy off with the astronomer Tycho Brahe. The boy learns Danish, and also astronomy.

"This was written *before* Hans worked with Brahe," she said. "It's spooky, right? He meant it as pure imagination." She covered her mouth with a kerchief and coughed. "But then it was like a prophecy."

There was some detail in the book which Susanna could not follow. The general story, however, was simple. After a number of years, the boy returns to his mom, who is overjoyed to see him. He tells her he's learned astronomy. She's even more delighted. She also knows astronomy, she tells him. She's learned it from some daemons she knows. She calls one of the daemons over to teach them more. The daemon—

"So it really is true that the mother is a witch?"

"Only in a story sort of way. Not a witch, even. But in touch with spirits."

I nodded.

"And the daemons aren't bad. They're not devils. They're more like ancient spirits. It's all imaginary, you see. Hans makes that very clear in the footnotes. He really, really didn't want anyone to misunderstand. One of the daemons describes how to get to the moon. What the geography is there. What the earth looks like when one is standing there. It's a story for a schoolboy, you see?"

She asked me if I, as a friend of Katharina's, thought people would take it the wrong way.

"I know very little about the book trade," I said.

She said she was unfortunately in a difficult place with money. So many revered Hans, but so few paid him what they owed.

I nodded.

She asked me what manuscript had I brought to the fair.

I panicked. "It's hard to say. It's a Christian testimony of a kind. I haven't figured out how to describe it. Maybe that's my problem." I laughed, like a dog. "I couldn't be a worse salesman." I felt the ghost of Katharina—the other widow Kepler, my first widow Kepler—sitting next to us. She rested her head in her hands and looked at me askance. "You were very kind to Katharina," I said. "She told me that."

The widow Kepler, the younger one, began to tear up. She said that she had spent a great deal of money on a respectable tombstone for Hans. She had hoped an office of the Emperor would help pay for it. Her pleas were never answered. He had been in Regensburg, trying to collect his pay, when he died. No one could give her details of his illness. The tomb was not marble, but limestone. On it was an illustration from one of Hans's books: *The Harmony of the World*. The tombstone maker charged her double what was appropriate, she knew what he was doing, but she had no energy at that time to argue. And then the soil was still soft when the gravestone was destroyed by soldiers. She couldn't even find it now.

YES, I WAS and remained a too-quiet witness. There is something else I haven't mentioned before, to anyone. I first met Katharina as a child. When I was twelve, my family had stayed for a short time at The Sun, the inn run by her father. We were looking for a home in the area. Kath-chen was a pretty young woman, and at her father's side more than any of the other children. I remember her handing him an embroidered kerchief for his breathing. He would sometimes be short of breath, and would then hold it to his face. I noticed the young woman's fidelity— that was how I saw it—because my father faced some hardship at that time, and I felt my own fidelity wavering. Another family ignominy had forced us to move: My father was said to have provided saddles to the Spanish Catholic troops. He denied it. I myself suspected that he had—he was not one to pass up a commission. I write this all now as if lightly. Yet it still makes me tremble, though the origin of the tremble is seventy years in the past. When we were at The Sun, it was with great vigilance that I and my siblings pruned back any weed of the rumor that followed us. Why were we moving? My father told a story that an angel had come to him in a dream, told him to bring his family to a clear spring, with day-moths visiting dark violets on the shores. Where he got that nonsense from, I don't know. He sounded like a pastor whose services were poorly attended—that was my unfaithful feeling at the time. He had no gift for lying. He had a gift for making saddles.

Katharina never recognized me from that short time I stayed at her father's inn. I never mentioned it.

That young Katharina, so attentive and faithful, is the one who remains most vivid to me. More than the old woman I came to know so many years later.

WHAT A FOOL I am to forget that a reader might not know the fate of Katharina. A fool too directed by his own memories and anxieties. The trial ended, but still there was no decision. The paperwork of the trial, including Hans's final defense, as well as the ducal advocate's final offense, were sent to the law faculty at Tübingen. I hardly understood the procedure, it was shifting one day to this, one day to that. Finally, it was another five weeks before a response came on the paperwork, and Katharina remained in prison for the deliberations. Five weeks was fast in comparison to our previous waits. I was at that time ready to die myself. The suitor Alexander had returned, but Anna had fallen to a terrible consumption. If faith is worth anything, shouldn't it make us not fear death?

On a Monday afternoon, Hans came to my home unannounced. I thought that he had heard word of Anna's illness, and maybe he had. But he came with papers in his hand and said nothing of my child.

What was the verdict? I couldn't read the expression on his face. He didn't look devastated. He didn't look triumphant. He looked distracted. He took a seat at my table.

"Did you know my first wife, Barbara?"

How would I have known her?

He said he had never hidden that it was a contentious marriage, but that didn't mean it was not also full of love. Barbara—there are so many Barbaras—had wanted to be

part of his scientific world. She had spoken to guests in
Latin and Greek, had asked after their work, as if she were
one of those Frenchwomen who present themselves as
most at home among men. That had annoyed him. Women,
he said, are even numbers, and men are odd. Then he said
he had strayed from what he wanted to tell me. He had a
question for me.

"Our son died of the flu." Barbara and the boy had
been constant companions; the boy had worn her shoes
around the house; he had tied her hair kerchiefs on his
own head; the two of them had hunted for mushrooms together, and drawn pine cones, and flowers. He was eleven
when he died. One loves all of one's children—but she
was the closest to this boy. "After that, Barbara devoted
herself to caring for soldiers sick from the same flu. She
soon succumbed."

I was listening.

"Would you call that a suicide?"

I didn't know what to say. "When will we hear your
mother's fate?" I asked.

"My God, I thought you already knew."

"I've been finishing a stirrups order."

"She will be freed. More than freed—the Reinbolds are
fined nearly a thousand thalers. You didn't hear? The judgment says Katharina will have to endure one last threat
of torture, for some salad logic reason they offer—but the
torturer is absolutely not permitted to put anything to effect. They want to scare her. They've hired some buffoon
with a knife to do so. But I gave her warning, she knows he
can't do anything. We've won, you see?"

Once freed, Katharina went directly from the prison to
live in Heumaden with Greta. She was not able to return
to her beloved, brutal Leonberg. Einhorn and the Reinbolds

had made it known that she would be killed in the street. They let it be known that her head would be put on a pike, her body roasted in the town square, that her blood would be used as an ink to make a sign warning others, that her corpse would be treated with none of the respect of a pig at market day, that the story of the evil she had done would live long, and survive as a tale to frighten children until the end of days.

THE DAY I resolved that I would walk to Heumaden to go to visit Katharina, I first went, deliberately, to Jerg Hundersinger's bakery. I wanted to buy something celebratory. Egg cakes, or a raisin loaf. Jerg appeared unusually bright and cheery. I'm no master of sly small talk or charmingly ambiguous phrases. But I said to Jerg, since other customers were around, that I thought I knew what had put a smile on his face.

He said that yes, he did indeed have good news, and how did I know?

Katharina? I asked in a quiet voice.

He looked confused. That's a different story, he said. He was smiling because his uncle had died. That was the good news. He, Jerg, had come into some money, and wasn't it just at the moment he needed it? Others wanted to complain of bad winters, of ill cattle, but look, even death had this bright underside, didn't it?

I bought a round milk loaf with raisins and headed out on my way, bewildered.

I can admit that I was somewhat anxious about not having made the trip to Heumaden to see Katharina earlier. I had meant to go in November, shortly after she was released from the Güglingen prison, and after Anna had so quickly recuperated. But surely Katharina needed that time to rest and recover, to have only her close family nearby. December was too cold for the long walk, I felt. The same thinking continued on into January and February. Easter, you may recall, came early. It was in March. And so it wasn't until the very start of April that I went. Anna encouraged me to go—I don't know why. Why didn't I write to Katharina in that time? Since she couldn't read the letters herself, I felt the scrutiny of eyes other than hers—that distressed me.

Now I will also mention that by this time in April I had heard rumors that Katharina was in a fury, that she was often seen wandering country lanes, shouting curses at magpies, at goats. That was not why I was avoiding her. I had heard reports that she scared children at the well with her dark mutterings, that she went about in velvet cloaks and lace headdresses, and that hound dogs whimpered and ran off when she came near. I didn't want to put faith in such stories. Even as a part of me wondered if my own name came up for gruff reprisals. When Katharina was grumbling about wrongs—if, indeed, she was grumbling about wrongs—was I one of those wrongs? It was selfish, I know, to be thinking in that way. And after all she had been through. As I walked the path, past cherry blossoms, I felt that I was walking to my own trial. I was looking forward to it, I realized, as the miles passed. It had been trying, waiting so long, to be heard out, to be issued a verdict. A brief drizzle was the only interruption to the long spring day's walk, and by the late afternoon I had arrived to Heumaden. I realized I was anxious about knocking at the door unannounced. But as it turned out, I didn't need to knock. Katharina was outside, in the garden.

She was wearing a simple dress, and had neither a velvet cloak nor a lace headdress on. She was not muttering, or cursing. But also she was not humming. She looked to be sowing seeds. She had not yet noticed me. When I got closer, I saw that she was working scraps of yarn and some broken buttons and a little bit of ash into the soil. Maybe it was some recipe for avoiding pests.

"I can't invite you in, Simon," she said, when she noticed me.

I apologized for surprising her.

"Let me rinse my hands, and I'll bring out another stool and we can sit in the shade," she said.

I said I didn't mean to interrupt her gardening. I said that I understood if she had no time for me. I held out the milk bread from Jerg's bakery. I told her about how he said he'd had some good luck with a relative dying. She laughed at that. Then she stepped away and into the house.

I don't know why I had believed the stories of Katharina fuming, or muttering, or being mad. But she did seem altered. What was it? It was more than a year since we had seen each other. Why had she not asked me straight off why I wasn't present at her trial? Or why I hadn't written to her? Why didn't she ask after Anna?

She came out carrying two small stools, with some difficulty. I hurried forward to help her and set them in the shade.

After some period of quiet, I suggested that we could play backgammon. We could have a makeshift board from pebbles and leaves, which was how I had played as a child.

She said she wasn't in the mood, if that was okay with me.

I told her that, for a while now, I had been wanting to say, I had been meaning to write, or visit—I wanted to say how relieved and pleased I was that she had been freed, that the correct thing had happened.

At first she said nothing. Then she said, "Yes, Simon, I know that you didn't put in a good word for me. That's troubling you, isn't it? You're coming here on this visit to tell me all about it, or explain your reasoning. I don't mean to offend you, Simon, but you're not the Duke of Württemberg. I don't know what difference your words would have made. I wonder if it's worth two old people spending time reassuring each other of this or that."

Was she trying to say that she wasn't angry because it was happy in the end?

"I wouldn't call it a happy end," she said. "To have nothing to give my children, to be unwanted in my own town."

"I've been a bad neighbor," I said. "You must despise me."

"My father used to call me his little scallion," she said.

I was confused by the change of topic. Then I saw that she was looking at the spring scallions, already making their way in the garden.

She said, "You liked me, Simon."

"I still like you," I said.

"Of course you do. And you wish me well."

I was waiting for the counterpoint of the argument. I was waiting to hear how little it would have cost me to visit her at Güglingen. Or to have spoken what I knew of her.

"I'm fond of you, Simon," she said. "I can see that you want me to be angry with you, but I can't do it. You have love in your heart. You've been a friend to me. In the ways that were available to you. You're not on trial. I won't convince you that you're not a witch, or that you are one." Then she said it was time for her to take Chamomile to pasture. I offered to walk with her. She said I shouldn't feel obliged.

She then apologized again for not being able to invite me in. She said Pastor Binder preferred not to see her, a position that she understood. It was his house.

I walked home with the feeling that I had been acquitted. Or that was the feeling at first. As the miles passed, I began to wonder if maybe it was simply that Katharina couldn't be bothered to convict me. That she was too morally exhausted. If I was tired, then she must have been all the more tired. She didn't seem like the same woman I had known before. Her apparent peace could as well be a sign of terrible defeat as a sign of the grace of God.

I SAW GERTIE at the tailor's, where I was having Anna's dress altered. Gertie told me that it was she who had walked Chamomile the distance so that Katharina could be reunited with her in Heumaden. Gertie told me that Katharina wept with gladness to see her cow—the first tears Gertie had ever seen her cry. And that Katharina had said of the cow that it had her father's eyes, and Maruschl's soul. Gertie also told me the sad news that in the middle of April, Katharina had died in her sleep. That I had seen her that one last time was a blessing.

The dark times that have been on my mind now seem like milk and honey. Not long after our meeting in Frankfurt, Susanna also died. I don't know where she was buried. I heard the news from someone who had spoken to her stepson. When the papal soldiers came through last fall, in faded greens and metal, Greta's husband, the pastor Binder, was beaten to death, and the soldier who beat him was soon dead of the plague, as was the nurse who cared for that soldier. I learned of that from Christoph, who became a criminal court judge. He held the position until only last year, when he died, too, also of the plague. Gertie and Agnes passed of an illness within weeks of each other. Greta is all right. Even well. She has married a distinguished poet. A friend of Hans's. It is rumored to be a happy match.

ACKNOWLEDGMENTS

This book is based on real events but is very much a work of fiction. Many names and details have been invented.

I am most indebted to the marvelous German historian Ulinka Rublack for her celebrated nonfiction book *The Astronomer and the Witch: Johannes Kepler's Fight for His Mother*. I initially read Rublack's book simply to learn more about Johannes Kepler. A detail in Rublack's book—a neighbor of Katharina's asking to be dismissed from serving henceforth as her legal guardian—caught my heart and opened up this novel for me. I have not used that neighbor's real name, Veit Schumacher, because his voice and life in this novel are wholly imagined.

The letters that appear in this novel are based on real letters. The language used in the depositions is largely imagined, the exception being the opening question used throughout, which is a straight translation of what is found in the trial records. That translation was done by Alex Bernhardt Beatty. Beatty provided numerous wise and nuanced translations of original material and authored the translations of the two Kepler letters.

The broader translation—that of Katharina Kepler's

world across language and time—has been done with the J. A. Underwood translation of Hans Jakob Christoffel von Grimmelshausen's *The Adventures of Simplicius Simplicissimus* as a spirit guide.

I have never enjoyed working on a book as much as I enjoyed working on this one, even as it is a sad book, written during a distressing time. I owe my happiness in large part to the works I read as part of my research. Many articles and books kept me in good company, most notably: *Reformation Europe: New Approaches to European History, Series Number 54*, by Ulinka Rublack; *Witch Craze: Terror and Fantasy in Baroque Germany*, by Lyndal Roper; *The Crimes of Women in Early Modern Germany*, by Ulinka Rublack; *Ideas and Cultural Margins in Early Modern Germany: Essays in Honor of H. C. Erik Midelfort*, edited by M. E. Plummer and R. B. Barnes; *Witch Hunting in Southwestern Germany, 1562–1684: The Social and Intellectual Foundations*, by H. C. Erik Midelfort; *Johannes Kepler and the New Astronomy*, by James R. Voelkel; *Florilegium: The Book of Plants*, by Basilius Besler; *Johannes Kepler: Life and Letters*, by Carola Baumgardt; *A Magical World*, by Derek K. Wilson; *The Holy Household*, by Lyndal Roper; *The Thirty Years War*, by C. V. Wedgwood; *Kepler*, by Max Caspar, translated by C. Doris Hellman; *Leonhart Fuchs: The New Herbal of 1543*, by Klaus Dobat and Werner Dressendörfer; *Opera Omnia*, by Johannes Kepler, edited by C. Frisch; *New Astronomy*, by Johannes Kepler, translation and introduction by W. H. Donahue; *Martin Luther*, by Lyndal Roper; *Fictions of the Cosmos*, by Frédérique Aït-Touati; *The Cheese and the Worms*, by Carlo Ginzburg; *Cardano's Cosmos*, by Anthony Grafton; and https://somniumproject.wordpress.com.

The records of Katharina's trial are available for the curious here: https://archive.org/details/joanniskeplerias08kepl/page/n9/mode/2up.

A partial translation by Pamela Selwyn of Johannes Kepler's defense of his mother is available here: http://www.keplers-trial.com/keplers-defence.pdf.

My editor, Eric Chinski, and my agent, Bill Clegg, both offered substantial and generous editorial guidance that helped me find this book's gravitational center. Robert Rubsam and Katie Schorr were a tremendous help in locating research materials. Columbia University's Hettleman Junior Faculty summer research grant provided essential support. Deborah Ghim's insights and shepherding have also been invaluable. Spenser Lee's early support of the book buoyed me. Rodrigo Corral designed the unforeseen and ideal cover. And I am grateful to the whole team at FSG, who not only helped me with this book, but have brought into being so many books that I love to read.

A NOTE ABOUT THE AUTHOR

Rivka Galchen is the recipient of a William Saroyan International Prize for Writing and a Rona Jaffe Foundation Writers' Award, among other honors. She writes regularly for *The New Yorker*, whose editors selected her for their list of "20 Under 40" American fiction writers in 2010. Her debut novel, *Atmospheric Disturbances* (2008), and her story collection, *American Innovations* (2014), were both *New York Times* Best Books of the Year. She received an MD from the Icahn School of Medicine at Mount Sinai. Galchen divides her time between Montreal and New York City.